WATCH
HER
SLEEP

BOOKS BY L.T. VARGUS AND TIM MCBAIN

LT VARGUS
TIM MCBAIN

WATCH HER SLEEP

bookouture

Published by Bookouture in 2021

An imprint of Storyfire Ltd.
Carmelite House
50 Victoria Embankment
London EC4Y 0DZ

www.bookouture.com

ISBN: 978-1-83888-837-4
eBook ISBN: 978-1-83888-836-7

PROLOGUE

He watches through the windows as he creeps toward the house. Sees the glowing panes of glass like bright and hollow TV screens flaring in the night.

Looking for her. Waiting for her.

The darkness shifts around him as he crosses the front yard. The night grows thicker the closer he gets to the shade of the building, the bushes running along its perimeter helping to conceal him.

The sharp October chill reaches right through his jacket, presses its iciness against his back, against his chest. Pulls his skin taut. Sucks down into his lungs in frosty plumes. The cold feels invigorating tonight, though. Adds a sense of exhilaration to the proceedings.

He's awake tonight. Alive. All the way.

Just as he rounds the corner into the side yard, he sees her skinny frame flit past one of the windows. A brief flash of her flutters in the big bay window, moving out of the living room and into the gaping maw of the hallway beyond.

His heart leaps. Head goes light and swimmy.

She is delicate. A fragile thing that appears gauzy in the half-light. Ghostly. Ethereal.

He stays low. Sidles past the overgrown shrubbery along the side of the house. Completely swathed in gloom now.

He can feel the shadows on his skin, the energy of those darker places seeping into his body, prickling bolts of electricity mainlining into his bloodstream. Power, raw and wriggling.

He reaches the corner at the back of the house where the bushes thin out some. Settles into his spot beneath her bedroom window.

Keeps his face lower than the sill. Head angled up to stare into the glowing space.

With her back to him, she peels off her shirt. Her milky flesh gleams like alabaster. Black bra straps truss the ribcage, draw a perpendicular line across her spine and two more up and over her shoulders.

And then that dainty bit of lycra and wire comes off too. Frees that sheet of pale skin down to her waist.

His fingers curl on the wooden lip of the window ledge. Flexing and stiffening.

His heart hammers in his chest. Breath sucking between his parted lips.

Tonight's the night. He knows that now. No more pane of glass between them.

He's watched her for so long. Now he gets to touch.

She turns before him. Her front not quite coming into view.

His face flushes with animal heat. Fever touching his temples, spreading over his forehead. Cheeks tingling with pinpricks.

Then she disappears behind her closet door.

He licks his lips. Ducks back into the darkness.

He shuffles out from between the bushes along her window. Renews his trek to the rear of the house. Finds his way to the back door. Kneels before it.

He grips the door handle. Tests the sliding glass door. Locked. Not a problem.

His fingers move lower. Seek the seam along the bottom of the doorway, where the door itself is mounted into a steel track. He finds the little grooved place in the metal there.

Then he slips the screwdriver out of his back pocket. Jams it home into the notch in the door frame. Lifts.

Quietly. Carefully.

The door rises. Pops out of the track. The lock surrenders, the L-shaped latch lowered from the bracket by the upward force.

He smiles at how easy it is. Euphoria bubbling like champagne in his skull.

So many times he has let himself in this way. Violated her space this way. And somehow the thrill of it never diminishes.

Tonight is different, though. Usually he came when she wasn't home. A few times when she was asleep, but this…

He lowers the slab of glass and wood back into its groove. The door slides open in slow motion.

The darkened kitchen lies before him, the dimly lit hallway stretching out beyond that.

He presses into the breach.

Visions of her whirl in his head as he crosses the threshold. Memories of all that creamy skin exposed. The curved contours of her hips and waist. The dimpled ridges running up the length of her spine. Those little swollen spots pouting on each side of her ribcage where he could glimpse the sides of her breasts, the skin there somehow paler still, milkier still. Everything tapering, dainty, sculpted just so.

He eases the door shut behind him and steps fully into the darkened kitchen. Soundless. Crouched low so he can just peer over the tops of the counters.

He drifts over the ceramic tile of the kitchen floor, and that tingle of power spreads from his arms into his chest with each step. Excitement swelling in him. Every pore throbbing and creeping with electricity, slicked with sweat.

So many times he's been in her place, in her room. Picked through her things. Sprawled naked in her bed while she was away. Watched her while she slept.

But it's different now. Knowing that he will touch her makes it different entirely. Makes that electricity in his blood burn hotter and brighter, so sharply it stings.

As he treads into the hallway, his senses heighten with a fresh rush of adrenaline, details sharpening around him. The stench of the potpourri in the vase on the console table becomes overpowering. Every creak and murmur of the floorboards underfoot makes him wince, makes his heart race faster and faster.

His eyes lock on that rectangle of light ahead—the glow spilling out of her bedroom door and over the hardwood planks of the floor.

Shadows move there, disrupting the glow. The light dulls. Her silhouette takes shape in the box of illumination.

He freezes. Watches.

She darts past. Shoots across the hall. Enters the doorway diagonal from her room. The bathroom.

But she doesn't see him. Oblivious. Just the way he wants it.

She'll have no clue he's there until it's too late.

He creeps forward a couple paces and tucks himself behind the console table the best he can—not really concealed there, but no longer out in the open either.

He peeks over the top of the table. Watches.

Watches as she trails back to her bedroom.

Watches as the light goes out a few moments later.

Hears the creak of the box spring beneath her mattress.

Licks his lips again.

He waits. Holds still. Breathes.

He wants to pounce. Touch her. Scare her.

But he needs to let the scene settle. Let her drift off toward slumber.

Blood thrums in his ears. Pulsing. Impatient.

Finally he slips out from behind the table. Ready now. Ready to take what's his.

When no one wants you, when no one cares, you have to take it. There's no choice in the matter.

He leans forward, about to take another step, but the floorboard squeals beneath him. A long, shrill squawk like a seagull.

Icy liquid surges through his veins.

He holds his breath. Maybe she didn't hear.

And then the box spring creaks again.

"Who's there?" she says, and there's fear in her voice, but strength too. Defiance.

That tingle of power thrumming in his limbs dies back all at once. Abandons him. Leaves him cold, empty, vulnerable.

And it feels wrong. It feels all wrong.

But he waits. Holds his breath. Listens. Waits for the lights to flick on, but they don't.

Maybe he can salvage this. Maybe she will settle back down. Maybe.

When headlights swing past the windows at the front of the house, he backpedals into the kitchen.

The car swerves into the driveway off to his right. Idles there, the engine rumbling. Then a car door slams. Someone is coming.

He retreats all the way to the back door. Waits there.

A knock rattles the front door, followed by the sound of her weight shifting on the bed. The whisper of bare feet on the floor.

Lights flick on in the living room, and the wooden front door pops and cracks as it's eased out of its frame.

Then he hears a second woman's voice, sharp and loud, apologizing for stopping by so late.

Interrupting bitch.

He hesitates there a moment. Listens to the babble of their two voices intertwining. Not quite wanting to leave.

He's disappointed, yes, but he's still somehow empowered to be here. Listening. Watching. Without anyone seeing, without anyone knowing.

When it feels right, he flees out the back door. Starts his crouch-walk journey back through the dewy yard, moving slowly but surely toward his car down the street.

Not tonight. But soon.

CHAPTER ONE

Charlie was wiping down the countertop in the back room when the bell over the front door jingled. A moment later, she heard Paige's voice.

"Welcome to A1 Investigations. How can I help you this evening?"

A woman's voice responded, but Charlie couldn't make out the words through the wall. She glanced at the clock. It was a quarter to five. Too late to start the whole rigmarole that went with a client intake. She'd have Paige take down her information, and Charlie would follow up in the morning.

Allie scoffed.

"Got big plans, do you?"

"I don't know," Charlie said, rinsing the sponge she'd used to clean up in the sink. "I thought maybe I'd call Zoe to see if she wanted to hang out."

"Liar," Allie said. "You've been daydreaming all day about vegging out with a pizza from Towne Square and that half-eaten pint of Ben & Jerry's in your freezer."

Charlie squeezed the sponge out, gritting her teeth. It was often irritating the way her sister always knew what she was thinking, but then what did she expect from a voice in her head?

"So what?" Charlie asked.

"Oh, nothing. It's not like you're wasting your life or anything. No, no. You're a real carpe diem kind of gal, you know? That's what I've always liked about you, Chuck."

Charlie tossed the sponge down and was about to tell Allie to shut her face, but she was interrupted by her assistant coming into the room.

"There's a girl out front with some questions for you," Paige said.

Charlie dried her hands with a paper towel. "The kind of questions I can answer in fifteen minutes and follow up on tomorrow morning?" she asked.

Paige chewed her lip. "I think maybe you ought to talk to her yourself and decide."

"Why? What does she want to know?"

"Well, the first thing she asked when she came in was how she could tell if someone was tailing her."

"'Tailing.' Is that the word she used?"

"Yes, ma'am."

That was unusual enough for Charlie to poke her head out to get a better look.

The girl was young. Under twenty-five, if Charlie had to guess. Definitely not the standard middle-aged lady convinced her husband was running around on her. The girl's eyes were trained on the plate glass windows at the front of the office, as if she were monitoring the street outside.

Charlie considered the time again, but what the hell? She supposed she could spare half an hour of her evening for a damsel in distress.

"OK. I'll talk to her."

Paige led the way to the front office, where the girl sat on the old beat-up sofa that had been a part of Uncle Frank's office decor for longer than Charlie had been alive.

The girl was dressed in a T-shirt, a hoodie, and a pair of black jeans with strategically placed rips along the thighs. Her posture ran in stark contrast to the casual attire, however. She sat rigid and upright, shoulders back, something stiff in her neck. Charlie might have interpreted the body language as a sign of confidence if it weren't for the way her eyes flitted about the room. *OK, then. An uptight achiever trying to pass herself off as more of a slacker than she really is*, Charlie thought.

"You can dress any which way you want, but you can't hide that kind of dorkiness. It's like trying to put lipstick on a nerd," Allie said. "You know all about that, don't you, Charles?"

Ignoring Allie's comments, Charlie put her hand out and introduced herself. The girl stood to shake her hand. Her fingers were ice-cold, and Charlie wondered if it was nerves or from being out in the October weather.

"Emma Jacobis," the girl said.

"Paige tells me you think that someone is following you?" Charlie asked, sliding into the chair behind her desk. "Is there a reason you can think of that someone might have hired a private investigator to look into you? Family drama? Boyfriend stuff?"

"Oh, no. It isn't like that. At least I don't think so."

Emma fiddled with the cuff of her sweatshirt. Her lips quirked as if she was about to go on, but no words came.

Charlie's brow furrowed. The word "tailing" conjured a very specific set of associations for her, all of them involving investigative purposes. If it wasn't that…

Emma's lips kept moving. It wasn't the quirk of someone about to speak, Charlie realized. The girl was trembling. When she finally spoke again, it came out in a jumbled rush, her eyes growing wider and wider as the words left her mouth.

"It's just… I hear things. Sometimes. At night. Bumps and thuds and… Someone's been in my apartment, I think. I mean, I'm pretty sure. I don't know. And… and… and… Well, I tried to tell the police, and I guess, you know, no crimes have been committed as far as they can tell, but I—"

She burst into tears mid-sentence. Her throat hitched for a second, a choked interruption to her speech. Sobs and whimpers pouring out instead of words, her lips still opening and closing like her mouth kept trying to talk, not quite aware that the rest of her body had been overcome. Water poured from her eyes, trailed down her cheeks.

Charlie had seen the girl's emotional outburst coming, but even so, the arrival of the crying fit took her breath away. A weepy feeling crept up Charlie's throat and into the corners of her eyes as though Emma's tears might be contagious. She blinked hard and swallowed, rendered momentarily speechless.

Charlie handed Emma a tissue and waited for her to calm down enough to be able to explain herself. But there was one thing Charlie knew all on her own: this girl was absolutely terrified.

"Here," Emma said when she was finally able to get words out again. She leaned over her bag, both hands digging frantically. "I found this."

She plucked a piece of lined notebook paper from her purse and handed it to Charlie.

There was a detailed pencil drawing on the page. A portrait of a woman lying on a bed with her eyes closed. It was a beat before Charlie recognized that the drawing was of Emma.

"There's more." Emma's finger shook as she pointed at the sketch clutched in Charlie's hands. "On the back."

The paper rustled as Charlie flipped it over.

Jagged text was scrawled on the back of the drawing in the black ink of a ballpoint pen, the letters traced over and over in spiky lettering that spelled out four words.

You could be mine.

CHAPTER TWO

Charlie's heart raced as she studied the page. Each letter had been traced several times over, and whoever had written it had pressed so hard with the pen nib at one point that they'd torn through the paper.

"Where did you find this?" Charlie asked.

"In my car."

Charlie raised her eyebrows.

"Someone broke into your car?"

"Not exactly." Emma shook her head. "One of my windows was open a crack while I was at work the other night. It was an accident, but he must have slipped it through the gap."

That's interesting, Charlie thought. Emma's gut was telling her the stalker was male. Charlie knew statistically that was probable.

As for the note, Charlie thought the placement was intentional. He could have left it anywhere. In her mailbox, tucked under her windshield wiper. But he'd made sure to cross a boundary by putting the drawing inside Emma's car. Violating a locked, private space.

It also showed that he'd been doing his homework. He knew where she worked. And while he may have simply gotten lucky by leaving the note on the night her window happened to be cracked, there was a chance it meant that he'd been waiting. Biding his time. Watching for an opening. Charlie didn't like that notion one bit.

"When did you find the note?"

"Two days ago." Emma fiddled with the straps of her purse. "And last night... I thought I heard someone inside my house."

"Inside?"

"Yeah. I mean, I've been pretty jittery since I found the note, so there's a chance it's just paranoia."

Charlie held up the piece of notebook paper.

"It's not paranoia when someone is leaving you things like this. You said you've talked to the police?"

Emma nodded.

"They took down a report. Scanned the note. But there's only so much they can do, I guess," she said, shrugging. "From their point of view, no serious crimes have been committed."

Not yet, anyway, Charlie thought. Her fists clenched, and she was overwhelmed by a sudden flash of anger. Of course the police couldn't help this girl. They were rarely able to do anything until after the fact, and by then it was often too late.

Almost twenty years ago, Charlie's twin sister had gone missing. All that time, and yet the case remained unsolved. Having studied Allie's case file over and over again, Charlie knew the police investigation had never even come close to finding an answer as to who or why or even how. They'd never found anything but the severed foot that had washed up on the beach, and that had pretty much landed in their lap.

Charlie felt her fingernails digging into the flesh of her palms and forced herself to release the tension. She inhaled deeply.

Don't get off-track, she told herself. It did her no good to wander the same old beaten path her mind went to whenever it got the chance. Charlie had a job to do, and if she was going to help this girl, she had to focus on the here and now. Not the past.

Emma fiddled with the cuff of her sweatshirt.

"I tried to tell them about Fred, but the deputy just shrugged and said maybe I had a secret admirer."

"Who's Fred?" Charlie asked, thinking how lucky she would be if she already had a potential suspect to look into.

Emma crooked a finger at the notebook page.

"The stuffed rabbit in the drawing."

Charlie flipped it over and peered down at the crosshatched pencil lines. She hadn't noticed the stuffed animal clutched to the girl's chest, but it was there alright. Clear as day.

"I've had him since I was a kid, and I still sleep with him most nights." The girl started to tremble again, and tears pooled in the corners of her eyes. "I just keep thinking that the only way someone could know that is if they've watched me, right? I mean, they even knew that Fred is missing an eye."

A chill ran up Charlie's spine at the thought of how closely someone must have been following Emma to know such things. She was suddenly very glad she hadn't told Paige to turn this girl away.

Flipping open her notebook, Charlie scribbled down Emma's name and a few quick notes based on what they'd discussed so far.

"Has there been anything else?" she asked. "Phone calls? Strange gifts left for you?"

"No gifts, but my phone has rung a few times in the middle of the night. When I've answered, no one has been there. I started putting it on 'do not disturb' while I'm asleep, so I don't know if it's still happening."

"The same number?"

"I'm not sure. I think it was at least two different numbers, because I remember figuring it was just some kind of telemarketing scam or something."

Charlie made a note to check Emma's call records. If he was smart, he was using burners or a number-spoofing app, but she'd check it out anyway.

When she glanced across the desk, Emma was crying again.

"I'm sorry," she said, sniffling. "I was so prepared for you to turn me away, just like the police. I felt like maybe I was being crazy. Just having someone listen to me is such a relief."

"Don't worry," Charlie said, passing her another tissue. "We're going to get to the bottom of this, OK?"

Emma nodded.

"Let's talk about your job, since that's where the note showed up. Where do you work?"

"The Laughing Raven. I wait tables and tend bar."

The pen in Charlie's hand scratched against the notepad as she wrote this down.

"Notice anyone strange hanging around the bar lately? Maybe a customer who pays you a little too much attention?"

Emma shook her head.

"No, but it's been so busy this month, I wouldn't have noticed anything like that anyway. We do events every Friday and Saturday leading up to the big carnival thing we always do on Halloween, so it's been packed the last two weekends. A few nights I felt like I barely had time to take a bathroom break in between pouring shots."

Charlie didn't love the sound of that. She'd probably have to check out the bar at some point, but she hated the idea of weeding through a few dozen college kids in search of the lone creeper. Even if she brought in Uncle Frank to help, the person stalking Emma could come and go in a crowded bar potentially without notice.

Pushing the frustration from her mind, Charlie moved on to the next possibility.

"Are you dating anyone?"

"Not right now."

"Have you had any bad breakups?"

"Nothing like that. I've only really had one serious boyfriend since graduating high school."

"And what happened with that?"

"We were both applying to grad school. I got into U of M. Tyler got into UCLA." Emma shrugged. "Neither one of us was willing to sacrifice our school of choice for the relationship so we… let it go."

Charlie got Tyler's full name so she could look into him later.

"So no hard feelings, and I'm assuming he's in California now?"

"That's right. Last I heard he was going out with a yoga instructor he met out there, so I doubt he's still hung up on me. And also, he has, like, no artistic ability, so I doubt he did that," Emma said, pointing at the drawing on Charlie's desk.

"What are you studying?"

"Psychology, but I'm taking a semester off. Well, hopefully *just* a semester, but it depends on how much I can make tending bar." Emma crossed her arms. "Speaking of which, I should come right out and tell you now that I don't have a lot of money. I assume something like this isn't cheap."

"Let's not worry about the money right now, OK? We'll figure that out later." Charlie peered out through the windows, trying to determine how much daylight was left. "I'd like to take a look around your place, if I can."

"Tonight?" Emma's eyes went to the clock on the wall. "I have to be at work in half an hour."

"That's fine. I can poke around on my own, and if I have questions for you, I'll give you a call."

"OK," Emma said, bobbing her head.

Charlie closed her notebook and lifted the drawing of Emma by one corner.

"And I'd like to get a copy of this before you go."

"Just keep it," Emma said, shuddering. "I'm sick of looking at it."

"I can imagine."

At the door, Emma turned back, and Charlie could see she was on the brink of tears again.

"Thank you," she said with a sigh. "Thank you for taking me seriously."

Charlie put her hand on the girl's arm.

"You're not alone in this anymore, Emma. We're going to get through this together."

CHAPTER THREE

The bottom edge of the sun was grazing the top of the treeline when Charlie pulled into Emma Jacobis' driveway. The house was a single-story duplex with yellow siding, set back from the road and partly shielded from view by a cluster of bushes that were reaching peak redness.

Charlie got out of her car and glanced around. She'd been hoping there'd be neighbors who might have spotted a stranger or an unknown vehicle hanging around in recent weeks, something that might lead to a description of the stalker or his car. But now that she was here, Charlie thought that was unlikely.

Emma's house was nestled in thick foliage. Even if he had been foolish enough to park in such a conspicuous place, he wouldn't have been able to see Emma from the street. Her unit of the duplex was almost completely concealed by the bushes out front.

No. He would have had to get closer if he wanted to watch her. And if he approached on foot, which Charlie thought the most likely, he could easily stay hidden in the heavy leafage of the terrain.

Charlie went to the side of Emma's unit, scanning for any little detail that might be out of place. A slit screen on a window. An errant cigarette butt. Her eyes fell on a matted patch of grass right at the base of the foundation. Charlie stopped and glanced around. The whole lawn was in need of a mowing, which made the trampled place even more noticeable.

As she got closer, Charlie could even make out vague footprint shapes around the edges of the flattened spot. Peeking through the window just above the disturbed area, Charlie saw a mirror over a dresser and, beside that, a bed. Emma's bedroom.

Had he been standing here, watching often enough to wear down this spot on the lawn?

The thought gave her a chill.

Charlie took a photo of the rumpled grass and moved back to the front of the house. Instead of grass, the space here had been planted with a row of ferns and rhododendron. Pausing before the window that looked in on the living room, Charlie studied the ground. Sure enough, the dirt here showed signs of being disturbed by foot traffic as well, and a few stalks of the nearest fern had been broken and crushed, as if someone had carelessly stepped on them as they tracked Emma's movements inside her house.

Charlie snapped another picture, wishing there was a clean footprint somewhere among the mess of crushed grass and exposed soil. She saw nothing that could truly be useful forensic evidence.

In the backyard, Charlie found that each unit had a sliding glass door that led onto a small wooden porch. The unit next to Emma's was equipped with a stack of plastic lawn chairs, a kettle-style charcoal grill, and a large plastic light-up palm tree. Emma's side had a small metal table with two bistro chairs and a pot of red mums.

Charlie climbed the six steps onto Emma's porch and tested the handle of the sliding door. It was locked, but when she peered through the glass, she saw no bar keeping the door from being pried open. Charlie lowered herself to one knee and ran her finger along the underside of the door. A few inches from the bottom corner she felt a very slight dimple in the frame. She bent closer and examined the dent. It was subtle. The kind of thing she wouldn't have noticed if she hadn't been looking for it. But the indentation was precisely in the place where you'd shove a screwdriver if you wanted to jimmy the door. Simply lifting the door up and off its track was usually enough to disengage the lock on most sliding doors, a fact that many homeowners didn't even realize. But plenty of thieves knew it. And Charlie thought that Emma's stalker knew it, too.

With practice, it could be done quickly and quietly. And it would explain how he might have gotten into the house.

There was a tightness in Charlie's chest now. It had started when she'd first noticed the trampled grass outside of Emma's window. But now that she'd figured out an easy way the stalker might have entered Emma's house, the feeling increased tenfold.

Charlie got a photo of the door before turning around and taking in the back of the property. Less than fifteen feet away, a line of cedar trees crowded the rear of the house. It would be the perfect place to lie in wait for the cover of night. Someone standing even a yard from the edge of the trees would be rendered almost invisible by all the foliage. He could be watching now, for all Charlie knew, and the thought sent the hairs on the back of her neck to prickling.

Charlie climbed down from the porch and approached the line of trees. Crickets chittered from their hidden places in the undergrowth, and the birds chirped out their evening songs. She slipped between two of the trees, getting a whiff of pine smell. Against the backdrop of the evergreens, sumac and sassafras offered pops of red and gold and orange.

It was an attractive backyard, really. Private and quiet and bursting with the colors of fall. And yet Charlie couldn't help but feel overwhelmed by that same sense of foreboding she'd had earlier. The fact that night was starting to fall didn't help, she supposed.

Charlie's gaze caught on something in the carpet of rusty-brown pine needles. Glinting in the last vestiges of twilight. Metallic and round. A coin? She stooped and plucked it from the ground.

Not a coin but a bottle cap. She flipped it around and read the logo. Coors Light.

Eyes downcast, she scanned the forest floor and found a few more. Four in all. Someone had sat back here drinking beers. Could be nothing. Or it could be proof that the stalker hid back here and watched the house, waiting for the right moment to get closer.

Behind her, a branch cracked, and Charlie whirled around.

She gasped.

Someone was there.

CHAPTER FOUR

Charlie's mouth went dry at the sight of him.

He stood just on the other side of the trees. A large man with a bulbous forehead and thick, juicy-looking lips that reminded her of two fat worms. One arm dangled at his side, and at the end of it, Charlie saw he was clutching a crossbow.

Her heart kicked against her ribcage. She gripped her phone a little tighter in her hand, swiping up with her thumb so she could hit the "Emergency" button. But she stopped herself just shy of it.

"Can I help you?" she asked.

The man raised one eyebrow and parted his slimy fish lips.

"Funny, I was just about to ask you the same thing." With the hand not presently gripping the crossbow, he lifted a beer koozie to his mouth and drank. "See, this here is my property."

Charlie relaxed a little. This was only Emma's landlord, who lived in the other half of the duplex.

"There some reason for you to be lurkin' around my place?"

"Emma hired me," Charlie said, approaching with her hand out. "Charlie Winters. I'm a private investigator."

The man set the crossbow down, leaning it against his leg to shake Charlie's hand.

"Roy Merriwether," he said. "What's Emma need a P.I. for?"

"Someone left her a threatening note."

"No shit?" Roy took another sip from the can of PBR swaddled in the foam koozie. "She didn't say nothing about that to me."

Charlie wasn't sure, but he almost sounded offended at that.

"You two are… close?" she asked.

"I mean, it ain't like we're bosom buddies or whatever. But we hang sometimes." He shrugged. "She's cool. Not like the last tenant I had. Stuck-up bitch thought she was God's gift, let me tell you."

He pitched his voice higher and did what Charlie assumed was an unkind mockery of his previous tenant.

"Roy, you got your video games up too loud, and I'm trying to sleep. Roy, you said you fixed my toilet, but it's still running at odd hours. Roy, the smoke from your cigars is coming in through my open window."

He scoffed, shaking his head.

"That last one, I told her, 'Then shut your damn window!' That shut 'er up. For maybe fifteen minutes, and then she was onto pissing and moaning about something else, I'm sure." Roy sighed. "Emma, though, she ain't like that, see. She barely makes a peep most of the time. You say somebody's been threatening her?"

"Yeah. Have you seen anyone around? Cars? People who don't belong?" Charlie asked.

"Nah. But I mostly mind my own business. Not the nosy type," Roy said, pausing to drink. "I can't figure why someone would want to harass quiet little Emma, though. That just don't make sense. Now if we were talking about that last one, I could see that. Probably woulda done her some good, to be honest. Put her in her place, so to speak. Little, uh, you know, attitude adjustment."

Charlie nodded, thinking this guy was sounding like a bigger creep the more he went on. She held out the bottle caps she still had in one fist.

"Do you ever hang out back here? Maybe have a few beers under the trees?"

Roy chuckled.

"Now, why would I go and do that when I got a perfectly good porch for drankin' on?" He gestured back at the grill and the artificial palm tree setup. "Speaking of which, I'm bein' awfully rude, standing here suckin' this brewski down and not offering one to you. Why don't you come up to Roy's Party Pad, and I'll get you a cold one."

"Thanks, but I only came out here to get a quick look." Charlie glanced at her phone as if checking the time. "I'm supposed to meet a friend in twenty minutes, so I should get going."

She wasn't sure why she'd invented that last bit about meeting someone, other than the fact that Roy was giving her major creep vibes.

"Suit yourself, party pooper," he said, shrugging and polishing off the can of beer.

When Charlie headed for the front of the house, Roy followed.

"Hey, why don't I get your number, in case I see anything, you know… suspect."

"Just google 'A1 Investigations,'" Charlie said, hurrying to reach her car. "We're the top search result."

"A1 Investigations," Roy repeated. "Got it."

Even though Roy was still standing there as she got into her car, Charlie felt an instant sense of relief once she was inside.

I'm being paranoid, she thought. A moment later, she realized that was exactly what Emma had been telling herself until today.

When Charlie got back to her apartment, she dialed Emma's cell number. The line rang three times before she picked up. Charlie could hear the sound of voices and clinking glasses in the background.

"Do you have a minute to talk?" Charlie asked.

"Sure. Just let me duck into the storeroom so I can hear you better," Emma said over the clamor of a blender whirring.

A door closed with a soft thud, and the ambient noise suddenly winked out to almost nothing.

"OK. What is it?"

"I don't want you to go back to your house tonight. Until we have a better grasp on this thing, I think it'd be best if you didn't stay there at all."

"Did you find something?" Emma asked, sounding concerned. "What happened?"

"I went over to your place and had a look around outside. There are signs that someone's been lurking around. Looking in windows. Hanging out in the woods behind your house. Possibly even evidence that someone's pried open the sliding glass door on the back porch."

Charlie had considered holding that last bit back. She didn't want to scare the girl too much, but she wanted Emma to know what they were dealing with.

"I knew it," Emma said, and to Charlie's surprise, she didn't sound frightened. "You know, for years, I've been trying to be less uptight. To quit constantly worrying about everything all the time. To not always leap to the worst possible conclusion. But for once, my gut was right."

Now Charlie worried that Emma wasn't taking this seriously enough. The voice on the phone seemed so nonchalant compared to the girl's demeanor back in the office. The tension Charlie had felt earlier returned, all the muscles around her ribcage constricting. Squeezing.

"Emma, I need you to promise me you won't stay there alone. Do you have somewhere you can crash for a few nights?"

"Oh, sure," Emma said. "I made plans to do that already. Finding that note and then hearing those noises last night, I knew there was no way I'd get a wink of sleep at home."

Charlie let out a big breath and felt the tightness in her chest recede.

"I'd like to set up some cameras at your house," she said. "If he's coming around at night, it will be hard to get a good shot of his face for identification purposes, but we might be able to use the footage to pinpoint a pattern for when he comes around—time of night, day of the week. Can you meet me over there tomorrow?"

"Sure," Emma said. "Would ten thirty be OK?"

"That'll be fine." Charlie had placed the bottle caps she'd found at the scene into a plastic baggie, and she looked over at them now. "What can you tell me about your landlord?"

"Oh." Emma chuckled. "You met Roy, huh?"

"I did."

"He's what I'd call an 'acquired taste.' The kind of guy who would think nothing of telling a dirty joke to a room full of Sunday school teachers. But he's pretty harmless," Emma said.

"You don't get any bad vibes from him or anything like that?"

"Not really. He's more obnoxious than anything else. Kinda crass. Mildly sexist in that 1950s way. But I can't really imagine him stalking anyone. And the way he tells it, he's Don Juan with the ladies. He's always telling me semi-graphic stories about his conquests."

"OK," Charlie said. She was willing to trust Emma's instincts for now, but she wouldn't write off Roy entirely.

Emma sighed.

"Is that everything? I hate to rush you, but we're really slammed tonight."

"Just one more thing," Charlie said. "I want you to have someone walk you to your car when you get out of work tonight."

"You really think he'd... I don't know... try to do something here?" Emma asked. "Right in public like that?"

"I can't say for sure, but we're not going to give him that chance, right?"

Emma inhaled sharply.

"Sorry. That gave me goosebumps. I've spent the last few weeks telling myself this was all in my head. Hearing you say it out loud makes the whole thing seem more real. And more scary."

"Having some fear is good, because the truth is, we don't know what this guy will try. Better safe than sorry, right?"

"Right," Emma said.

When she finally ended the call, Charlie looked down at the open file in her lap. The angry black letters on the back of the page stared back at her, frenzied and menacing. Charlie closed the folder and breathed easier knowing that Emma would be safe, at least until morning.

With that knowledge soothing her worries, she grabbed a slice of pizza from the box on the counter and settled in to relax for the night.

CHAPTER FIVE

The autumn wind rips at the windshield. Rattles the last of the leaves still clinging to the branches. Shakes some to the ground, where the crispy brown things scrape over the concrete.

Inside the car, all is still. Quiet. Motionless.

He stares at her windows. Dark. She isn't home yet. Isn't here.

What if she doesn't come home tonight?

He swallows. Smears sweaty palms at the thighs of his jeans. He needs to stay calm. Stay patient.

Headlights flicker. Draw his eyes to the next intersection.

Fresh hope bobs to the surface of his chest. Lifts his posture into a fully upright position as though sheer excitement has inflated his body into something bigger.

But the car races past. Doesn't turn down her street. The lights gone as quickly as they appeared.

A little breath pops as it exits his lips.

He should have gone through with it last night. Shouldn't have pussed out.

She would be his already. For now and forever, she would belong to him.

Possession.

He squirms in his seat. Fingers flexing on the steering wheel. *You could be mine.*

His gaze flicks to his reflection in the rearview. His own scared eyes staring back at him. Gaping pupils. Something powerless in the expression, like a beaten dog.

No. He shouldn't think that.

You will be mine.

Yes. Better. It is a question of *when* not *if.* And the answer is soon.

He thinks back to last night. Shadowy movies projecting themselves in his mind.

Such excitement as he thrust the screwdriver under the door. Breath hot against his lips, against his teeth. He jimmied the lock and let himself in with barely a sound.

He remembers the slight give of the tiles under his feet as he crossed the kitchen. The sharp scent of laundry detergent as he passed the utility area and moved into the hall. The way the light made slanted boxes on the wall where it gleamed in through the windows.

And then he remembers how it slipped away from him.

His retreat as he trailed back the way he came. Fled through the back door.

He should have stayed the course. Seen it through.

She would already be his. To have and to hold. For now and for always.

Headlights flare again at the intersection. This time the two beams wheel around the corner. Creep his way. The brightness makes him squint his eyes down to slits.

It's her. He knows even before the Jetta parks along the curb out front. Feels it.

His heart beats faster.

She jumps out. Jogs toward the house. Her feet kick up dew as she crosses the grass, little flecks of wet that glisten under the harsh glow of the streetlights. Spraying and glittering. She climbs the porch steps and disappears through the front door.

This time when he looks in the mirror, his eyes have gone hard. Wolfish. He can just make out the faintest smile in the folded skin surrounding them.

CHAPTER SIX

The sides of the Jetta's tires scraped against the curb as she parked, grating out an unpleasant sound, and Emma killed the engine a beat later. She sat a moment in the dark, taking a long slug of lukewarm cocoa from a styrofoam cup before she gathered the keys and stepped out of the car.

The night air enveloped her, a wet blanket with that bracing October chill to it. She hugged her hoodie against her chest and knifed her body into the wind, hustling for the apartment door.

Five minutes and this would all be over.

A yawn formed on her mouth as she climbed the steps of the front porch, reminding her of how tired she was. No sleep for the stalking victim, right? No *real* sleep, anyway. Instead, she'd spent the last several nights listening to the sounds of the house, drifting halfway under and then startling herself awake. She scrubbed the heel of her hand into her right eyelid as though the friction could remove the exhaustion.

She only needed to stay awake long enough to grab her toothbrush and a change of clothes before heading over to Cindy's for a night of real sleep, someplace safe. That was all she wanted.

She fumbled with the keys. Unlocked the door. Stepped inside.

A twinge of fear roiled up from her subconscious as she moved out of the streetlight's glow and into the gloomy interior of the living room. She chewed on her bottom lip, half expecting to find the place trashed. Some threat or warning spelled out in vandalism, in the destruction of her things, in the chaos of a wrecked living space.

The light switch clicked at her touch, and the bulbs overhead blinked on a fraction of a second later.

The living room stared back at her. Neat and tidy, as always. Untouched.

She let out a breath. OK. Nothing to worry about.

The apartment still felt like home, a feeling that resurfaced as soon as the lights came on. Even after all the time she'd spent cowering in fear here, feeling watched and tampered with and increasingly violated, it still felt like home. She was thankful for that.

She strode to her bedroom and started piling clothes into a duffel bag, mentally running through all the things she'd need. The clothes were the easiest thing to remember. She'd bring her buckwheat pillow, too. And then of course there was the toothbrush. She couldn't forget that. Should probably drop everything and grab it now, even.

Her stomach fluttered as she reached the dark bathroom and grabbed her toothbrush from the mug at the back of the vanity. But she felt better once she held it in her fingers—a solid object, angular plastic. God, she was being such a baby about all of this, wasn't she? Terrified of every shadow.

She couldn't help but feel like she was imposing on Cindy, slipping over to her place in the middle of the night like this to sleep on the couch. She knew it was a silly thought. Cindy had insisted, had even given her a key so she wouldn't need to wake anyone when she got there.

She got back to the bag and put the toothbrush inside. Almost done now.

She was so busy packing, she didn't notice the face hovering outside her bedroom window.

CHAPTER SEVEN

As soon as the door closes behind her, he's out of the car. Moving toward the house.

His footsteps sound catlike on the asphalt. Light patters. He hears the grit of dirt pressing into the textured surface of the street, a tiny sound even in the quiet.

He blends in with the shadows alongside the house. One more dark blot among a mess of them. Keeping low. Keeping his movements smooth.

At the back corner of the building, he nestles himself among the shrubs. Crouches to his knees as he reaches the area outside her bedroom. Ducks in his usual spot to watch her through the window.

His heart punches at the walls of his chest. Sweat weeps down from his hairline, and giddy little tremors twitch at his lips. Life courses all through him as it always does when he watches her. Awake with it. Thrumming with it.

The light leaps on in the room as he knew it would. The fixture on the ceiling quite visible from his kneeling vantage point. A dome of frosted glass spilling its glow in all directions.

He lifts himself to peer over the precipice. To drink her in. He blinks hard. Feels his eyes go wider.

Her back fills the pane of glass like it's a TV screen, just like it did last night. She leans over the foot of her mattress. Working at something.

When she turns and dips a hand in her dresser drawer, he sees what's happening. The socks in her hand enter the open mouth of the duffel bag resting on the bed.

She's packing. Seems in a hurry about it.

She moves to the doorway. Vanishes into the hallway. Reappears moments later with her toothbrush in her hand. A plastic cap covers the head of the brush like it's wearing a helmet.

This, too, disappears into the zippered lips of the duffel bag.

His throat constricts. Rejects the saliva as he attempts to swallow.

She's bailing out. Leaving him.

He doesn't think.

He moves for the back door. No time to hesitate now.

Tonight is the night.

CHAPTER EIGHT

With the packing complete, Emma zipped up the bag, velcroed the two straps together, and hefted the thing onto her shoulder. Part of her exhausted mind had expected it to be heavy and was pleased to find that it wasn't.

OK. All done here. She double-checked her pocket for Cindy's key. It was still there.

Time to get some damn sleep. She moved for the door.

Something thudded and startled her, a solid sound reverberating from the back of the house. She stopped a couple paces shy of the hallway. Froze mid-step with one foot on the threshold.

A tingle crept up her spine in slow motion. Goosebumps dotted her upper back, which she had hunched instinctively at the violent thump, some involuntary wince lifting her shoulders.

She waited. Listened. Breath held. Lips pinched between her teeth. Eyes darting everywhere.

A vast hollowness opened in her belly. She anticipated the crash of a broken window or the groan of the door hinges as it drifted open. Something. Anything.

Instead the silence stretched out. Emptiness. Nothing but the faint buzz of the light bulbs burning overhead.

She was imagining things. Her warped mind hearing threats in every crack and crunch of the house settling. Anxiety and exhaustion distorting her perception.

She took a breath, the wind dry and cold in her throat. Relaxed her shoulders.

The thud came again, louder, followed by the familiar whoosh of her back door sliding open.

Her heart thundered.

She dropped the duffel bag and hurried out into the hall. Turned to her left, looking through the kitchen into the gloom beyond.

The dark silhouette. Motionless. Broad shoulders filling the open doorway. She could just make out the glinting specks of his eyes in the silvery moonlight, cold and black.

She moaned as their eyes locked. The whisper of a scream mewling from the hollow of her throat. Icy tendrils coiled inside, froze her body to the spot.

The figure rushed for her.

CHAPTER NINE

Electricity surges into his hands as he wraps them around her shoulders. Current twitching and spitting under his skin.

So long he has waited for this moment. Touching her. Holding her. Never letting her go.

He shakes her. Watches her head flop around her limp neck. Eyes so wide, so wet. Lips peeling back in a grimace to reveal rows of glistening teeth that glow almost violet in the half-light of the hallway.

He smells the stale beer stink on her from the bar. It clings to her clothes.

But the odor of her body persists beneath the Budweiser stench. The lavender scent of her deodorant cannot disguise the sharp tang of her perspiration. He can smell the oil of her scalp, earthy and pungent. He has smelled it many times while alone in her apartment, wafting upward from the beanie she wears on the coldest nights.

He lifts her up on her tippy toes. Shakes her again.

Pins and needles spread into his wrists, prickle in the meat of his forearms. Power. Raw power gushing out of her and into him. Taken. Transmitted by touch.

His breath shudders.

An evil smile splits the bottom half of his face.

He shakes her a third time. Watches those exposed teeth as her head flops around again.

She feels bony. Fragile beneath her hoodie. Birdlike and small.

She makes no move to fight back. She just submits. Surrenders to what he wants. What he needs.

Gone floppy in his arms, her body is clay for him to mold as he wishes.

And it makes sense. It makes perfect sense to him. This is the only way it could have been. The only way. Her total submission is the only way.

Her elbow appears out of nowhere. Smashing him in the nose like a hammer.

Stars explode inside his skull. Bright motes bursting across his field of vision.

He staggers backward. Releases her. Cups his hands against his battered face.

Blood jets down from his nostrils. Sluices over his lips.

And water flushes his eyes. Blurs the world around him.

He falls back into the wall behind him like a boxer on the ropes.

Pictures go crashing down around them. Plucked from the wall. Glass shattering to the hallway floor.

His hands flail for her. Find her shoulders again. He grips her so hard he can feel his nails dig into her skin even through her sweatshirt.

She resists. Plants her feet wide. Tries to wriggle out of his grasp.

They grapple in the narrow hallway. Glass crunching underfoot.

He bulls forward. Presses his torso into hers. Backs her against the opposite wall. Crushes his bodyweight into her and drives his legs to pin her there, to keep her there.

His right hand lets go long enough to swing a fist at her. A hook headed for her jaw.

But she bobs out of the way.

And his fist sinks into the drywall. Punches a neat hole in it. The wall seeming to swallow his hand.

He teeters again. Legs going wobbly.

He jerks his arm. Wrenches his balled hand free of the drywall.

Just as his fist comes free, the heel of her hand catches him under the chin. Pushes his head up and back and into the wall.

Her hand tightens under his chin. Cinches around his throat. Constricts his breath.

He thrashes. Rips free of her grip and bucks his hips.

But another solid forearm to the face knocks him right back. Bounces the back of his head and then the rest of him off the wall again.

Dark again. Stars again. Dizziness spiraling where his thoughts should be.

Instinct takes over and he lunges after her.

His chest collides with her side. Sends her into the console table, which topples over, spilling knickknacks everywhere.

A house plant plunges to the floor. Potting soil flung like confetti.

A vase goes down. Shatters. Shards skittering over the wooden planks.

A dim night light winks out as debris rains down on it.

He belly-smacks the floor. Gravity pulling him down with a savage jerk.

He slams his chin on the floorboards. Bites his tongue. Tastes his own blood as it floods his mouth.

He skids among the fallen soil and bits of crockery. But he never takes his eyes off *her*.

Can't let her get away. No matter what.

She stumbles, the impact of his shoulder ramming her side knocking her pretty good, but she regains her balance. Darts away.

He struggles to get his hands and knees under his bulk. Limbs scrambling over broken bits to push himself up. Fingers sliding around in a wet puddle where blood has leaked from his head. But it's no use.

She's impossibly fast. A blur.

She zips down the hall. Across the kitchen. Disappears through that open door into the blackness beyond.

CHAPTER TEN

Emma sprinted across the backyard. Found the parted place in the hedges and turned sideways to slip through the gap, moving onto the neighbor's property.

She picked her feet up higher as she moved into the open. Speed building. Dew kicking around again.

Her eyes locked on the back door of the house before her. Some distant part of her noted that no lights were on, that the house was utterly dark, utterly still, but that was to be expected. It was late. Two thirty in the morning. Maybe later.

She leaped up the three concrete steps of the back stoop, and she yelled, a shrill voice catapulting out of her, its pitch lurching and strange from the adrenaline. In no way did it sound like her voice.

"Help!"

She pummeled on the screen door with both fists. Metallic bangs reverberated in the silent night, pounding out a panicked rhythm, and the door rattled in the frame, squawking and tapping out of time with the beat.

"Please! Someone help me!"

She threw open the screen door and pounded on the wooden door beyond it. Beat at it with her fist, her rhythm slowing as the force of each blow increased.

THUMP.

THUMP.

THUMP.

She stopped a second to listen. Waiting for that damn light to come on inside the house. Waiting for the curtains to part.

Nothing.

She sucked in a breath and held it. Eyelashes flitting. Tears threatening to spill from the corners.

Could this really be happening to me?

Another eight heartbeats raced past. No one came.

Everyone was asleep. No one would get out here in time. No one. Even if someone called the cops, it'd be too slow to matter.

She needed to move. Now.

Noise behind her.

She swung her head around to see him crashing through the bushes between the houses. Headed right for her.

She ran.

CHAPTER ELEVEN

He sees her. Standing on the narrow concrete stoop behind the house next door, her body made grayscale like a pixelated picture in a newspaper.

She turns. Looks at him.

Even in black and white she is beautiful. The dainty elfin nose. The milky skin glowing where sweat slicks her cheeks and forehead and top lip. The shape of her petite body only just discernible in silhouette. Fragile. Like if he were to grip her too hard he might crack her in half.

Their eyes connect.

Her mouth opens. The shock of seeing him dropping her jaw.

And he loves it. Loves scaring her. Having this power over her. Mattering to her. It's the first step toward the life they'll spend together.

Before all this, she never would have noticed him. Never ever.

But now he has her full attention. In this moment, he is the only thing that matters to her. She has eyes for no one else.

And then she's gone. Darting away again, always just out of reach. All those sharp details soften as soon as she's in motion.

She bounds down the steps and hurtles into the next yard. Picking up speed with every step.

He gives chase. Smears a wrist at his bloody nose and lip. Tries to lock his eyes on the blur, but it keeps moving, keeps shifting.

She screams, and he cringes.

"Help! He's trying to kill me!"

This voice rasps out of her. Harsh and shrill and full of fright. And loud. Too loud.

He swallows, and his left ear pops. He needs to catch her. Quiet her. Before someone calls the police.

A chain-link fence takes shape in the dark ahead. Forms a barrier between them and the next yard. It's only about four feet tall, but maybe it'll slow her.

She maintains her speed until she's right against it. Then her hands latch onto the bar running along the top of it, and she hurdles it. Effortless. Graceful.

Shit.

She scampers onward. Her blur moving into the deeper dark again.

He approaches the fence. Goes to mimic her vault.

But his toe catches. He tips. His forward momentum falls away all at once. Gravity ripping him down.

He drops to the cold ground on the other side of the fence. Lands on his chest. Feels the wind *woof* out of his ribcage. Every muscle in his chest drawing taut as a wire.

He blinks. Water fills his eyes. Pink splotches blot his vision.

Can't.

Breathe.

His hands paw at the wet grass. Fingers curling and uncurling like claws.

It takes him a second to push himself up onto hands and knees.

He gets to his feet. Forces himself forward. Races after her again.

He scans everywhere. Eyes swiveling in his head like marbles. But he can't see her.

His stomach clenches. Fear and loathing and dread stirring within.

What if she gets away? What if she saw my face?

He whimpers. Just louder than a whisper.

Then he launches himself over a wooden fence. Plops down on the other side. He's almost certain he saw her scrabble over it as he writhed on the ground. Almost.

This yard is darker than the others. Enclosed by trees on three sides, most of them pines. Something feels off.

He stops. Listens.

Quiet.

Nothing.

No footfalls pattering in the distance. *Where the hell did she go?*

He creeps forward. Instinctively lowers himself into a crouch as he proceeds.

Cast-iron lawn decorations jut up from the ground, twisted black things like spindly trees. He stares past them, through them. Scans over the small vegetable garden swaddled in chicken wire, over the wood stacked along the fence, over a small shed with a padlock securing the door.

A doghouse in the far corner of the lot catches his eye. Hopefully Fido is inside his human house or deep asleep. He doesn't need to deal with a territorial Rottweiler just now.

And then instinct pulls his eyes back to the woodpile. The shadowy edge of the rectangular stack of split logs. That'd make a good hiding spot. Maybe she figured he'd race by. Leap the other side of the fence and keep moving.

A porch light clicks on a few houses down. A dark shape appears beyond the glass of one of the doors, a face shoving between curtains. The neck cranes to the left and then to the right.

He lowers himself further. Lets the fence line conceal him.

And for a second he thinks she must have gotten there. To the house up ahead. Banged on the door. Drawn someone out to help.

But no. There was no movement outside the window where the peering face pivoted to look out.

She has to be close. Hiding. Here. In this yard.

The porch light clicks off. Its glow snuffing to black.

He licks his lips again. Tastes the blood. Shuffles for the woodpile. Needs to be quick now.

Her tiny figure squats in the shadows. Back tucked against the stack of wood. Knees hugged into her chest.

She jerks up as if sensing his presence. Torso levering. Soles of her shoes toeing at the dirt.

He lurches for her. Curls his arms around her. Feels the warmth of her slight frame press against the knotted muscles in his abdomen and chest. She's more rigid than before, more tense than before. Not quite as soft.

She opens her mouth to scream.

Too late.

His fist crashes home above her right eye.

And then he feels her go slack in his arms.

CHAPTER TWELVE

Charlie lifted a stainless-steel travel mug to her lips and took a drink. The coffee was hot enough that she winced slightly as it hit her tongue.

The car bumped through a pothole, and the jostling motion caused some of the gear in the passenger seat to rattle and jangle. She glanced at the bag filled with her surveillance equipment, wondering if her collection of indoor nanny cams and motion-activated outdoor trail cams would be enough to cover most of Emma's house.

Charlie figured she'd put one outdoor camera near where she'd found the bottle caps and another pointed at Emma's bedroom window. That left one exterior camera, and she wasn't sure if she should point it at another location on the house or perhaps focus on the road. If Charlie tracked the traffic going by Emma's house, she might be able to identify the stalker that way.

Charlie checked the time as she pulled onto Emma's road. It was only a quarter after ten, and she worried that Emma might not be at the house yet since they'd agreed to meet at ten thirty. Not to mention that the poor girl had worked late.

But as she rounded the bend in the road, Charlie saw Emma's Jetta parked in front of the house. She pulled in behind it and shut off the engine, then gathered up her camera bag and climbed out, crossing the yard to Emma's front door.

Charlie knocked and waited. A US postal service truck chugged past on the street behind her, its engine loud and throaty.

Adjusting the bag of gear slung over her shoulder, Charlie rapped her knuckles against Emma's door a second time. And suddenly her gut clenched.

Something was wrong.

She held her breath, angling her head closer to the door to listen for sounds coming from inside. A muffled, "Just a minute!" or footsteps approaching the door. But all she heard was the chittering of a squirrel in the oak tree across the way and the distant rumble of the postal truck as it continued on its route further down the road.

Charlie slid over to the window next to the front door and cupped her hands to the glass, trying to peer through it. The curtains were drawn, gauzy fabric blocking her view.

She dropped her bag on the front stoop and went around to Emma's bedroom window. It looked the same as it had the previous evening, and there was no sign of Emma.

As she skirted the back corner of the house, her eyes snapped to the sliding door.

It stood open like the slack mouth of a corpse.

Charlie hurried to the door, a voice in the back of her mind saying it could be nothing, that maybe Emma left the door open sometimes to get some fresh air. But she knew in her gut that something had happened. Something bad.

At the door, Charlie paused.

She called out, straining to hear over the sound of her own heartbeat thudding like a kick drum in her ears.

"Hello?"

Please answer, Charlie thought. *Please be OK.*

Silence blared inside the house. The stillness made Charlie's skin pucker on the backs of her arms.

She nudged the door open a few inches wider with her foot and then hovered there on the threshold, not wanting to enter but knowing she had to. Her gut cinched itself tighter, turned to a full-on gnawing dread, twisting and flexing.

Charlie forced herself to take that first step into the house, one foot coming down on the tile floor and then the other.

"Emma?"

Her voice sounded so normal. Impassive and almost casual, without a hint of the anxiety that felt like it was trying to claw its way out of her stomach.

The blinds in the kitchen were closed, casting the room in shadow. Charlie blinked as her eyes adjusted to the sudden shift from bright sunlight.

It was a small but tidy space, smelling faintly of lemon dish soap. Nothing out of order.

Her eyes moved beyond the kitchen to the hallway.

Broken glass flecked the floor, glittering where the light caught on the points of each shard. Clusters of potting soil dotted the places surrounding the glass, and then she spotted the toppled plant. The overturned table. The framed photos that had fallen from the wall and shattered.

The hole in the drywall caught Charlie's eye next. She held her balled fist next to the rough cavity. It was just about the right size.

She got out her phone and dialed Emma's number. The line rang as she went from room to room. Living room first, then down the hall to the bathroom. And lastly, the bedroom, which was just as empty as when she'd peeked through the window minutes ago, though a duffel bag sat on the floor.

When Charlie got Emma's voicemail, she hung up and hurried back down the hall.

And that was when she noticed it. A dark pool shimmering among the debris in the hall. Round, but slightly irregular.

Blood.

CHAPTER THIRTEEN

For the next several hours, Charlie milled around the back of Emma's property, watching the police and crime scene techs work the scene.

They started at the sliding door, the likely entry point for the attack, dusting the edges of the frame for prints. After that, they moved inside, and Charlie could see the camera flashes light up the space in bright blue-white bursts as they photographed the tacky puddle of blood on the floor, the overturned table, the broken picture frames.

A detective came over and took an official statement, and Charlie directed him to the place in the woods where she'd found the bottle caps, the trampled grass near Emma's bedroom window, the area at the front of the house where the dirt was disturbed by layers of footprints.

Charlie followed the movements of the men and women, frustrated at how slow the process was. She knew it was purposful, that each piece of evidence had to be painstakingly photographed, swabbed, bagged, labeled, and logged so that the integrity of the scene was preserved. And while Charlie appreciated the concept of the chain of custody, in the meantime, Emma could be anywhere. Hurt. Scared. Fighting for her life.

Her eyes strayed to the line of trees at the back of the house where the forest began and wondered if Emma was out there somewhere, even now.

A hand clasped Charlie's shoulder, and she jumped.

"Whoa there," Zoe said. "Didn't mean to startle you like that."

Deputy Zoe Wyatt was one of Charlie's oldest and closest friends, and she was the first person Charlie had called upon finding the blood in Emma's apartment.

"Any news?" Charlie asked.

"Talked to the folks over at the Laughing Raven and managed to work out who Emma was staying with last night. Or maybe I should say was *supposed* to stay with last night." Zoe glanced down at her phone. "Cindy Agostino. Another gal that works at the bar. She said Emma had needed to grab some things from home before heading to the Agostino girl's house to sleep."

"I told her not to come back here," Charlie said, closing her eyes. "I thought she understood how dangerous it would be to come here alone."

Zoe hooked her thumbs around her gun belt.

"Probably figured she was only going to be in and out." Zoe rocked back and forth on her heels for a few seconds. "Anyway, we found evidence that there was somewhat of a chase, if you want to take a look."

"Show me," Charlie said.

She followed Zoe to the hedges along one side of the backyard, where still more law enforcement personnel swarmed.

Zoe gestured at where two crime scene techs huddled near a gap in the bushes.

"The bushes here have been disturbed," Zoe said. "And there were some fibers stuck to the branches."

They crunched over the gravel of the driveway and took the long way into the neighbor's yard so as not to disturb the scene. A chain-link fence bordered this side of the property.

"We found a few drops of blood on this fence here and a smear on that wooden one over yonder."

Charlie craned her neck to look back the way they'd come.

"He chased her all the way down here?"

Zoe nodded.

"We think she was trying to call out for help, maybe get to one of these back doors."

They marched on, and Zoe lifted her arm and pointed to the yard beyond the wood fence. Cameras popped as more techs photographed a woodpile in the far corner.

"There's a bit more blood by the woodpile. Not a lot, but it's obvious there was a struggle there."

Charlie glanced around at the houses. Two split-levels and a small log-cabin-style home with an American flag flapping in the wind. The chase had taken place in their backyards. Why hadn't anyone helped her?

"And no one heard anything?" Charlie asked.

"Actually, there was a call logged down at dispatch at about two forty-five in the morning. The people in that house reported hearing a woman screaming and yelling on the street."

"And?"

"When the deputy arrived at approximately three, all was quiet. He figured it was probably just some kids screwing around. You know, some early Devil's Night activity and whatnot." Zoe shrugged. "Anyway, he sat out here for about half an hour, just in case the hooligans decided to come back, but there was nothing to report. He didn't see so much as a porch light come on."

Allie had been quiet for some time, but now she spoke up.

"Funny how when Emma went to the cops in the first place, they told her there was nothing they could do." Her tone was pointed and full of bitterness. "And then once this guy actually does enough to get the cops called out, they're too late. Salem Island's finest."

Charlie said nothing. She could empathize with Allie's point of view, but she wasn't sure if playing the blame game was the best use of her energy. The damage had been done. What mattered now was finding Emma.

When they turned around and headed back toward the duplex, Charlie spied Roy, Emma's landlord, talking with one of the detectives on the scene.

"Well how long is this all gonna take?" Roy demanded, arms waving in the air. "Because I need to get in the unit and assess the damage to my property. Speaking of which, I see you guys dusting that black powder all over the place, and you best hope that gets wiped up good and proper. I'll be damned if I foot the bill for cleaning up this mess."

"When did her landlord show up?" Charlie asked.

"Oh, he pulled up maybe twenty minutes ago," Zoe said. "Ran right past the line of tape we got strung up out there. Demanded to know what the hell we're doing on his property."

Charlie crossed her arms.

"There's only a wall between her unit and his. All that broken glass. The hole in the wall… He must have heard something." She frowned over at her friend. "Was he here last night?"

Zoe shook her head.

"Works overnight at Meijer, part of the stocking crew. He was on shift from eight last night to four this morning."

"Then what?" Charlie asked.

"He was, quote, 'At the home of a special lady friend, if you know what I mean, and I think you do.'"

Charlie rolled her eyes.

"But hey, we do have some good news," Zoe said.

"What is it?"

"Did you know that Emma is diabetic?"

"No."

"Well, we talked to her doctor, who said that Emma could be experiencing either high or low blood sugar, which could make her weak and disoriented," Zoe said.

"Holy hell, Zoe." Charlie's eyes were wide. "That's the *good* news?"

"It could explain why we haven't heard from her, is all. We're thinking that if she got spooked and ran out into the woods, then got dizzy and confused, she might be lost out there."

Charlie made a sound that was half sigh, half grunt.

"What about her phone?" she asked. "I know you said the sheriff already talked with the phone company, and her phone has GPS location tracking disabled, but there are other ways to track a phone. Wifi, cell tower triangulation… they're not as precise, but it's possible."

"We're working on it," Zoe said.

Dragging a hand down the side of her face, Charlie took in the scene again from the street. The cop cars and the tape and the bustling techs with their cameras and tweezers and evidence baggies and the little yellow markers pointing out a spatter of blood here and a disturbance in the shrubbery there.

Categorizing. Taking inventory. But none of it told them what they really needed to know: what happened to Emma?

Charlie ground her teeth together, knowing that every second they wasted lowered their chances of finding her.

Perhaps sensing her thoughts, Zoe reached out and squeezed Charlie's shoulder.

"Don't worry. We'll find her."

Charlie wanted to say, *That's what everyone said about Allie, and look how that turned out.*

Instead she kept her mouth shut and prayed that Zoe was right.

CHAPTER FOURTEEN

When the police released the scene later that day, Emma's landlord was the first inside. Charlie followed him in.

"Do you mind if I look around?"

"As long as you don't add to the mess," he said, a scowl on his face. "Just look at this. There's a hole in the sheetrock. Broken glass and frickin' soil everywhere. This'll take forever to clean up."

Charlie clenched her fists, tempted to pointedly remind him that a girl was missing and perhaps his priorities were a bit off. But technically she was on Roy's property, and it would be stupid to get herself kicked out before she had a chance to look around.

Roy suddenly froze.

"Jesus H. Is that blood?" He stomped over to the dark spot on the wood and gaped at it for a full two seconds before he spoke again. "That's great. Just had these damn floors refinished, too."

That was it. Charlie couldn't take it anymore.

"You know that could be Emma's blood, right?" she snapped.

Roy looked over at her. Squinted.

"Well, I figured as much. What's your point?"

"She could be out there somewhere, bleeding. Right now."

"Not like there's anything I can do about it." He shrugged. "If you'll excuse me, I have to go call my insurance company, see if this is covered or not."

He brushed past her, and Charlie considered saying more, but what was the point? His apathy was the least of her problems.

Charlie was glad when he was gone, but after a few seconds, the silence of the empty apartment began to unnerve her. All morning the place had been bustling with the various levels of law enforcement. Practically buzzing like a hive of bees. Now, alone in Emma's home, the quiet was almost oppressive.

Charlie flipped on a light, thinking that making it a little brighter might help. The effect was microscopic at best.

Stepping around the broken glass in the hallway, she headed for the most personal space here: Emma's bedroom.

Pale lilac paint coated the walls, glossy and smooth, and the bedspread was a patchwork of grays and purples. Fred, Emma's one-eyed stuffed rabbit, sat propped against the pillows. A few pieces of framed art suggested that Emma's favorite animal was the elephant.

In the bedroom closet, Charlie discovered a dozen or so small boxes on a shelf. They were all under ten inches in height and width, and each one held an incredibly detailed scene in miniature. A tiny bookstore with books smaller than Charlie's thumbnail. A minuscule greenhouse with microscopic plants. A coffee shop with itty-bitty stacks of cups and a teensy espresso machine.

A bundle of copper wire ran from each box to a switch at the side of the shelf. Charlie pressed the switch and each scene came to life with real lights. A crystal chandelier in the box made up to look like a Parisian bakery. Gas lamps lining the street of a long narrow box designed to look like a nineteenth-century alleyway, complete with cobblestones and hand-lettered signs over the shops.

On the floor of the closet Charlie found a plastic storage tub filled with craft supplies: paints, rulers, craft knives, tweezers, glue. And that was when she realized that Emma had made the miniatures herself.

Charlie's eyebrows lifted as she thought about the time it would have taken to make these. The hours Emma must have spent huddled over these creations, positioning each piece just so. Holding things in place while glue cured and paint dried.

"Good God. I could tell she was a nerd the second I laid eyes on her, but this is ridiculous," Allie said.

"Don't be mean." Charlie stepped closer to admire the detail in each one of the scenes. "Besides, I think it's kind of cool."

Allie let out a belly laugh.

"No surprise there. You're as dorky as they come, Chuck." There was a thoughtful pause. "Actually, you're kind of lucky I disappeared. Being a private detective is probably just about maxing out your potential coolness. If I was still kicking around, you would have come up with something even nerdier than this to do with your life."

There was a shoe box next to Emma's tools, and Charlie lifted the lid to peek inside. It was another miniature, though this one was only half completed. Judging by the tiny bottles on the walls, Charlie thought it would be a Victorian apothecary.

Something twisted in her chest, and she felt the sting of oncoming tears in her sinuses.

"Dude. Get a grip," Allie said. "They're just miniatures."

"I know." Charlie wiped the corner of her eye. "But what if... what if she never gets to finish this one?"

Allie had nothing to say to that. No snarky response or sardonic witticism.

Charlie took a deep breath and gathered herself. She should keep searching, even if she wasn't sure what she was looking for. Emma hadn't struck Charlie as the type to be hiding some kind of dark secret, but there wasn't much else Charlie could think to do at the moment.

Searching under the bed turned up an old tin *Powerpuff Girls* lunchbox. Inside, Charlie found a dried rose, a necklace with a small gold heart pendant, a Polaroid photograph, and a stack of handwritten letters. Charlie pulled out the photo. It featured a man wearing a pair of novelty New Year's Eve glasses, holding up a bottle of champagne. He was young. A college kid by the look of him. Charlie unfolded one of the letters and quickly confirmed her suspicion that this was the ex-boyfriend Emma had mentioned. Tyler Nelson, the one who'd moved to California for school.

Despite Emma's insistence that he had a new girlfriend and thus couldn't possibly be hung up on her, Charlie knew it was always better to confirm with facts over gut feelings. She got out her phone and dialed Frank.

"You find your girl yet?" he asked.

"Not yet." Charlie picked up the dried rose and spun it between her finger and thumb. "I'm going through her apartment now, and I found a breakup box."

"Uh-huh," Frank said. "Five bucks says it was under the bed."

"It's always under the bed," Charlie said.

"No. Sometimes it's in the closet."

Charlie rolled her eyes.

"OK, smart guy. Cigar box or shoe box?"

"Mmmm… normally I'd say shoe box for a girl this age, but based on what you told me, she could be the type to hit up thrift shops or yard sales. I'm gonna go with cigar box."

Charlie made a buzzer sound.

"Neither. It was a metal lunch box."

Frank scoffed.

"That's cheating."

"In any case, the ex-boyfriend is supposed to be in California at school."

"And you want me to make sure he is where he says he is, as opposed to lingering in the bushes of our fair island town?"

"Exactly. His name is Tyler Nelson. He's in grad school at UCLA."

"I'm on it," Frank said. "I'll call you back when I've got something."

"Thanks."

Charlie hung up and the silence closed in on her once again.

One of the love notes from Tyler stood open on the floor in front of her, and she read the first line.

Emma, I want to sit with you and watch the sun set. I want to kiss you under the glow of a streetlight as snow tumbles down around us. I want...

Charlie blushed, feeling a sudden sense that she was invading Emma's privacy. Going through someone's personal belongings like this always made her cringe a little. These were things Emma had never intended anyone else to see. That was why they were hidden away in a box and shoved into the darkest corner beneath the bed.

She placed the items back in the lunch box as closely to how she'd found them as she could. If they found Emma, she wouldn't ever have to know Charlie had snooped into these places.

Charlie gave the rest of the bedroom a quick once-over. On top of the dresser, Emma had a small lamp, an elephant figurine draped with a few necklaces, and a large bowl-shaped pot planted with succulents and cacti. Neatly folded clothing and undergarments filled the drawers. A fantasy novel resided on the bedside table along with a pair of reading glasses.

In the bathroom, Charlie found a tube of prescription acne cream and a retainer box with a set of invisible braces. The feeling that she was prying returned full force.

Charlie was in the kitchen sifting through the cabinets and drawers when her phone rang. It was Frank.

"Tyler is a dead end," Frank said. "I used the special delivery ruse. Said he needed to be home to sign for something this evening with a photo ID. He said he'd be there and confirmed his address."

Charlie sighed.

"I figured. But I wanted to be sure."

"Sure is always better than a guess," Frank said. "Do you know what time it is?"

"Not really," Charlie said, glancing at the clock on Emma's stove but not really registering what she was seeing. "Why?"

"Because if you're anything like me—and I know you are—you've been going all morning without a break and probably don't realize it's well past lunchtime."

"Oh."

"I take it that means you haven't eaten."

"No, but I don't really want to leave." Charlie leaned over so she could rest her elbows on the counter. "I might find something if I keep looking."

"So I'll send Paige over with some grub," Frank said, as if he'd already known she'd refuse to stop working. "Any requests?"

"Not really. Whatever's easy."

There was a pause.

"How are you handling this?"

"I'm fine," Charlie said, shrugging even though he couldn't see the gesture.

"Because this kind of thing hits close to home for you. It can be tempting to think you can right the wrongs of the past with a case like this. And that's not really how it works."

"I know that. And I'm handling it fine," Charlie said, realizing too late that her tone was overly harsh.

After a moment's hesitation, Frank's voice came back, quieter than before.

"OK. Well, I'll let you get back to it."

They hung up, and a rising tide of guilt rolled over Charlie in a wave. She'd hurt Frank's feelings, she knew, and he'd only been trying to help. On top of that, he had a point. It was hard to keep the emotions surrounding Emma's disappearance separate from what had happened to Allie. The one inherently made her think of the other. Had her drawing comparisons. Everything always came back to Allie in some way or another.

Charlie let out a sigh, her shoulders slumping. She blinked a few times, staring down at that patch of blood on the floor.

But Emma wasn't Allie. And that meant there was still a chance to bring her home safely.

CHAPTER FIFTEEN

Charlie was still rifling through Emma's belongings when she heard the crunch of tires on gravel in the driveway. She moved to the living room window and saw Paige climbing out of her car with a bag from Dionysus, a local Greek restaurant that had the best subs in town.

Figuring she'd violated Emma's private space enough for the time being, Charlie pushed out through the door and met Paige outside.

They sat on the hood of Charlie's car and ate. When Frank had first mentioned sending over food, Charlie hadn't thought she'd have much of an appetite. But once she got a whiff of the toasted bread and melted swiss cheese and the tang of the Greek dressing, Charlie realized she was starving. Maybe part of it had to do with being out of the house. There was something about being inside with all of Emma's things—not to mention the lingering destruction of the attack that took place there—that had kept Charlie's stomach in a permanent state of queasiness. Outside, she had a chance to clear her mind a bit.

"Have you heard anything from the police?" Paige asked. "Any updates, I mean?"

Charlie shook her head.

"Zoe said she'd let me know when they had something solid to go on. They're trying to use cell tower data to narrow down the location of Emma's phone, but in a place like Salem Island, they might need to search an area of several square miles. It'd be like trying to find a needle in a haystack."

They ate in silence for a few moments, and the only sounds were the crunch of potato chips and the slurping of fountain drinks. When they'd finished eating and gathered up their trash into the bag their food had come in, Paige stared out at the woods crowding both sides of the road and shuddered.

"You OK?" Charlie asked.

"Yeah. It's just kind of unsettling, you know? The idea that someone could be watching you, and you might never know it." Her eyes scanned the forested terrain. "Especially in a spot like this. Even though there are more houses just down the way, it seems so isolated. Sitting here just now, it feels like we could be out in the middle of nowhere."

Charlie nodded.

It was the same thought she'd had the night before, and it was part of the reason she'd told Emma not to come back here. If only the girl had listened.

"And earlier this morning, I was looking at that drawing of Emma again, thinking about how there's this line between creepy and sweet. Like, someone obviously took such pains rendering Emma in that picture. Each freckle. Every eyelash. It looks just like her. And if it was her boyfriend who drew it, it'd be this sweet gesture, you know? But the fact that it's a stranger, leaving it in her car?" Paige shuddered. "That's just not right."

Charlie's bag buzzed, and she reached in to retrieve her phone. When she saw Zoe's name on the screen, she couldn't help but feel hopeful. Maybe they'd found Emma. Maybe she was OK, and all of this had been some sort of terrible misunderstanding.

Charlie bulldozed past any sort of formal greeting when she answered.

"Is it good news or bad?"

"Not sure yet," Zoe said. "But we found her phone."

CHAPTER SIXTEEN

Emma's phone had been discovered roughly five miles from her apartment, in an overgrown field alongside the Potawatomi Bay Nature Preserve, just a few hundred yards from the turnoff for the public beach. The phone was found nestled in a briar of wild raspberry bushes approximately fifty feet from the edge of Walleye Road. Most of the surrounding area was state land, over 300 acres of untouched, uninhabited forest and marshland bordering Lake St. Clair.

The Salem County Sheriff's Department had issued a call for volunteers willing to help search the area for any sign of Emma Jacobis, and already a few dozen people had arrived at the beach parking area. Nervous energy oozed from the group as they murmured among themselves and milled around awaiting instructions.

Even Charlie wasn't immune to it. She'd checked the time on her phone non-stop over the last twenty minutes, anxious for the search to begin. But Sheriff Brown had requested that people arrive by 4 p.m., and there were still a few minutes before the hour.

Beside her, Paige rocked from her heels to her toes, no doubt also feeling tendrils of anticipation slithering through her veins.

Charlie stared into the woods, trying to see through the tangle of branches and turning leaves, and she had a sudden sense of déjà vu. When Allie had gone missing, there'd been half a dozen searches like this. All of them fruitless. Charlie remembered thinking she knew Salem Island like the back of her hand before that. But once they'd started sifting through the more remote stretches of the island, she'd realized how much wilderness there was out here. How many places someone might be lost and never found.

A handful of additional cars carrying search volunteers wheeled into the parking lot in the final minutes before the clock struck four. At 4:05 p.m., Sheriff Brown stepped to the front of the fidgeting mob and signaled for quiet.

"If I could have everyone's attention for just a bit, we can get on with the task at hand. Firstly, I want to thank every one of you for coming out here today to help us search for this missing woman. Emma Jacobis was last seen yesterday leaving her place of work at approximately two in the morning. Given that she's only been missing for approximately fourteen hours, we have every reason to hope for the best, but Emma is a Type 1 diabetic, meaning she needs insulin or there could be dangerous, potentially life-threatening side effects. Complications relating to her illness could mean she's out here now, weak, dehydrated, and confused. The sooner we find Emma and get her medical attention, the better."

Sheriff Brown raised his arm and pointed at the forest that served as a natural border of one end of the parking lot.

"A few words about the area we'll be traversing this afternoon. Some of the terrain is rough, and the undergrowth in this particular stretch of wilderness is quite thick. It's not an easy hike. Everyone should be mindful of that. Also there's a lot of thorny stuff back here—wild roses, blackberries. Folks should exercise caution when encountering that type of growth, as it can be nasty. Now, the southwest corner of our search area is marshy. Very wet, lots of cattails. There's also a creek on the western edge. We're going to hold off searching there for now, but some of our groups will be adjacent to those areas. If you end up in the wetter parts of our search grid, please watch your step. We don't want anyone falling headlong into a swamp or what have you."

Charlie's gaze strayed from the sheriff as he spoke, peering again into the dense woodland and wondering if Emma was stranded somewhere in there, lost and afraid. As her eyes swiveled away from the woods and traveled from face to face in the crowd, she paused on a familiar figure.

It took a moment before Charlie realized the man she was looking at was Will Crawford, a lawyer in town and another old friend from her youth. He'd grown a beard since she'd last seen him. She almost hadn't recognized him.

She was still squinting at the coarse hair along his jaw when a burly man in a camo hunting hat shifted his position, effectively blocking Will from Charlie's view. She refocused her attention on Sheriff Brown.

"We have a helicopter coming in from the state police, who'll be able to give us eyes on some of the more hard-to-access points of our search grid. And the same dogs that helped locate Miss Jacobis' phone will continue aiding us in our search. The handlers have asked that I remind everyone that these are working animals, so please do not approach the dogs or attempt to pet them while the search is underway."

As if to emphasize this point, Sheriff Brown hiked up his gun belt and gave the crowd a hard look.

"If this is your first search, you'll want to be cognizant to not just have your eyes on the ground but your surrounding areas as well. Trees, bushes. Sometimes bits of fiber get tangled up in the thicket, so don't be fooled into thinking you'll only find something at ground level. What we're looking for is any sign of Emma Jacobis. Jewelry. Clothing. Et cetera. Anything that might give us an indication of where Emma was or in what direction she might have headed is of interest. Now, this close to a roadway and the beach, there's liable to be some manner of trash strewn up in there. Takeaway containers and drink cups from Mickey-D's and the like. Generally, we're not interested in random litter, but I trust you all to make the determination of what's trash and what ain't."

Someone toward the front of the huddle of volunteers spoke up.

"What should we do if we find something?"

The sheriff tugged at the corner of his salt-and-pepper mustache.

"That's a good question," he said, nodding. "If something looks suspect to you, I want you to give a holler. Which brings me to the next important point: what to do if you hear someone shouting that they found something. There's a tendency for everyone to come a-runnin' to see what the fuss is. To want to gather around the commotion. But what happens then is we have to start over with the fanning out and spacing ourselves properly, and in the meantime, the whole search grid is compromised from all the foot traffic trampling over hill and dale. So just stay put until the professionals among us can make a determination."

The sheriff swept a hand out to indicate the deputies and other first responders in attendance, each one wearing a neon-yellow vest.

"I'd like to direct your attention to these folks here in the ever-fashionable hi-vis vests. These are our group leaders. Judging by our numbers at the moment, I think we'll be in groups of five or six. Each group will be led by one of these fine individuals. They'll have a map and will set the pace for your group, and any questions you might have during the search can be directed to your group leader."

There was a loud clap as Sheriff Brown brought his palms together.

"Now if our volunteers will please form into a line here in front of Deputy Wyatt, she's going to take down your name and assign you to a particular area of the grid and tell you who your group leader is."

CHAPTER SEVENTEEN

A soft murmur of voices babbled as the tight crowd of people attempted to form themselves into a line. After a few moments of confused shuffling, they sorted themselves out. Charlie and Paige found themselves toward the head of the line and didn't have to wait long before reaching Zoe.

She grinned over the clipboard at them.

"One Charlotte Winters and Paige Naughton… Looks like you two somehow wound up in my group." Zoe winked and scribbled their names on her clipboard. "What a coincidence."

"Blatant favoritism," Charlie teased. "Mass corruption in the Salem County Sheriff's Department? Business as usual, I see."

"Hang tight, guys," Zoe said, smiling. "I'll be with you as soon as I'm done handing out the rest of the assignments."

Charlie nodded, stepping off to the side. She glanced back at the line snaking out from behind them and wondered if Will was back there somewhere. She was tempted to ask Zoe about it, ask if she'd talked to him lately, but then she stopped herself.

She and Will hadn't spoken in months. Why would she open that can of worms now?

"It's the beard," Allie said. "It's a scientific fact that beards almost always add an additional ten to twenty percent of extra hotness, and Will is no exception. In fact, the beard might have pushed him into the zone of physical attractiveness that rights all past wrongs."

Charlie rolled her eyes at that thought. It would take a lot more than looking good with a beard for her to forgive Will's past wrongs.

After everything that had happened, after what he'd done… she wasn't sure she could truly forgive him, no matter what she'd said at the time.

They'd gotten so close during the Kara Dawkins case, rekindled old feelings between them that they'd never acted on all those years before. But he'd violated her trust. Spied on her.

"Tit for tat," Allie said. "You falsely accused his cousin of murder, he installed spyware on your computer in an attempt to clear the guy's name. Even-steven."

The corners of Charlie's mouth turned down. It may have been that simple for Allie, but it wasn't for her. Will's transgression may have been in the name of justice for his client, but it didn't change the fact that he'd willfully and intentionally taken advantage of her.

She asked herself again: could she forgive him? She didn't know.

Charlie's eyes searched the crowd for his face, but the knot of people that had been pressed so close together during Sheriff Brown's speech was now unraveling. Some of the search groups had already entered the forest, heading for their assigned place on the grid. Will might very well have been one of them.

"Ms. Winters?" a voice called from behind her.

Charlie turned and saw a familiar face approaching, but it wasn't Will. He'd grown leaner than the last time she'd seen him, and his dark hair was longer and slicked back with some kind of oily goop.

Robbie Turner grinned when their eyes met.

"I thought that was you," he said.

Before Charlie could respond, Robbie had thrown his wiry arms around her, wrapping her in a bear hug.

"I bet you're surprised to see me," he said, releasing her but keeping an arm slung around her shoulder.

"Well… yeah," Charlie said.

At their last meeting, Robbie had held a knife to Charlie's throat. The fact that he'd moments later dropped the knife and started blubbering like a baby was worth noting, but Charlie wasn't sure when their relationship had progressed to the level where hugging was the greeting of choice.

More to the point, Robbie had been caught with a felony quantity of illicit drugs around the same time as the knife incident, and last Charlie heard, he was looking at a prison sentence of at least seven years.

"I thought you were in prison," Charlie said, not sure how to put it any less bluntly.

"Oh, I was. Served nine months of a two-year sentence."

"They only gave you two years?"

"Yeah, I got me a sweet plea deal, thanks to you." He pulled her closer and lowered his voice. "The DA offered plain old possession if I agreed to testify against Silas Demetrio. First I was like, 'Man, I ain't no snitch,' you know? But then I thought about it. Only a fool would take the fall for Demetrio. I mean, what's in it for me? So I was like, 'Hold up. I *am* a snitch.'"

"You were smart to take the deal," Charlie said.

The muscles along Robbie's jaw bunched, his face uncharacteristically solemn.

"Fuck yeah, I was."

"How long have you been out then?" Charlie asked.

Robbie twitched his shoulders into something like a shrug.

"Little over a month," he said. "Feels good to be back in the real world, I'll tell you what."

"And you're staying out of trouble, I hope?"

"Now, what kind of question is that, Ms. Winters?" Robbie let out a hissing laugh. "I've been on my best behavior since I got out."

Robbie's wild brown eyes flitted away and zeroed in on Paige. He ran a hand through his wet-looking hair and jutted his chin out.

"Who's this? You got a little sister you never told me about?"

"She's my assistant," Charlie said. "Paige, this is Robbie Turner."

"Well, hello there, Paige," he said.

The smile Robbie aimed in the girl's direction somehow straddled the line between flirtatious and predatory, a thought that made Charlie uneasy. A dozen disastrous scenarios flitted through her mind when she considered the idea of someone as innocent as Paige getting mixed up with someone as chaotic as Robbie.

"Yeah, you better break this up quick, sis," Allie said. "If Robbie were to get his claws into this supple young lamb, there'd be nothing left. Not even scraps for the vultures."

Charlie cleared her throat and angled herself in a way that cut off the direct sight line between the two.

"So what brings you out here?" Charlie asked. "Do you know Emma?"

Robbie shoved his hands into the pockets of his leather jacket.

"Why else would I be down here helping out in the search? You think I'm one of those weirdo ambulance chasers who listens to their police scanner and watches Court TV nonstop?" Robbie removed one hand and slapped her on the back. "Not judging, of course. I got an aunt who's like that."

Now Charlie was curious. Emma didn't strike her as the type to hang out with convicted felons.

"Do you know her well?"

"Sure. We used to have Thanksgiving at her house every year when I was a kid. She makes this pumpkin pie that's just..." He brought his fingers to his mouth and made a kissing sound.

Charlie frowned.

"Not your aunt. I'm asking how well you know Emma."

"Oh. Right." He chuckled. "We're not super tight or anything like that, but I see her around."

"Where?"

"The Laughing Raven. She tends bar up there."

"And you hang out there sometimes?"

"Try *all* the time. The Laughing Raven is *my* bar." Robbie put a hand to his chest. A moment later, he was squinting suspiciously at Charlie. "Hey, wait a minute. Are you interrogating me?"

"No," Charlie said, though she wasn't sure if that was completely true or not. "But I haven't really had a chance to talk to anyone who knows Emma. What's your impression of her?"

Robbie lifted his eyebrows, no longer dubious.

"She's hilarious. Sort of quiet and awkward. And super easy to embarrass. If you say something dirty in front of her, she turns beet-red. She's like your buddy's emo little sister, except, you know… hot."

"Does she get a lot of attention at the Laughing Raven? From guys, I mean."

Robbie shrugged.

"I'm sure she gets some, but there are a couple girls that work there that probably get more, given their, uh… natural talents?" Robbie pantomimed a pair of large breasts in front of his chest.

Charlie sighed and rolled her eyes. She was about to sarcastically thank him for offering such a helpful bit of insight, but he pivoted away from her and held up a hand, signaling a cluster of people standing at the edge of the treeline.

"Well, shit. My group is heading out, so I gotta jet," he said. "But it was good catching up. We should hang out sometime."

"Definitely," Charlie said, though she didn't think he caught the sarcasm.

She wondered if he even remembered the knife incident. Maybe that was how someone like Robbie Turner made friends, for all she knew.

Her gaze followed his slim form as he jogged over to join his search party. Was he as unaffected by his time in prison as he'd suggested or was it an act? She had a sudden flash of him sitting in the police interrogation room, eyes still moist from his tears.

She remembered thinking he'd looked like a little boy then. Chin quivering. Nose running. She had a hard time reconciling that image with the knowledge that he'd recently done a nine-month stint in prison.

As his group moved into the trees, Charlie watched him pause and light a cigarette. He cupped his hands to his face and took a puff, and for just a moment, before he turned and disappeared into the forest, he stared out at the water in the distance with an absolutely dead look in his eyes.

CHAPTER EIGHTEEN

The crowd thinned as most of the volunteers followed their leaders into the woods to begin searching. Charlie and Paige hung back, waiting for Zoe to complete her task, and soon there were only a dozen or so people left in the parking lot.

The two older women who would round out their group introduced themselves as Pat and Karen. They both wore tracksuits and had their hair dyed the same unnatural shade of carrot-orange.

Eavesdropping on their conversation, Charlie formed an impression that they were the type of tabloid addicts that Robbie had described earlier.

"You see this sort of thing on TV, but you never really think you'll get to be so up close to it in real life," Pat said. "I keep getting goosebumps!"

Karen nodded in agreement.

"And just imagine if we were to actually find something? I bet we'd get interviewed on the news."

Pat reached out a hand and grasped Karen's arm.

"Oh my Lord, I never even considered that! You know, I keep thinking that if only Nancy Grace was still on… She made such a difference in cases like these. Getting them the attention they needed."

"You didn't hear? She's got a show on another channel now," Karen said. "I knew she'd be back. No one has even half the poise and charisma Nancy has. No one."

"We should find a way to get in contact with her. Make it go viral. I saw some of this girl's pictures on Instagram. She's very pretty."

"What pictures?" Karen asked. "I didn't see any pictures."

Pat pulled a phone from her pocket and tapped at the screen.

"All the kids these days have their stuff just free for all to see on the internet," she said with a disapproving shake of the head.

The two women bent over the screen.

"You're right. She *is* pretty," Karen said. "Exactly the kind of girl Nancy would take an interest in."

"That's not all," Pat muttered, lips pursed.

"What do you mean?"

Raising her eyebrows, Pat sighed.

"I mean that it's the pretty ones who always end up dead." Pat swiveled around, and Charlie suddenly found herself the object of her attention. "But of course you know all about *that*."

Charlie was startled by the abrupt manner in which she'd been dragged into the conversation, but a few of the cases she'd worked had received some media attention, especially locally. She supposed she shouldn't be surprised they recognized her.

Before Charlie could respond, Pat amended her earlier statement.

"Because of what happened to your sister."

"Yes. That must have been awful," Karen said, but the expression on her face didn't match the words. Her eyes were wide and hungry. Excited.

Both women edged a little closer to her. Leaning in. Holding their breath in anticipation.

Charlie's mind went blank. She had no idea what to say. She'd had uncomfortable moments before relating to Allie's disappearance, but no one had ever been quite so blunt. Or so eager to pry.

"What?" was the only thing she could manage to force out.

Zoe elbowed her way into the huddle then.

"I think you must have Charlie here confused with someone else," she said.

"Well… but…" Pat sputtered. "You said your last name was Winters."

Karen nodded emphatically.

"Surely that would make Allison Winters your sister?"

"Oh, I see the confusion," Zoe said. "See, Charlie's last name is actually *Winterz*. With a z."

Pat's mouth hung slightly ajar.

"But…"

"Don't worry about it. She gets it all the time," Zoe said, nudging Charlie's arm. "Isn't that right, Charlie?"

"Oh yeah." Charlie bit down on her cheek to keep from smiling. "All the time."

The two women exchanged a befuddled look, but neither one apparently had the gumption to confront a uniformed deputy.

Zoe pointed to the narrow path leading from the edge of the beach parking lot to the woods.

"Why don't you ladies lead the way? We're heading right up that footpath there." When Pat and Karen were far enough ahead to be out of earshot, Zoe grinned over at Charlie. "That shut 'em up, huh?"

Charlie chuckled.

"'Winterz with a z.' I kinda like that. You think Frank would change the sign on the office?"

"Can't hurt to ask."

Leaves crunched underfoot as they made their way into the forest proper. Zoe took point, leading the group deeper into the woods. The Nancy Grace Fan Club veered off to her right, and Paige stayed close to Charlie as they picked through the foliage, staying on Zoe's left.

The trace of a smile Charlie had retained since talking with Zoe faded from her face. Being under the gloom of the canopy and seeing the various search teams in the distance reminded her of the task at hand: finding Emma.

Despite what the two busybodies in their group had hinted at, she was hopeful that Emma was still out here, alive.

Everyone fell quiet for a bit, trudging through stalks and stems. Somewhere on the island, someone was burning leaves. Charlie could detect just a hint of the acrid, smoky scent in the air, and it reminded her of Halloween as a child.

Eventually Zoe veered off the beaten path and led them deeper into the wilderness.

The path was narrow and overgrown in places. They had to hold branches out of the way and duck under low-growing tree limbs. Charlie glanced down and noticed her ankles were covered in the seedpods she and Allie had always called hitchhikers for the way their Velcro-like surface clung to fabric and hair.

The faint trace of wood smoke faded, and an earthy fragrance took its place. A wet, peaty smell like damp soil, as if the dirt here could never quite get dry.

At one end of a natural clearing, Zoe finally halted.

"OK. This is the southwest edge of our search zone." Zoe spread her arms wide. "We're gonna fan out in a line about arm's-length from one another, and then we'll walk from this side of the clearing all the way down and over that ridge at the other end. When we reach the edge of our search area, we'll stop, shuffle a little further down, and then start the process again, heading back to this side here. Kind of a big zigzag, if you will. And we'll keep doing that until we've completed our entire section of the grid or until it gets dark, whichever happens first. Makes sense?"

The rest of them nodded, and Zoe pointed at the ground.

"I see some decent walking sticks lying around here. If you want to pick one up, it can be a handy tool for poking into brush piles and bushes and whatnot. It's not mandatory, but it beats bending down every time you think maybe you spotted something."

Charlie joined the other women in arming herself with a suitable stick, and then they spread out as Zoe had directed.

Zoe was positioned in the middle, the best vantage point for keeping track of everyone and setting the pace. Charlie took the far-right end, with Paige sandwiched between herself and Zoe.

And they began. Zoe set a measured pace, perhaps one step per second. Long enough to hopefully scan one scrap of the forest floor before moving on to the next.

The trees here had shed most of their leaves already, their branches gray and lifeless. But there were still splotches of fading green here and there. A fern and a patch of dead nettles that hadn't been hit by any of the early frosts yet. Soon, winter would come and kill all of it, turn it brown, and then cover it over with snow.

The dry autumn leaves swished and hissed as they were whisked aside by feet and sticks. Charlie jabbed at a snarl of wild roses, checking the thorns for anything that might have gotten caught—a scrap of clothing, stray hairs. But there was nothing.

"I can't imagine being lost out here," Paige commented from a few yards over. "I know we're only a mile at most from the nearest road, but it feels like it could be ten miles or twenty."

"I know," Charlie said. "And if Emma came out here in the dark, it'd be even more disorienting."

"Gosh, I hadn't even thought about that."

A pair of crows flew overhead, calling to one another or perhaps protesting the sudden invasion of their forest. The cawing sounded like they were laughing, and Charlie shivered.

"Have you ever been in the woods at night without a light?" she asked.

"I went camping a few times as a kid," Paige said. "But we always had flashlights and lanterns."

"It's spooky. And dark," Charlie said, thinking about the time Allie swore she knew a shortcut through the woods near Uncle Frank's house. "If the moon isn't out, it's almost pitch-black. You can't see your hand in front of your face. You're tripping and stumbling along, feeling plants and branches around you. But the dark itself is the worst part. It feels like there's no end to it."

Paige scrunched her face into a scowl.

"I have a terrible sense of direction, so I'd probably end up walking in circles."

They reached the far end of the clearing and proceeded up a slight incline into the trees. Charlie's feet kept slipping as she trudged up the slope. Gouging muddy slashes into the ground here and there. She glanced about, wondering if Emma might have left a trail somewhere, a dotted line in the mud that would lead straight to her. If only it could be so easy.

Another hundred yards or so into the trees, there was a shrill whistle. Zoe stopped and waved her arms.

"Alright, this is the edge of our zone of the grid. Everyone feeling OK?"

There were nods all around. Pat and Karen appeared to be a bit out of breath after the hike up the small hill, and the hair at Karen's temples was glued to her head with sweat.

Charlie felt a slight sense of disappointment at not finding any sign of Emma yet. She tried to tell herself that was a good thing, but was it?

"Good," Zoe said. "We're all going to slide down that-away to get into our new position before we sweep back to the other side. Charlie, take about twenty paces that way, if you don't mind. I'll tell you when to stop."

As Charlie pushed on, weaving through the trees, Zoe jogged forward to catch up with her.

"It seems the nosy twins struggled with that hill a little," she said, keeping her voice low. "As much as I'd love to make them suffer a bit, we should probably take a quick break before we start up again."

"Sounds good to me."

When Zoe brought them to a halt again, she jabbed her stick in the ground.

"Let's pause here for just a minute, ladies," Zoe said. "This is a marathon, not a sprint. So catch your breath. Hydrate. Answer nature's call if you need to."

Looking relieved, Pat and Karen drifted over to a large oak tree and leaned against the massive trunk.

"She was only kidding, right?" Paige whispered.

"About what?" Charlie asked.

"Answering nature's call?" Paige's eyes were wide as she glanced around.

"Why, do you have to go?"

"No, but… one time, at summer camp, we were on a hike, and one of the parent chaperones was helping all of us girls go in the bushes, and somehow I ended up peeing all over my pants *and* her."

When she saw Charlie trying not to laugh, she shrugged.

"I know. It's kinda funny now, but it was so embarrassing. I've had a phobia about peeing in the woods ever since."

"Just don't chug all your water at once," Charlie said. "You'll be fine."

When their time was up, Zoe stuck her thumb and forefinger in her mouth and whistled again.

"Everyone ready?" she said. "Let's get spaced out again. We got kinda bunched together during our break."

Charlie took a few steps further along the line. When Zoe was satisfied, they began again, marching slowly and methodically back in the direction they'd come. Eyes on the ground. Sticks jabbing the undergrowth.

They reached the top of the ridge and started their descent. At the bottom, Charlie sniffed the air. There was a new smell, something different from the decaying leaves or distant smoke. It was weak at first, enough that she thought she might be imagining it. She tried to ignore it until Paige spoke up.

"Do you smell that?" Paige asked.

Charlie nodded.

"What do you think it is?"

"Something dead."

Charlie tried to tell herself it couldn't be Emma. That this smelled too ripe. Too far gone. But the odor got stronger with each step, and her dread increased along with it. Every snap of a twig made her flinch.

The root ball of a large fallen tree blocked Charlie's path forward, so she skirted around it. On the other side, she stopped abruptly and let out a groan.

The smell of rot was overpowering now, so thick she could practically feel it on her skin. And finally she discovered the source.

The body lay before her in the tangle of broken twigs and brown leaves. Mouth opened wide. Eyes narrowed to slits.

It was a dead cat.

CHAPTER NINETEEN

Relief flooded through Charlie. She closed her eyes, shuffled back several steps from the dead animal, and took a few breaths. The tension in her chest and shoulders let go.

Just a cat. That was all. Finding the poor thing's corpse out here was creepy, yes, but it was, after all, just a cat. Part of her had expected something worse, was thankful it wasn't Emma.

Zoe knelt over the cat, leaning left and right as she inspected it.

Despite the deputy having reminded Pat and Karen to stay where they were, the two women stomped over for a look. At the sight of the mangled animal corpse, Pat's face went almost green, and she hustled away to vomit in a nearby snarl of honeysuckle bushes.

Meanwhile, Paige had taken one look at the dead cat and burst into tears. Charlie pulled her away, handing over a tissue from her bag and trying to calm the girl down.

Finally, Zoe straightened, tugging at her gun belt as she approached.

"What do you think?" Charlie asked.

"I think it's a dead cat."

"What's it doing way out here?"

Zoe shrugged.

"There are ferals all over the island."

"Yeah, but it's weird, right?" Charlie asked. "If it was by the road, I'd assume it'd been hit by a car or something. What could have happened to it out here in the woods?"

"Could be anything," Zoe said, adjusting her deputy's hat. "Old age. Ate a poisoned rodent. Hell, we've had reports of coyotes more and more over the years."

She guided Charlie and Paige a few paces further from the carcass.

"Look, I know it's upsetting, but there's no reason to think this is anything but a random dead animal. If it was a groundhog or a raccoon, you wouldn't think anything of it, would you?"

Charlie scratched the back of her neck.

"I guess not."

"Let's regroup and keep going," Zoe said.

A sudden yelping came from the vicinity of the two older women. When Charlie glanced over, Pat was still in the same spot, bent over at the waist, eyes watering but no longer retching.

The noise was coming from Karen, who'd wandered around to the far side of the bushes Pat had been throwing up in.

"For the love of God," Zoe muttered. "Is everyone going to lose their shit over this cat?"

Karen stumbled back toward them, hands to her face in an almost comical portrayal of shock. She babbled, her voice so high-pitched Charlie could only understand a word here and there.

"—nothing—" and then, "—trash—" and then, "—bad."

"What's she saying?" Zoe said. "She found some trash?"

It was only when Charlie saw Karen's eyes that she understood. The way they stretched wide but were utterly blank. Unseeing.

She took off in a sprint toward the place Karen had come from, her feet crashing through the leaves and dying plants.

"Charlie, wait!" Zoe called.

But Charlie didn't stop. She bounded past Karen, not slowing until she'd reached the far side of the thicket.

She stopped when she saw it. Gaped at the form on the ground.

The figure sprawled among the fronds and stalks of the ferns that hovered all around her person, reaching leaves and petals out over her, almost concealing her.

Emma.

The girl's broken body lay there in the weeds. Utterly still. Her eyes were closed as though sleeping, the flesh around them gone purple. The rest of her skin shone ghostly white, almost glowing against the yellowing ferns.

CHAPTER TWENTY

Everything went still as Charlie gazed down at Emma. The sounds around her suddenly seeming dull and far away.

The girl lay on her back, neck cocked at an angle, chin tucked, lips parted. Nestled here in the leaves, she looked almost like a lost princess from a fairy tale, lulled to sleep by some strange magic in the enchanted forest.

Charlie knelt next to the girl. Brushed aside the plants so that she could see Emma's face more clearly. Pale gray had overtaken the flesh of her cheeks. The lifeless gray of the bare tree branches. Of ashes. Of weathered bone.

That was when Charlie spotted the wound. A deep gash across the delicate skin of the girl's throat.

Flies buzzed around the raw flesh, lighting on the dried blood that looked nearly black.

And even though Charlie knew it was too late—before she'd even reached the body, she'd known—she pressed her fingers to Emma's wrist, feeling for a pulse.

The skin was cold, the flesh strangely firm to the touch. Charlie held her breath, knowing and yet hoping still. But there was no patter of life in Emma's veins. No thrumming beneath the surface. She was cold and still now forever.

And suddenly a vision of Emma flashed in Charlie's mind. Sitting in her office. Alive and vibrant. Filled to the brim with hopes and dreams and ambitions. Charlie remembered the miniatures she'd found in Emma's bedroom closet. The tiny chandelier and minuscule tea set. Each one of them created by this girl's hands.

But whatever spirit or soul or magic or electrical current in the brain that had energized this body was gone. Drained. Taken.

Charlie removed her hand from the girl's wrist, falling backward from her crouch until she sat on the ground.

She heard Zoe swear from behind her, then she was talking into her radio.

"This is Deputy Wyatt. We're at the northern edge of grid A-three, and we've got a code seventy."

Tears welled in Charlie's eyes, spilling over and running down her cheeks.

Zoe reached down and took Charlie by the arm, hauling her to her feet.

"You OK?"

Charlie nodded and wiped her face with her sleeve.

"Where's Paige?"

"I told her to stay over there with the others." Zoe gestured over her shoulder. "Figured she didn't need to see this, if it was what I thought it was."

They stared down at the corpse, and neither one of them spoke for several seconds.

The sound of men's voices could be heard in the distance now. The rustle of feet kicking through the thicket. The barking of the search dogs. Charlie glanced up, thinking she might be able to see them coming, but they were still a ways off. Her eyes returned to Emma.

"I really thought we'd find her alive," Charlie said.

"Me too," Zoe agreed, sighing. "Sometimes we think if we want something hard enough, it will just happen."

CHAPTER TWENTY-ONE

Just outside a perimeter marked with bright yellow crime scene tape, Charlie bid farewell to Paige, who was being escorted back to the beach parking lot with the rest of their search group. The sheriff had tried to kick Charlie off the scene as well, but he owed her one too many favors to make it stick.

"I don't think you should come in tomorrow," Charlie told Paige. "Take the day off, OK?"

Paige sniffled and nodded. Her eyes were puffy and red from crying, and Charlie wondered, not for the first time, if this fragile creature might be better off in a different line of work.

As Charlie watched Zoe lead Paige, Pat, and Karen around a bend in the trail not far from where they'd discovered Emma's body, she couldn't hold back a few final bitter thoughts for the two busybodies. They'd gotten what they'd wanted, hadn't they? To find the prize, the red meat relating to the case, to be front and center at the grisly climax of the search, something Nancy Grace could milk for ratings. Only Charlie suspected they were now coming to terms with the fact that it was a lot more than they'd bargained for.

Charlie felt her cheeks redden with anger at the women, but she knew it was misplaced. It wasn't for them, not really. Charlie's rage was for whoever had done this to Emma. Whoever had stolen this girl from the world.

Her eyes shifted over to where the girl still lay, though Charlie could barely see her now with the various crime scene techs, detectives, and coroner's assistants swarming around in booties and gloves, snapping photos and processing the scene.

When Zoe returned a few minutes later, she handed Charlie a fresh bottle of water.

"Paige made it back alright?" Charlie asked, taking a sip from the bottle.

"Yeah. She's a trooper," Zoe said. "Tougher than she seems."

Sheriff Brown huddled nearby with the county coroner, and Charlie could already envision the sheriff's press conference for the evening news. He'd hold his hat in his hand and tell the public how he wouldn't rest until justice was served. His voice would be calm and reassuringly firm. He'd look straight into the camera and deliver some kind of tough message to Emma's killer. He'd put on his little show, and then the media would take their turn. They'd flash smiling photographs of Emma while a random neighbor or acquaintance went on about how she was such a sweet girl.

They'd all talk and talk and talk about poor Emma Jacobis. She'd become tabloid fodder for women like Pat and Karen, just like Allie had. A cautionary tale to bring up when it was time for re-election or ratings were starting to dip.

And Charlie was sick of it. Sick of all the talk. She wanted people to shut the hell up and do something for once.

"This shouldn't have happened," Charlie said.

"Nope," Zoe agreed.

"No, I mean it was preventable," Charlie said. "Emma was being stalked. She went to the police. She came to me. And she still ended up dead. We failed her."

"No one could have known this would happen."

"Well, someone should have," Charlie insisted. "*We* should have."

Two men in white suits maneuvered Emma into a black vinyl body bag, and Charlie shook her head.

"We failed her, Zoe."

The anger came again. Charlie would find the one who'd done this. She would find him and make him pay.

CHAPTER TWENTY-TWO

Alone.

Empty.

He picks his way through the last of the woods and moves into the clearing. A vast expanse of ankle-high grass stands between him and the area where most of the cars are parked.

The crowd still gathers in the gravel lot off to his right. The aftermath of it all. They all came out here to search for her.

The girl. His girl.

The one he murdered in the deepest dark of last night.

These clusters of humanity seem strange to him. Foreign. Behaving almost more like a pack of chimps than human beings.

Too many people congregating in the parking lot. Touching. Hugging. Crying. Cooing out words of comfort to each other, words of love. Some collective outpouring of grief.

There's something overwhelming about all of that emotion being displayed in one place.

Caring is creepy. Makes his skin crawl.

He peeks over his shoulder, not really wanting to watch them but unable to look away for very long.

They're now lighting candles for the makeshift vigil. Some members of the crowd hold up the lights on their smartphones instead.

It's almost night, almost dark. Even here, some 150 feet away from them all, the little fires burn so bright. Blazing and brilliant and dancing atop their wax tubes.

They look like night lights somehow from this distance. Fires lit to keep the dark at arm's length.

He moves away from all of them. Walks toward the silvery stuff in the opposite direction.

The moon is out. Big and bright. A glowing white dome shining down on this scene. It paints the ground in pale shades, frosts the tips of the grass.

He keeps his head down. Stares at the blades of green as the wind shoves them around. And then the grass is gone, and he's stepping over a concrete divider into the paved section of the parking lot.

He climbs into his car. Closes the door behind him. Hears the way the cabin shuts out the ambient noise of the world outside. Muffles reality.

Instantly he feels different now that panes of glass separate him from the search crew. Still alone, yes. But safe somehow.

Apart.

Again his eyes shift to the distant crowd, to all those little spears of flame reaching upward. But something is different already.

The number of candles dwindles. The crowd is breaking up. Streams of them pouring his way. Ready to go home, to try to sleep after what they've all seen. He wonders if any of them will rest well tonight. He knows he won't.

It wasn't supposed to be this way.

And then the pictures open in his head. Little movies of the night before flickering on the insides of his eyelids. Fragmented. Spliced together.

The struggle. The knife. The blood. He relives the moments one by one. His stomach lurching with nausea as he does.

The girl turns into a rabid thing before his eyes. Thrashing. Flailing. Clawing and biting and spitting. Her skin looks all mottled under the harsh glow of the fluorescent bulbs.

He fights with her. Tries to overpower her. His big hands latching around her bony wrists. Tugging. Wrenching.

But he can't secure the chains with the way she's thrashing. Can barely keep her in the chamber he's set up for her.

He watches her bash herself into the cinder block walls as though she means to run right through them. Watches her break herself that way. Skin flaking open where the concrete turns her away. Still she picks herself up. Hurls herself into the cement. Again and again and again.

His face flushes. Floods with heat. Some vaguely swollen feeling accompanying the warmth in his cheeks.

He is powerless. Against the sheer forcefulness of her will, he has no control.

He tries to tell her. Tries to tell her that he doesn't want to hurt her or anything like that. Tries to tell her that they could be together forever now.

But she won't listen. Eyes all wide. Lips peeled back. It's like trying to communicate with a wild animal. A terrified cat climbing the walls to get away.

She comes at him. Claws out. Lurching. Grabbing. Hissing.

And he panics. Reacts without thinking. Sticks her with his blade. As much as he doesn't want to. Never wanted to.

He jabs the metal into her neck and rips. Opens up the flesh flaps there like another crooked mouth beneath the original. Lets her blood come streaming out.

Crimson spills on the blue tarp laid over the floor. Splatters audibly. Smacks the vinyl like water from a hose bib slapping at wet soil.

Steam coils off the wet red draining from her. Puffs of it heaving out of that hole in her neck. Rising from the scarlet puddle.

She drops to her knees. Then to her belly. Skin going so cold. Face turning pale blue.

If only he'd given her a hard tap on the head instead. A little attitude adjustment administered with the handle of his blade. If he'd knocked her out again, he could have secured the chains, no problem. He sees that now. But in that panicked moment, it had felt like stabbing her was the only choice. Like he needed to show her once and for all who was in charge here.

A car door slams just outside his vehicle. Rattles him out of the memories.

He opens his eyes. Blinks a few times. Watches the crowd filter into the lot around him. Climbing into their cars. Headlights winking on. Taillights moving away.

He follows suit. Starts his car. Falls in with the mob. Pulls out onto the road.

He puts the window down a few inches. Lets the crisp autumn air come spilling in to ruffle his hair.

And he tries to forget. Tries to erase the images flitting in his skull. Tries to make his mind go blank.

At a stoplight, he rolls his long sleeve back, examines the gouges on his arm. Long slashes where her fingernails scraped away flesh. Ragged along the edges. It took scrubbing with a wire brush to get the tattered bits of his body out from beneath her nails.

He imagined it all a million times. Fantasized. Dreamed. He always figured she'd learn to accept him, learn to accept living there, to be brought out when he wanted her. Would learn to enjoy his company if only out of boredom, being stuck so long by herself chained up. She would see, in time, that he, and only he, could give her the life she'd always wanted.

The fantasies always followed that same trajectory. Painted pictures that veered toward dark romance.

But real life doesn't work that way. Not even close.

The light turns green, and he drives again. Strives forward. But what for? What comes next? He doesn't know.

The future is empty now. Hollow. Black seas of infinity too big to even fathom.

It's not the killing that affects him, the taking of a life. He has hunted since he was a kid. Slayed rabbits and squirrel and deer and so on. And he's grown hard to the spilling of blood, callused to the snuffing out of life's light.

Killing is just the way of this world. The way that the strong express their power over the weak. As natural as eating a juicy steak. Medium rare.

Meat on the plate. Blood on the teeth.

No. Taking a life hardly affects him. What purpose does guilt ever serve?

It's the loss of what was rightfully his that kills him.

She was his. Belonged to him. And she was ripped away like pliers getting at one of his teeth, leaving a gaping hole in his person.

It hurts to lose her. She was supposed to be his forever. Not dead.

He sees it again. The blood draining from her neck. Thick red puddling on the blue vinyl tarp beneath her. Her skin going icy.

He pulls over to the shoulder. Tires juddering over the gravel. Kicking up dust everywhere.

He stumbles out of the car and vomits on the side of the road.

No matter what anyone might think, he never wanted this.

CHAPTER TWENTY-THREE

As darkness began to fall, the activity surrounding the crime scene became frenzied. Even though they'd brought in lights, Charlie sensed that none of them wanted to be out here processing the scene into the night.

Charlie watched the men from the coroner's office zip Emma into the body bag and lift the dead weight between them. Saying goodbye to Zoe, Charlie followed them through the woods.

The sky had cleared over the course of the evening, and the moon was already visible in the pale twilight.

At the edge of the parking lot, a gurney waited. It looked strange there with the beach in the background. Some sort of avant-garde photograph Charlie could imagine seeing at a student art show.

The men hoisted their burden on top of the stretcher. After securing it with straps, they wheeled it the rest of the way across the lot, where a van waited to take Emma's corpse to the county morgue.

Charlie hovered there under the canopy of skeletal trees and let her gaze track the van out of the parking lot. Only when the taillights disappeared from view did she move again.

The weight of it hit her as she walked back to her car. The moment she plopped down in the driver's seat, she let out a sob that shook her whole body.

Emma was dead. Twenty-four years old, and she'd stay that age forever. No more birthdays. No more breakups. She'd never laugh or cry or love again. She'd never become a psychologist. She'd never have a family or buy a house or get a dog.

Charlie had been holding it together for the better part of the day, and the crying was out of frustration as much as it was out of grief. She'd been worried when she'd discovered the disarray at Emma's house, but she hadn't wanted to admit how much to herself. She'd wanted to stay hopeful. As if that ever did any good.

If she was honest with herself, she'd known it was bad once she saw the blood. And finding the phone in the woods had been another indication that there wouldn't be a happy ending for Emma Jacobis. And yet Charlie had clung to hope. Just like she had with Allie.

Tears streamed down Charlie's face, and she was glad it was mostly dark now so no one could see her.

"That's definitely a good thing," Allie said. "Because you give new meaning to 'ugly cry.'"

"Go away," Charlie grumbled.

"Make me."

Charlie ground her molars together, annoyed that she had zero control over the voice in her head.

Except there was *one* place where Allie never made a peep. One place where Charlie could have some peace.

She started the car and flipped on the headlights. A few minutes later, she was parking in the driveway of her childhood home.

The house was dark, and Charlie knew she'd find it empty. Her mother was still at Cedar Grove Healing Center, a long-term care facility a few hours away.

Charlie let herself in through the front door and flipped on a light. Even though she came by once a week to open the windows and make sure rodents hadn't moved in, the air smelled slightly stale inside.

Her mother kept saying they should think about putting it up for sale, but Charlie had mixed feelings. This place was her last direct tie to Allie. There was the nick in the kitchen tile from the time Allie had dropped a cast-iron skillet on the floor. Downstairs in the basement, a dent in the wall from when Allie had tried to teach Charlie how to do a cartwheel, only to land with the side of her foot in the drywall. A smear of tangerine on the bathtub where Allie had broken a bottle of nail polish. Charlie was afraid that if they sold the house, she'd lose those memories, one by one.

In the kitchen, Charlie realized she was starving. It made sense considering she hadn't eaten since Paige had brought her lunch at Emma's house.

She found a sleeve of crackers and a jar of peanut butter in the cupboard and took them into her old room. The room she'd shared with her twin, from birth to premature death.

Shared.

The word echoed in Charlie's mind as she plugged in the strand of Christmas lights over Allie's old bed.

It had always been more Allie's room than hers, hadn't it, though? Allie's posters on the wall. Allie's favorite perfume wafting from the bottle on the dresser. Allie's CD in the stereo.

Charlie had only ever been a bit part in *The Allie Show*. No wonder she'd never quite known what to do with herself once Allie was gone.

But even as she came to that conclusion, Charlie missed it. She would have been Allie's sidekick a thousand times over if it meant she could have her sister back.

Sitting on the corner of her bed, Charlie ate a cracker smeared with peanut butter and cried for Allie and Emma and all the other girls who were stolen away before their time.

CHAPTER TWENTY-FOUR

Charlie woke in her old room sometime after dawn. The clock on the dresser said it was almost 9 a.m., but she had no idea if the time was accurate or not.

This was becoming a habit. Coming here anytime she had something on her mind or whenever she was in the mood to sit in this shrine to Allie and think about the old days.

She sat up and rubbed her eyes. It was funny, really. She'd spent the last eighteen years trying to keep her distance from this place, and now that she was back on Salem Island, she couldn't seem to stay away. The house she'd grown up in pulled at her like a rip current. If she stopped fighting it, how could she be sure it wouldn't pull her out to sea?

But that was enough ruminating for one day. There was work to be done. Emma Jacobis needed justice. Charlie forced herself up and out of her old bed, unplugging the Christmas lights and grabbing her purse from where she'd left it in the kitchen the night before.

Charlie grabbed coffee and a breakfast burrito on the drive home. The morning was clear and sunny. At her apartment, she ducked inside long enough to shower and change into fresh clothes before heading downstairs to open up the office. She drained the to-go cup of the final dregs and started a fresh pot. She had a feeling she'd need it today.

Armed with a steaming mug, Charlie settled in front of her laptop and googled Emma's name. She found the girl's Instagram profile near the top of the list and started there.

The sight of Emma smiling shyly in her profile photo caught Charlie by surprise. For a moment, she just stared at the screen, chest tight, nose stinging. She took a deep breath and scrolled down the page, bracing herself. But Emma's Instagram page was light on selfies. The majority of her photos had no people in them at all. A sunset on Lake Huron. A field of sunflowers. A tree frog on a flowerpot.

But the main focus of Emma's page was her miniatures, which appeared to have somewhat of a following on Instagram. Over a hundred comments on each one and even more likes. Charlie would have to sift through all of them at some point, but for now she was looking for people closer to Emma than just a pseudo-anonymous commenter on Instagram.

Charlie navigated to Emma's Facebook profile, which was similarly lacking in self-portraits, but there were dozens of photos that Emma had been tagged in. That actually worked better for Charlie's purposes, since she could easily see who had posted photos in the first place, which allowed her to assemble a list of friends and acquaintances.

She clicked through the images, writing down the names of everyone in the photos, bookmarking their profiles for later perusal.

A fair share of the pictures had been taken at the Laughing Raven. Charlie had already been planning to canvass the bar as soon as possible since it was clear Emma's stalker had known she worked there. But the list of names she was gathering from the Facebook photos would give Charlie a good starting point when she went there tonight.

Charlie had already gone through most of the pot of coffee when the bell over the door jangled and Paige bustled inside. Before Charlie could say anything, Paige held up a hand.

"I know you said I shouldn't come in today, but I want to help."

Charlie raised her eyebrows.

"Help with what?"

"Emma's case."

Charlie sat back in her chair, swiveling side to side.

"Well, Zoe promised she'd send over a copy of Emma's phone records, and I'm putting together a list of all of her contacts on social media, so between the two, I can definitely use the extra pair of eyes."

"Of course," Paige said, chewing her lip. "I can do all that. But I'd also like to be more hands-on, if I can. Hit the streets or whatever."

A vision of Paige's tear-streaked face after they'd discovered Emma's body in the woods the previous day flashed in Charlie's mind.

"I don't know if that's a good idea…"

Taking a step closer to the desk, Paige clasped her fingers together.

"It's just that being here when she came in and when we found her, I don't know… there's just something personal about it all. This probably sounds weird, but I feel some kind of connection with her, I guess." Paige closed her eyes. "Anyway, I'll help in any way you see fit, even if that means shutting myself up here in the office and handling paperwork. But if there's something more I can do, well… I'm ready."

Charlie didn't love the idea of bringing Paige into the field. But there'd probably be a full crowd of people at the bar. Even if she got Uncle Frank and Zoe to come along, it would be useful to have help canvassing the place. And all things considered, the Laughing Raven wasn't exactly a high-risk location. What was the worst that could happen?

"OK," Charlie said. "How would you feel about coming with me to the bar to interview anyone there who might have known Emma? Co-workers. Regular customers. So on."

"Really?" Paige beamed. "Of course! Gosh, I thought for sure you were going to say no."

Charlie found herself smiling at the girl's enthusiasm.

"In the meantime, what do you say we make a fresh pot of coffee and start with a bit of light cyberstalking?"

*

After refilling her coffee, Charlie returned to her computer and found that Zoe had emailed Emma's phone records to her. She had Paige print them out and then go through the pages, color-coding the numbers and doing reverse look-ups to figure out who each one belonged to.

Meanwhile, Charlie tracked down some of Emma's friends and classmates from college on the off-chance that Emma had picked up her stalker at school. Talking with Emma's former roommate, her best friend, and her faculty adviser gave her three strikes in a row. None of them remembered anything strange. No mysterious notes. No crank calls. No mention of anything off from Emma herself.

When the last call was finished, Charlie hung up and rubbed her temples. The fact that there seemed to be no evidence of Emma having been stalked at school meant it had most likely started here, on Salem Island. It was a tiny step forward in the case, but Charlie couldn't help feeling frustrated. She'd wanted more.

Paige wheeled over to Charlie's desk, papers fluttering. The pages were a rainbow of highlighted phone numbers and names scribbled in the margins.

"I finished organizing Emma's cell phone records."

"What have we got?" Charlie asked, flipping through.

"Her most-called number is her mother. Second is her friend Gretchen Beattie, who I heard you talking to earlier. After that it's a mish-mash of restaurants, the financial aid office at her school, her cable company. The standard stuff."

"OK," Charlie said. "What about incoming calls?"

"Mostly the same, except for one thing."

Charlie raised a questioning eyebrow, and Paige pointed out a set of numbers highlighted in green.

"This number here called several times a week for a few weeks starting the end of September. The duration of each call was always short. Ten or twenty seconds. And always at odd hours, like one or two in the morning."

Charlie started nodding. Emma had mentioned the late-night calls.

"But two weeks ago, the number disappeared. Stopped calling." Paige pointed at another set of numbers in purple. "Then a few days later, a different number started up the same pattern. Several calls a week. Short duration. Always in the middle of the night."

"Let me guess," Charlie said. "Neither of these numbers is in the reverse look-up?"

"Right."

Charlie drummed her fingers against the desk.

"So the stalker used a burner to call her for a while. Maybe a month or so. Then he got a new one." Charlie snatched up a pen and jotted both numbers down. "That's good work, Paige. I'll make sure to pass this on to Zoe. If we're right, and he keeps using the most recent number for a while, the sheriff's department can try to trace it. I doubt it'll lead to anything, but it's worth a check."

After forwarding the suspicious phone numbers to Zoe and making a few more dead-end phone calls, Charlie's eyes drifted over to the clock on the wall. She was surprised to see the workday was over.

"OK. Head home for a while, get some dinner, and we'll meet up at the Laughing Raven at eight."

"Are we supposed to be incognito? Do I need a disguise?"

Allie chuckled.

"Tell her to wear some of those Groucho Marx glasses with the fake nose and mustache."

"Um… no. We're just going to be talking to people."

"Yeah. Sure. Right." Paige blushed and laughed. "It's just that one time I got invited to a bridal shower for an old friend, and I showed up in some jeans and a sweater. Nice jeans, though, you know. Not ratty or anything. I thought that'd be OK, because it's what I wore when I went to my cousin's shower when I was in high school. But I got there and everyone else was all dressed in these cute dresses with hats and gloves. No one told me there was like, a dress code, you know?"

Paige flapped her hands in the air, and her face went a shade redder.

"And now I'm rambling. Sorry. I guess I'm just a little nervous. It's a good nervous, though. Excited, I guess."

Paige turned and headed for the door, but Charlie stopped her.

"I forgot to mention that there's one really important rule when you're in the field."

"Oh. What is it?"

"You have to do whatever I say, without question. Sometimes things get hairy, and I need to know you won't turn into a liability."

"I can do that," Paige said, looking relieved.

She was smiling as she went out the door, and Charlie felt a tightening in her gut. She wanted to call out, to tell Paige to stop being so giddy because this wasn't a game. But Paige was only a kid, and there was a part of Charlie that was envious of the fact that she wasn't jaded yet.

Because it was only a matter of time before the world showed her what it was really like: an uncaring, cruel place that was just waiting to kick you in the teeth.

CHAPTER TWENTY-FIVE

A decent-sized crowd lurched around the Laughing Raven in swells and eddies that reminded Charlie of the sea. They pressed against the bar, clogged the area in front of the stage, and huddled around most of the tables spread out over the floor.

This was good. A mostly full house was just what Charlie had been hoping for. She needed enough regulars available to increase the odds of finding someone who might have seen something, but not so packed that interviewing people would be made impossible through either congestion or noise.

She finished talking with a couple at the bar who were charming but ultimately unhelpful, as they'd never actually come to the Laughing Raven before tonight.

Charlie had just hopped down from her stool when a tall, redheaded girl with dark lipstick barged out from the kitchen to deposit a basket of fries at one of the tables nearby. Charlie saw her chance to get a word with one of Emma's co-workers.

"Miss?" she called, but at the same moment the man onstage finished his song, and Charlie's voice was buried under the applause.

She chased after the woman, hoping to catch her before she disappeared back into the kitchen, but the redhead's long legs easily outpaced her. The swinging doors parted and swallowed the woman up before Charlie managed to get her attention.

"Damn," Charlie muttered to herself.

She searched the room, looking for another waitress or bartender, but they were all busy.

Her eyes lingered on the reflections in the mirrored bar, scanning for the rest of her crew.

She spotted Zoe talking to a group of old-timer barflies at the tables farthest from the stage. There were two leather-faced women playing darts and some flannel-clad guys that looked like seasoned alcoholics. The patrons of the Laughing Raven tended to skew a little younger, so she figured these were the types that came in to get loaded during happy hour and then tried to nurse their drunkenness through the end of the night.

She didn't see Frank, which meant he was probably still shooting the shit with the bouncer at the door. Apparently they were old acquaintances, which could be useful if they ended up needing a favor at some point.

Charlie's gaze floated over to where Paige was interviewing a mixed group of younger customers by the pool tables.

Charlie hoped they were having more luck than she'd had so far.

On the stool next to her there was a burly guy in a black Carhartt jacket with "Schnell Shipping" embroidered on the back. She was pretty sure she'd seen the jacket in the periphery of a few of the Facebook photos Emma had been tagged in. A regular. That was something, at least.

Charlie spun around to face him.

"Hi there," she said.

Without looking her way, he took a drink of his PBR.

"Beat it."

Thinking she misheard him, Charlie leaned closer.

"Excuse me?"

Carhartt heaved a sigh, as if speaking was the most laborious task he'd ever attempted.

"I've seen you approach everyone sittin' at the bar, which means you're soliciting for something. And I don't care if it's drugs, pussy, or Girl Scout cookies. Whatever you're peddlin', I ain't buyin'."

Allie chuckled, and Charlie forced herself to move past the implication that she was a drug dealer or prostitute.

"I'm not selling anything. I just want to ask you a few questions."

"Ah. So you're a cop." He nodded and took a long pull on his beer. "Well, I know my rights. I don't have to talk to you."

"You don't even know what it's about," Charlie said, starting to argue and then closing her eyes. "Look, I'm not a cop. I'm a private investigator, and I just want to know if you come here often."

Up until now, the man hadn't even looked at her. But now he opened his eyes wide and turned to smile at her.

"Wow, a private investigator?" Just as quickly as it had appeared, the smile was gone, replaced by a scowl. "Answer's still the same as before. Fuck off."

"Hey!" A man wearing a Laughing Raven apron dropped a bus box filled with dirty glasses on the bar with a thud. He aimed a finger at Carhartt. "You've been warned about your mouth before. If you can't play nice, you can find somewhere else to drink."

The man in the Carhartt jacket scoffed and angled himself away from Charlie, returning to his task of glaring into the mirror behind the bar.

"Wow, I haven't seen a guy shut you down that hard since, like, pretty much all the guys you had crushes on in high school," Allie said, sounding far too amused.

Charlie ignored her, turning her attention to the bar employee. He was a few inches taller than her with a tangle of dark hair that fell in his eyes.

"Thanks," she said.

"Don't mention it." He gave a curt nod before hoisting the tub of glassware in his hands and turning to go.

"Wait," Charlie said. "Can you help me?"

"Sorry, I only work in the kitchen," he said, shaking his head. "You'll have to wait until one of the bartenders or wait staff can put in your order."

"Actually, I was hoping to ask you a few questions."

The man straightened, frowning. Charlie thought he seemed vaguely familiar somehow but couldn't place where she might know him from. Given that he worked here, he'd probably been in some of the photos she'd looked at today.

"Questions about what?" he asked.

"One of your co-workers. Emma Jacobis."

The man inhaled and set the bin of dirty glasses back down.

"Emma," he said, his face pained. "Of course. I heard about… what happened to her."

"Did you know her well?"

"Not really. I just started working here maybe a month and a half ago." He gestured over his shoulder, in the direction of the kitchen door. "You should talk to Cindy. She and Emma were pretty tight."

"Oh yeah?"

He nodded once before glancing around. "She must be in back. I can go get her, if you want."

"That'd be great," Charlie said. "Thanks."

As he turned, Charlie spotted the name tag pinned to his apron that said, "Craig."

Charlie snapped her fingers.

"Craig Rattigan!"

The man froze, looking startled.

"That's me," he said, blinking rapidly.

"You went to Salem Island High School." Charlie pointed at herself. "Charlotte Winters. I was a grade ahead of you."

A sheepish smile spread over his lips, and he stared down at the floor.

"I know who you are."

"Why didn't you say something?"

He shrugged, cheeks reddening.

"I didn't think you'd remember me."

"Of course I do. We had French with Mr. Bonneville together, right?"

"Oh, right." He nodded and scratched the back of his neck. "That was the class where Ivan Walsh superglued Bonneville's chair to the floor, wasn't it?"

Charlie laughed.

"Yeah. And Mr. Bonneville got so mad his face turned purple." Her laughter faded, and she frowned. "And then we all got detention because no one would tell who'd done it."

The silence stretched out between them, that awkward lull when two people who didn't know one another well ran out of things to say. Craig locked eyes with the dish towel he was fidgeting with while Charlie struggled to come up with some mundane topic to fill the void. A question about his family? But then she knew from experience how questions like that could be a hidden minefield. And she couldn't ask about work because they were *at* his work.

Charlie was still wracking her brain when he tossed the dish towel over his shoulder and shrugged.

"Anyhow, I'll go find Cindy for you."

"I appreciate it," Charlie said. "It was good seeing you."

He pushed through the kitchen door, untying the strings of his apron as he went.

"That was some solid socializing, Chuck," Allie said.

"Be quiet."

"I'm serious. I really felt a spark there when the two of you were avoiding eye contact and gulping for air."

But Charlie wasn't listening. Talking with Craig had dislodged a buried memory. Of that half hour she'd had to stay after school for detention with the rest of her fifth-hour French class.

She remembered sitting in that hard plastic chair, working on her math homework, and seeing movement out of the corner of her eye.

Charlie had glanced out the door and spotted someone doing the funky chicken down the hallway while wearing the giant pirate head that belonged to the school mascot.

Other students around Charlie had noticed, too, and they struggled to stifle their laughter as the person in the mascot head MC Hammer-danced past the open door in the other direction.

Charlie was pretty sure she was the only one who knew it was Allie under the pirate head. She would have recognized the ridiculous dance moves anywhere, but also, Allie was wearing a tie-dye shirt Charlie had made in her textiles class.

It was when Allie paused just outside the door and began a series of pelvic thrusting motions that Tina Mower lost it and let out a high-pitched giggle. Mr. Bonneville's head snapped up.

"Run!" Charlie hissed.

And Allie took off down the hall with Mr. Bonneville in hot pursuit. He returned half a minute later, out of breath and with his face his trademark shade of purple.

The acoustic guitar jangled to life onstage again, jarring Charlie from the memory. She blinked a few times as if awakening from a dream.

She hadn't thought about that day in years, but it was still so sharp in her mind. So vivid that she had practically felt the rock-hard chair under her ass and smelled the musty funk of the schoolroom carpet mixing with the acrid odor of dry-erase markers.

Charlie wondered if there was someone out there with memories like that about Emma. She hoped there was. There was a kind of magic in those vivid memories of the lost, because for just a moment, it felt like they weren't all the way gone.

CHAPTER TWENTY-SIX

The bar flutters with life and light. Activity. Motion.

He watches the crowd from the corner. Nestled to one side where the lights don't really reach. Eyes snapping back and forth between the mob and the windows.

She is there. Two tables away from him. The girl he saw on the search out in the woods.

The light over the bar spills into her hair. Puddles a glared spot on the curved slope of her forehead.

A beautiful creature. Fragile. Angelic.

The kind of beauty that makes him think of a flower pressed in a book to dry and preserve. To save. To keep forever.

In some ways, she reminds him of Emma. Beautiful Emma. Gone for good.

She talks now. Smiles. Her teeth glistening with a thin sheen of saliva.

She's flitted around the room striking up conversations then moving on. He can't help but notice that she talks almost exclusively to men. Smiles at them. Bats her eyelashes at them.

He squirms in his shadowed place. Clenches his jaw. Smears his fingers against his sweaty palms.

The beautiful preen themselves inside these walls. Admire each other. Strut around. Pair off to mate.

And he sits alone on the edge of it all. An outsider. In the dark. Where no one is looking. Where nobody cares.

Rage bursts in bright flashes inside of him.

Hatred detonates in his head.

Violent fantasies blossom in his heart.

All he wants—all he's ever wanted—is to find the perfect girl and trap her and keep her until she loves him back.

And she will. Eventually, she will.

She will love him. If he never gives up, someone will love him.

He can feel it in his heartbeat. Taste it on his tongue. Like something that has always been there, always been true. As sure as fate.

In school they talked about human psychology and the criminal mind. Impulse control. That's the biggest difference between a man in prison and a free man walking the streets. Brain scans have shown a spike in activity in such deviant brains, plain as day, the moment when the dark impulses take over. An urge to destroy. A lust for violence.

And he knew, listening to the teacher drone, that the textbooks were talking about him. Telling him how to stay out of prison. Telling him how to hide his darkness. Telling him how to beat the system.

So he reined in the impulses. Planned everything. Exercised caution. Meticulous. He fought his nature, fought his appetites, to stay hidden among the crowd.

And what has all the planning gotten him? No Emma. No love. Nothing.

He is no one. A loser. Invisible.

Maybe the time for planning is over now. Maybe it's time to let the impulses take over. Time to chase the fantasies with all of his heart. Let predator instincts get him what he wants.

Maybe he's learned, though. Maybe he can master both worlds. Follow his gut, unleash the beast, and keep hidden still.

His eyes flick over all those smiling faces clustering around the bar. Glistening teeth. Glowing skin.

He stands to walk among them.

CHAPTER TWENTY-SEVEN

Charlie leaned against the bar while she waited for the elusive Cindy to come out from the kitchen, watching the activity surrounding her in the mirrored wall again.

Robbie Turner sauntered into view, emerging from the throng. He paused a few feet shy of the overpopulated bar stools, scanning the place. His gaze froze on the gathering near the pool tables, where Paige had just approached a new group to interview.

"That was fast," Allie said. "Dude's like a shark smelling blood. I bet he could sense Paige was in here from outside."

Eyes still locked on Paige, Robbie waggled his shoulders a little and ran his fingers through his hair. He veered that way, moved on the group, more swagger in his step now.

"So you're just throwing Paige to the wolves now?" Allie asked.

"She's an adult. What do you want me to do?"

"Get over there and hurl yourself between them as if Robbie is a speeding train and Paige is a cartoon damsel tied to the tracks. Chop, chop, Charlie."

Charlie wriggled down off the stool, thinking that Allie was right. Robbie had an almost childlike charm which tended to put her at ease, but the fact of the matter was, he was someone who made chronically bad choices in life.

But just as Charlie's feet hit the ground, the kitchen door swooshed open and the tall, redheaded waitress from earlier whisked through it. Her hair was bobby-pinned into a long fauxhawk style, and up close, Charlie could see a tiny nose ring in her right nostril.

"You the one asking around about Emma?" she asked. Her voice was deep and slightly husky.

"Yeah. I was told you two were close."

Cindy crossed her arms.

"What are you?" she demanded, snapping a piece of gum between her teeth. "A reporter or something?"

"I'm a private investigator. Emma hired me the day before she died."

"Why would Emma need a P.I.?" Cindy asked.

"Because she was being stalked."

"You mean that drawing she found in her car or whatever?" Cindy said. "I kind of thought that was just a stupid joke."

Charlie raised an eyebrow.

"It wasn't only the drawing. She thought someone had been in her apartment, too."

"She didn't tell me that." Cindy's shoulders sagged, the tough-girl act crumbling before Charlie's eyes. "Oh my God. You think the stalker killed her?"

"It's early to say for sure, but that would be my guess."

"I had no idea she was so worried. She never said anything. I knew she needed to stay at my place, but when I asked her why, she said she didn't want to get into it." Cindy shook her head, and her eyelids brimmed with tears. "But that was classic Emma. She was always making sure everyone else was good, you know? Never wanted to make a fuss about her own problems."

Charlie grabbed a cocktail napkin from the bar and handed it to Cindy.

"Thanks," she said, wiping her nose. "I still can't believe she's gone. She was such a sweetheart. She didn't deserve this."

Suddenly the man in the Carhartt jacket barked at her from down the bar.

"You think I could get a fresh one sometime in the next century or should I take my business elsewhere?"

Cindy turned and gave him a withering look. The kind that maybe wouldn't kill but would definitely cause his balls to shrink a little.

She reached down into a cooler under the bar and grabbed a fresh bottle. In one motion, she removed the cap on a built-in opener on the wall and slammed it down in front of him.

"Drink up, asshole."

"Guess it's that time of the month for ya, huh?" Carhartt said.

"Fuck you, Neil!" she yelled.

He smiled, but it wasn't what Charlie would call a happy expression. There was a coldness in his eyes. After a few seconds, he swung his gaze away to glare into the mirrored glass of the bar again.

"Is he a regular?" Charlie asked when Cindy returned.

"Neil?" Cindy asked. "Yeah, I guess he'd qualify. But he's a trucker, so sometimes he's gone for weeks at a time for work. When he's in town, he's here most nights, getting shitfaced."

"And is he always that charming?"

Cindy snorted.

"I'd say this is a neutral night for Neil. Sometimes he's sweet and almost kinda flirty. Other nights he's like a damn rattlesnake waiting to strike. Tonight I'd say he's just his regular old grouchy self."

"Did Emma ever have any run-ins with him?"

"Not that I know of," Cindy said, shrugging one shoulder.

"What about your other regulars? Any of them known to cause problems?"

"Depends on what you'd call a problem, I guess." Cindy pointed at a man swaying drunkenly near the stage. "Scott Mackay is in here most nights. And most nights we have to scrape him off the floor and hustle him into the back of an Uber to get him home. It's a good night if he hasn't pissed himself. Robbie Turner over there is our crybaby. If he has too much to drink, he gets weepy and starts recounting all of his life mistakes. I don't see Jerry Bimpson, but he has a tendency to get a bit handsy, albeit only with the fellas."

Cindy shrugged and heaved a sigh.

"But it's a bar. We have to cut people off, call rides when they're too wasted to do it themselves, throw them out if they get too rowdy. I'd be more suspicious if a night went by and there wasn't some kind of drunken shenanigans."

"So you never saw anyone giving Emma a hard time? Or maybe too much attention?"

Cindy shook her head.

"I don't know if you know this, but Emma had anxiety. Some social phobia. And I thought of her like my little sister. Tried to watch out for her, you know? If there were any customers I either knew to be problematic or just had that gut instinct for, I steered her away from them."

Charlie couldn't help but think of the way she'd sent Paige on the light assignment by sending her to talk to the college kids at the pool tables instead of the rough-looking men sitting at the bar.

At that thought, Charlie's eyes slid over to where she'd seen Paige last. Robbie had one arm slung around the girl's shoulders.

"Oh, brother," Allie said. "They are looking awfully chummy."

"What about other girls?" Charlie asked. "Have any of them ever complained about a customer giving them the creeps? Gotten threatening notes? Been stalked?"

Cindy started to shake her head then stopped, a line forming between her eyebrows.

"You know someone else who was stalked?" Charlie asked.

"Not exactly," Cindy said, eyes sliding sideways to stare at an empty place on the bar. "I mean, I don't know why I'd even connect the two things, really. They're completely different."

"Tell me what happened."

"Olivia, one of the other waitresses… she was drugged or something. Woke up in a creepy basement and just barely managed to get away." Cindy shivered and rubbed her arms. "God, just thinking about it gives me the chills. But this happened over a year ago."

"You say she was drugged… Did this happen here?" Charlie asked.

"No. She was at one of those boat parties on the lake. You know, the kind of thing where you go from boat to boat, just picking up drinks from whoever. So like, there was no telling who'd slipped her what. Could have been anyone."

Charlie leaned in.

"Is she here tonight?"

"Nah, but lemme check the schedule." Cindy bustled over to a chart hanging on the wall next to the kitchen door. "Looks like she's not on until tomorrow night. Could you come back then?"

"I'd prefer to talk to her sooner than that, if I can."

Cindy snapped her gum.

"I guess I could give her a call. See if she has time to talk before then."

While Cindy pulled out her phone to make the call, Charlie craned her neck to check on Paige again. She was relieved to see that Robbie was no longer clinging to her. In fact, Paige was talking to a new trio who'd just come in. Two guys and a girl.

"I can't believe Robbie let her slip out of his grasp so quickly," Allie said. "I thought he had more gumption than that."

Charlie searched the room for him and found him in the darkest corner, chugging a beer. She watched him polish it off before wiping his mouth and dropping the bottle on the nearest table on his way to the door.

He took long strides, and Charlie thought he looked like a man on a mission. Then he pushed through the door and disappeared into the gloom outside.

"She wants to talk to you," a voice said from over Charlie's shoulder.

She whirled around and found Cindy holding her phone out with an expectant look on her face.

Charlie took the phone and plugged her free ear to hear better over the noise in the bar.

"Hello?"

"You're the one that was helping Emma with the stalking thing?" Olivia asked. Her voice was so light and soft, she sounded like a little girl.

"Yes."

"And you think what happened to me might be related?"

"I'm not sure," Charlie said. "But the more information I have, the better."

There was a long pause, and for a moment Charlie thought the call had disconnected. Then Olivia sighed.

"Do you know where the Cardamom Cafe is?"

"On Vine Street?" Charlie said. "I know it."

"Can you meet me there in twenty minutes?"

"Sure."

When the call ended, Charlie handed the phone back to Cindy.

"Olivia agreed to talk?"

Charlie nodded.

"Do me a favor," Cindy said. "Go easy on her. She was in rough shape after that. Not physically, but emotionally. Had a few panic attacks here at work. On a really crowded night, the noise and all the people would just, I don't know, set her off."

"I'll be gentle," Charlie said. "Thank you for putting me in touch."

Charlie picked up her bag from where she'd dropped it on one of the bar stools and turned to go, but Cindy caught her arm.

"One more thing."

"Yeah?"

"Don't let whoever killed Emma get away with it." Cindy's face was hard and fierce, but tears gathered at the corners of her eyes. "Find him and make him pay."

Charlie stared into the girl's eyes and bobbed her head once.

"I will," Charlie promised.

CHAPTER TWENTY-EIGHT

He climbs into the car. Plops into the driver's seat, which has gone cold while he was away.

His eyes flick to the window. To her.

She is still inside the bar. The girl. His girl. Still smiling. Still batting those eyelashes.

He closes his eyes. Clenches his teeth. Tries to shove the frustration away.

When he opens his eyes, he sees the rectangular package tucked in his hand. Yes. That might help.

He whacks the fresh pack of cigarettes against his palm. Three firm strokes.

Then he peels open the cellophane. Flips the lid. Plucks a cylinder from the neat rows. Wedges it between his lips.

That tangy tobacco stench fills his nostrils. Striking. A little acrid. Reminds him of the smell of light-roast coffee beans.

The lighter appears there under his chin. Flame bursting to life as he flicks the wheel around.

He breathes smoke. Holds the whirling fog in his chest for a beat. Then lets it jet out of his nostrils.

She moves closer to the window, and his view of her sharpens. The texture of her skin comes into focus. Soft. Supple. Flawlessly smooth.

She glows.

His jaw tightens. A faint gritting sound emitting from his molars.

He hits the cigarette again. Hears the cherry sizzle. Watches it burn a brighter shade of red.

The pack of jackals in the bar seem to circle around her. Spiraling. Spiraling.

Men. So many men orbit her brightness. Bask in her glow. Looking for an opening. A way in.

Another clown sidles up next to her. A frat-boy-looking chump with a baseball hat on backward. He grins like a chimp. Exposes bleached teeth.

She smiles back.

In the car, his hand trembles as he ashes the cigarette. A tremor assailing his outstretched arm.

And another wave of nausea roils in his gut. That sickness he felt walking back to his car after the search.

Fuck this.

Why focus so hard on one girl? The world is full of them. Overflowing with them.

No more planning, right? No more planning.

He pries his gaze away from her. Lets his eyes scan the rest of the bar.

Feminine forms move everywhere. Breasts and legs and hips that all seem to fit together just right. Skinny in some places. Thick in others.

He feels like a kid in a candy shop. Struggling to choose among all the bright colors. Wanting to possess everything.

He sees the private investigator. Charlie Winters. She's not bad. Not bad at all.

He pictures her in chains. Hung by her wrists. Mouth wrapped in duct tape. A terrified look in her eyes.

It could work, he thinks. But she's dangerous. Everyone's heard the stories. Why go after a hellcat when there are so many bleating sheep around?

Then he sees a college girl drinking some kind of pink-looking concoction. Tipping her head and letting the slush slide over the glass into her mouth. A daiquiri most likely.

His imagination places her in bondage. Naked on the concrete floor. The harsh glow of the fluorescent lights shimmering on her tear-stained cheeks, her face splotchy from crying.

Yes. Better.

He sifts through all the faces. Through all the body parts. Any of them could work. He could learn to love any of them.

And they could learn to love him.

He stubs his cigarette in the ashtray. Smells that astringent odor of the filter scorching against the crushed ember.

The next girl who walks out that door will be his. No more planning. No more sitting on his hands.

No need to be picky. No need to be precious about it. The next girl will be his.

A prickle crawls over his sweat-slicked body. Makes his scrotum shrivel into a peach pit as his own words replay in his head: *The next girl will be mine.*

Jesus, it could be anyone.

He starts the car. Lets it idle. Ready to move.

CHAPTER TWENTY-NINE

The Cardamom Cafe was a moody little coffee shop lit with string lights and colored lanterns. It had been a popular hangout spot when she and Allie were teenagers. The perfect place to go with a brand new driver's license, where they could order cappuccinos and pretend to be more adult than they really were.

"Wasn't there a whole thing in high school where if a guy brought you here on a date, it meant you had to go to at least third base?" Allie asked.

"I wouldn't know."

"Well, I would," Allie said, chuckling low in the back of her throat. "And so would Mark Zalenski."

"Ugh," Charlie said.

"Hey! Don't slut-shame me, Charles. That's totally uncool."

Charlie found Olivia Smith at a table near the front windows, sipping a cup of tea. She was small and curvy with almond-shaped eyes and shoulder-length black curls.

Charlie introduced herself and took the seat opposite Olivia.

"Thanks for meeting me here." Olivia absently traced random swirls on the tabletop as she spoke. "I have this new boyfriend, and I haven't really told him anything about what happened."

"No problem," Charlie said.

"It's not that I don't think he'd be understanding or whatever," Olivia blurted. "It's just... I don't know. Everyone says it's not my fault and all that junk. But people still look at you different. Like even if it's not in a damaged goods way or whatever, they end up pitying you or treating you like you're fragile or something. That might be worse. I'd almost rather be judged and just write someone off altogether than have them treat me like some kind of charity case."

"I think I know what you mean," Charlie said. "My sister died when I was younger. And for a long time, everyone acted different. They were always sort of artificially upbeat and peppy. But then they also wouldn't laugh around me or tell jokes, so it all felt… fake."

"Exactly!"

The conversation was put on hold when the waitress brought over the hot cider Charlie had ordered. When they were alone again, Charlie looked Olivia in the eye.

"Can you tell me about what happened?"

Olivia took a deep breath and closed her eyes.

"It was last year. Labor Day weekend. I went with some friends to the lake. I've done it a million times. And I work in a bar, for Christ's sake. I know how to pace myself. I can remember most of the day pretty clearly, but once it started getting dark out, that's when things get blurry. I have a hazy recollection of seeing some fireworks, but I don't remember if I was still on the lake or not. The people I was with lost track of me once it was dark."

"What happened after that?"

"I woke up somewhere. Lying on this gross musty mattress that stank like mildew. Smelled like my grandparents' old basement, you know? Someone was… *he* was trying to tie me up."

"But you got away?"

Olivia swallowed. Her eyes stared off into space, unblinking. Her voice came out flat.

"I went straight for his eyes. I wasn't thinking, really. It was all instinct. I knew I had to hurt him… or die trying."

"Where did he take you, do you know?"

"I was out cold until I woke up in that room. All I really remember is the smell and the white cinder block walls. I thought maybe it was a cellar or something, but I don't think there were stairs. Maybe a garage?"

Her eyelids fluttered, and then she fell quiet for a few beats before she went on.

"It was still dark when I got out of there. I wasn't thinking right, you know? Drugged. Panicked. I had no idea where I was. There were no lights. No cars."

She made eye contact with Charlie for a split second, and then her eyes darted away again.

"I ran. I ran for the trees, through the woods, and then I hit the beach. I figured from there, I could follow the coastline until I knew where I was, but I was afraid to go out in the open. So I stayed hidden in the woods. Tried to keep the sound of the waves within earshot. It felt like I ran forever in the dark, but…"

The girl's eyes flickered back and forth now. Back in those woods in the dark, Charlie figured, old nightmare movies playing in her head. She probably hoped they'd go away someday, those flickering images that hurt her over and over, but they wouldn't.

Charlie knew that better than anyone.

CHAPTER THIRTY

He sits forward in his seat when she appears.

A petite silhouette taking shape in the doorway. A shadow stepping out under the streetlights.

She is the one fate has selected for him. Together forever.

His arms and legs throb with pins and needles at how clueless she is right now.

Her whole life has led her to this moment—led her to him—and she has no idea. Oblivious.

He squints. Watches the details of her sharpen.

A circle of light glints around the top of her head as she passes under a street lamp. Chestnut hair spills down the sides of a heart-shaped face. Pouty lips. Sharp cheekbones.

His heart flutters. His tongue slathers wormy lips. Sweat leaks from every pore on his body. He lets his gaze drift lower.

A micro-waist tapers her torso into a cello shape. Something delicate in the contours. Slender arms and legs discernible through her clothing.

And he knows. He knows right away that she is in love with him. Or will be soon enough.

Eternal love. Unconditional. Strictly enforced by ropes and chains.

He smiles at the thought. Wets his lips again with the tip of his tongue.

Her clothes themselves winnow into focus only after he's taken her shape in. Skinny jeans. A tank top with a cardigan slung over it.

She walks to the parking lot. Feet shuffling in her stiletto heels. Scuffing and clicking against the concrete.

She moves away from the orangey streetlights surrounding the bar, and the moonlight paints her a lilac shade. Glows where it touches her flesh.

Her sweater peels back, and he catches just a glimpse of her collarbone as she climbs into her car. He lets out a shaky sigh as his eyes crawl over her skin.

She pulls out of the lot, and he follows. Heart thundering as he steers the car out onto the road.

Her headlights sweep around corners. Push through the darkness.

He keeps a bit of distance between them. Doesn't want her to notice.

And the night seems a vast emptiness that stretches out around them. A vacancy. Oblivion.

Just over eight blocks away from the bar, she pulls into a driveway outside of a small house of brick and pale gray siding. No light gleams out from beyond the curtains.

He slows. Watches.

Her brake lights flare there a moment. Bright red spilling over the concrete slab of the driveway, reflecting off the vinyl siding. Then the purr of her engine cuts off and the lights wink out.

This is it. Home sweet home.

He kills his own lights. Parks in a shaded spot a couple doors shy of her place. Smears his clammy hands on the thighs of his pants. Takes a deep breath.

OK. Go time.

He climbs out of the car. Quiet now but for his heart still hammering away in his ribcage.

He presses his wrist against the bulk tucked down in his belt. The blade. Ready now to come out and play. To press itself to that soft skin just off the center of her throat, the place where the vein makes the flesh quiver.

He'll get her just as she climbs out of her car. That moment of vulnerability as she unfolds herself. One arm will loop around her shoulders. The other will jam that cold metal to her neck just hard enough that she'll feel the sharp edge of the blade kiss her flesh.

The dome light glows inside the car. She leans to her right. Fiddles with something in the passenger seat. Probably gathering her things.

She has no clue that he's there. No clue how close he is now.

His lips twitch upward. Excitement roiling in his chest. A laugh threatening to come ripping out.

And his eyes open wider. He wants to scare her. Wants to hurt her.

But not yet. Not yet. One step at a time.

He stalks up behind the car. Staying off to the opposite side of her door for now. Keeping out of the line of sight of her rearview mirror as long as he can.

He's rounding the rear bumper as she moves to open the door. Needs to close the last few feet quickly. Grab her now.

The door pops open. The dome light slices a wedge out of the gloom.

He moves into that glow. Feels his jaw clench. Slides a hand over his belly, into his belt.

His fingers tremble as he pulls the knife free. His mouth goes dry.

One stiletto extends out over the concrete driveway. The shoe grits faintly as it touches down on the cement.

He lunges as the rest of her comes into the open. Loops his arms to grab her.

But she stops halfway out of the car. Dodges him. Ducks to keep just out of reach. Eyes wide and wet and staring straight at him.

She shrieks. A sharp sound spluttering from her lips and then piercing the night.

And he knows now that he's dragging this out on purpose. Toying with her and savoring it.

How could he resist? She looks so beautiful when she's terrified. The thrill of the hunt gets to be too much.

Again, the urge to laugh overwhelms him. Lurching and spitting in his abdomen. He wants to bend at the waist and let the giggles come launching out of him. Laugh until he cries. Never stop.

Instead he raises the knife. Leans for her. Reaches for her.

A small pink canister in her hand suddenly comes to life. Spits at him. Hissing and spraying. It spritzes a fine mist over his eyes, nose, lips, chin, and chest.

He didn't see it until it was too late.

He stumbles into the side of the car. Blinks. Tries to clear the blur.

It takes a fraction of a second for the effects of the pepper spray to take hold.

And then the whole world is on fire.

CHAPTER THIRTY-ONE

Searing pain grips his face. The pepper spray burns brighter in the wet places—the edges of his lips, trailing into his nose, and, worst of all, his eyes.

Gleaming. Blistering.

Tears flood his eyelids until they run over. The flesh around them instantly goes hot and puffy as though deeply sunburned—that sun-charred kind of burn that peels the top layer of skin away like leathery paper.

He whimpers. Brings the heels of his hands to his eyes. Tries to take a deep breath to steady himself but feels the burn spread to his throat, which only makes him gag and cough.

The chemical blaze assailing his face can't get worse, can't intensify. But it does.

Hurt. Blind.

Feels like his eyeballs are melting in their sockets now. Liquefying into an opaque goo that will weep down over his cheekbones like milky tears.

He grits his teeth.

Some instinct tells him to attack. Inflict damage. Leave a mark. Even if he's fucked beyond hope for the moment, he can still leave a mark.

He swings his blade at her. Feels some kind of contact made. Metal touching her. Opening her.

She gasps. Sucks breath over wet lips, through clenched teeth. *Good. Fuck you.*

He staggers a step forward. Slashes out with the knife again.

But she's gone. He can feel it, even if all he can see are smears of dark and light. Her footsteps trail away, a soft clap on the driveway.

He wheels around. Moves for the road.

He can barely see. Eyelids swelling so fast that he looks out at the world through little slits, angry folds of flesh that form red borders at the top and bottom of his field of vision.

Blinking rapidly, he tries to peer through the flowing tears. Can just make out the seams in the concrete driveway. Can see the place where the pale cement gives way to the black asphalt of the road.

He lurches that way. Hard to focus with all the fluid draining from his face.

Snot flows like water from his nostrils. Gathers and gushes from the tip of his nose.

He stumbles as he gets to the street. Scurries for his car.

The sedan becomes a huddling dark shape that distorts and clears over and over again as he blinks the endless tears away.

But he reaches it. A moan escapes his lips as he manages to work his fingers under the blurry crease of the door handle and falls inside.

He speeds away just as the sirens start to wail in the distance.

CHAPTER THIRTY-TWO

Olivia tried to keep going, to finish her story, but Charlie could see she was becoming more and more distressed as she went on. Her voice was barely more than a whisper now.

"I have no idea how long I was out there in the woods. It was cold and dark, and…" She put a shaking hand to her mouth. "And I thought…"

Her voice broke, and Olivia angled her face away, blinking rapidly. Trying not to cry.

"Olivia, if this is too much right now, we can stop," Charlie said.

Olivia swiveled back to stare at her, and there was a hardness in her gaze now.

"No. I need to do this for Emma. Even if it isn't the same guy. I can't stand the idea of something like this happening to anyone else. Because it leaves a mark. Being that scared, that close to the edge…" Olivia wiped at the corner of her eye and shook her head. "I still have nightmares that I'm back in that room. On that mattress. And waking up is barely any comfort, because I know he's still out there somewhere."

"I only mean that we could stop for now and talk again tomorrow," Charlie said. "Maybe it would be easier to think about this stuff in the daylight."

Olivia sniffled.

"I'll be OK in a minute. I can do this."

Charlie nodded her understanding, taking a drink of her cider while she waited. It was hot and tart on her tongue, with a warm spicy note that lingered long after she'd swallowed.

Across the table, Olivia hitched in a big breath and let it out slowly. When she went on, some of the tension had drained from her voice.

"All I know is that once it got light out, I could see the old Ferris wheel off to the south of me. And then I spotted someone jogging down the beach. At first I thought it was him, and I ducked into the weeds for cover. But it was a woman. So I scampered out there screaming and waving my arms, and I think I probably just about gave her a heart attack."

Charlie scribbled the details down in her notes. Even as vague as they were, the fact that Olivia could see the Ferris wheel from the beach was somewhere to start.

"The man who took you. Did you see his face?"

"Only in my nightmares," Olivia said, rubbing her eyes. "But that night? No. I can't even tell you if he was wearing a mask or not. It was dark, but I think the drugs made it even worse. It's like his face was a gray smear. No discernible features. I felt half blind running around in those woods. The one detail I can remember about him is his smell."

"What'd he smell like?" Charlie asked, hoping it might be something distinct, like a particular brand of cologne.

Olivia's nose wrinkled.

"Cigarettes. My grandpa smoked like a chimney, so I used to find that smell somewhat comforting." She swallowed. "But not anymore."

"And the police never caught him?"

"No. They took my statement. Did a rape exam. But they never found anything. They said there were so many people on the lake that day that it could have been anyone."

"But this guy clearly had a plan. He took you somewhere on the island, tried to tie you up, like the whole idea had been to kidnap you and keep you there. That makes it way more likely that he's a local. He had to know the area."

"That's what I said." Olivia shrugged. "I called every few days for like a month and a half, asking if they were making any progress."

"And?"

"Eventually I realized they weren't going to catch him." Olivia's chin quivered slightly. "And I can't blame them, really. I could barely tell them anything other than a vague description of the location. I couldn't remember anything about him, other than the smell."

"You were drugged and scared."

"But what if he's the one who killed Emma?" Olivia asked, her voice beginning to shake. "If I'd given the police something to go on, there's a chance she'd still be alive."

Charlie reached out and put her hand on Olivia's wrist.

"You had one job, Olivia." She waited until Olivia's eyes met hers. "To survive. And you did that."

Olivia wiped a tear from her cheek. Charlie gave her a moment to collect herself before the next question.

"Have you ever had any problematic customers at the Laughing Raven? Or maybe a psycho ex-boyfriend?"

Olivia winced and hesitated before speaking.

"There was this one guy. He wasn't exactly a boyfriend, but he was kinda psycho."

"How so?"

"We went on a few dates, and he got, like, really clingy really fast. Big turn-off." Olivia cocked her head to one side and pursed her lips. "So I told him it wasn't working out. And then he slashed my tires."

"Yeah, I'd say that qualifies as psycho," Charlie said. "What was his name?"

Again, Olivia hesitated.

"I just… feel bad pointing the finger at someone who might be innocent," Olivia said, crossing her arms. "Don't get me wrong. Darren is a douchebag, but I don't think he'd go this far."

"Don't worry. I'll be discreet," Charlie assured her. "What's Darren's last name?"

Olivia sighed.

"Nesbitt."

Charlie scribbled the name in her notes and then insisted on paying Olivia's bill as well as her own.

"I know this wasn't easy to talk about," she said, shaking Olivia's hand. "Thank you."

Outside, Charlie caught a glimpse of Olivia still inside. The girl gazed out the window overlooking the street, staring at nothing. Charlie knew her mind was still wandering those dark woods she'd gotten lost in, and she hoped that hunting down the man who'd hurt her would give the girl some peace.

As Charlie ducked into her car and turned on the ignition, her phone rang. It was Zoe.

"Are you still making the rounds at the Laughing Raven?" Charlie said. "I was about to head back over there now."

"No, there's been a... development."

"What's that mean?"

"He attacked another girl."

CHAPTER THIRTY-THREE

He drives. His car knifing through the vacant streets of Salem Island. Headlights sweeping around corners, pushing through the darkness.

Police chatter blares on the speakers. His scanner tunes into them. Lets him spy on them.

Nosy neighbors called in the scuffle in the driveway. A fight between a man and a woman. Yelling. Possible violence.

So far the officers arriving at the scene have yet to locate the girl. They don't seem terribly concerned.

His car swoops through another intersection as the idle chatter plays on the radio. He presses deeper into the night.

Anyway, he can't go home. Not yet. He needs to know how bad he hurt her before he can sleep. Can still remember the feel of his blade sinking into her flesh. But where? If he opened her neck up, the wound could have been fatal. If he got her in the hand or arm, the odds were worse.

His eyelids twitch. He lets his gaze sweep to the rearview mirror, sees the sunglasses that shroud his swollen eyes.

The hiss of the pepper spray replays in his mind. That first bright flare of the chemicals igniting his eyeballs.

Searing pain.

And then searing rage at having failed again. But had that really been his fault? How could he have known she'd use a dirty trick like that against him?

Stupid bitch.

He blinks a few times and fresh tears creep out from beneath the sunglasses. The moisture refreshes the burn somehow.

Brightens it anew. He dabs at his raw face with the sleeve of his sweatshirt.

Sleepy voices on the scanner grab his attention. A slow-talking deputy reports that the officers got no answer at the girl's front door. They're checking out the backyard now. They sound bored. Sluggish. Salem Island's finest.

At a stoplight, he swipes at the condensation on the windshield. The warmth in the car stands in glaring contrast to the crisp October night outside. He keeps fogging up the windshield. Wiping at it to clear away a small circle to look through like a porthole.

Block after block of empty streets and dark windows stare back at him through that clear spot in the glass.

The city sleeps at night. And he watches. A creeping shadow. A restless soul that walks among them.

Sometimes it feels like it all belongs to him after dark. When all is still. When nothing moves but him.

Mine. After dark, it's all mine.

He swims down the streets. Circles it all like a shark. Some creature who can never stop moving, who can never know rest, whose hunger is never sated.

An excited voice barks on the scanner, crackling with nervous energy.

"We've got something. Caucasian female, approximately twenty-five years old, here in the backyard. She's here."

"What's the subject's condition?" the dispatcher asks, voice still mostly neutral.

"I'm checking now. There's… there's blood."

He sits forward in his seat. Hunches over the steering wheel. Subconsciously presses his foot down on the accelerator so the car picks up speed along with his heartbeat.

After a long pause, the dispatcher follows up.

"What's the condition of the subject? Over."

The radio crackles once. Then falls quiet again.

"She's fine," the officer finally says, relief obvious in his voice. "She was assaulted with a knife in the driveway and managed to flee here to the backyard, where she hid. Suffered a minor laceration on the heel of her hand, but she's going to be OK."

CHAPTER THIRTY-FOUR

Cop cars swarm the driveway. Lights twirling red and blue.

He rolls toward the scene, going neither fast nor slow. Careful to seem inconspicuous, knowing he probably shouldn't have chanced this drive.

If any cops working the scene were to get a good look, they might notice the passing driver wearing sunglasses at night. And if he were to get pulled over, one look at the snarled-up flesh around his eyes glowing as red as a pair of lobster claws would tell them all they needed to know.

But it is too late for caution now. He watches the scene out of the corner of his eye, not wanting to appear any more interested than a random passerby might be.

The Podunk police cluster on the concrete, standing shoulder to shoulder. Many hook their hands in their belts as though it's something they learned at the academy.

A husky deputy points at the girl's car door, which hangs open like a mouth, the dome light still slicing its wedge out of the night where it spills at their feet.

He expects one of them to turn to see the oncoming vehicle, if only to give it a passing glance, but none of them do. Too engrossed in whatever the husky cop is yammering about.

And then he sees *her*, and his heart stops.

Not the girl who pepper sprayed him. The detective. Charlie Winters.

She ducks under the flapping yellow police tape and hustles over to the deputies. Hair fluttering behind her like a scarf as she moves.

The husky deputy has put his meaty hand away at last, and now it's Charlie doing the talking. Everyone leaning in a little to listen. Looks like a quarterback in the huddle. A natural leader. The kind of person people flock to. The kind of person who gets results.

He narrows his eyes as he looks at her. His swollen eyelids finding a way to crease even tighter, though it hurts.

And then she's gone. Somewhere behind him in the dark.

He drives on. Watches the scene transform into a shrinking smudge in the rearview mirror. And then it's gone, disappearing into the night.

CHAPTER THIRTY-FIVE

It wasn't difficult to locate the scene. Charlie spotted the strobing police lights from several blocks away. The residential street where the attack had occurred was peppered with Halloween and harvest decorations: a cluster of pumpkins and gourds on one porch, a trio of ghosts dangling from another.

Zoe intercepted her as she parked across the street from the commotion and beckoned her beyond a line of police tape stretched between two trees.

"Tell me again what happened," Charlie said.

Zoe nodded toward a young blond girl being interviewed by two detectives from the Salem Island Sheriff's Department. She was barefoot, clutching a pair of high-heeled shoes in one hand. The other hand was swaddled in white bandages.

"Rachel Shumway, twenty-five years of age, was parking her car in her driveway when a man approached from behind and tried to grab her. He had a knife. They struggled, and she managed to nail him full in the face with the can of pepper spray she has on her keychain. He went down, scrambled away, and drove off. And here's where it gets interesting." Zoe's eyebrows danced up and down. "Guess where she was earlier this evening?"

Charlie glanced over at the girl. She was gesticulating wildly with her hands, swinging the shoes this way and that, no doubt relaying some detail of her story to the detectives.

"No idea," Charlie said.

"The Laughing Raven."

Charlie could practically feel the synapses firing in her brain as she connected the dots.

"That means we can connect all of the attacks to the same bar."

"Yes, ma'am." Zoe leaned back on her heels. "So that's something, right? We figured out where he likes to hunt."

A chill ran up Charlie's spine, causing her to shudder.

"What is it?" Zoe asked.

"It's just that if we figure he followed her home from the bar, that means he was there tonight, at the same time we were." Charlie blinked. "One of us might have talked to him."

"An unsettling thought," Zoe said, crossing her arms.

"I'm assuming she didn't recognize the man who attacked her." Charlie gestured at the barefoot girl across the way. "You would have mentioned that."

"No, but we did get a description," Zoe said and started rattling off the details. "White male, dark hair. Mid-twenties. Above average height and slender build. But he was wearing a black sweatshirt with the hood pulled up, which kept her from getting a good look at his face."

"Kinda generic but better than nothing." Charlie sighed. "She's one lucky girl."

"It's not luck if you kick the guy's ass," Allie said. "That's called balls."

Charlie supposed Allie had a point, but she wasn't about to admit that. The last thing Allie needed was encouragement.

The lights on the nearest police car were at the perfect angle to shine directly into Charlie's eyes. She turned herself away from them and resumed her conversation with Zoe.

"So this other waitress from the Laughing Raven, Olivia Smith…" Charlie said. "She says she was drugged and kidnapped from one of the Labor Day boat parties last year."

"Oh, right." Zoe bobbed her head. "Yeah, I remember that."

Charlie's eyebrows shot up. From Olivia's statement, Charlie had expected to hear that her case had gotten shelved for lack of evidence. She didn't think Zoe would have heard enough about it to remember any of the details.

"You do?"

"Of course. It was pretty awful. I'm almost always there for the rape kits if I'm on duty, because they figure I'm less threatening than any of the male cops." Zoe sighed. "Just another perk of being a lady in uniform."

"What happened? Olivia got the impression you guys were blowing her off because she hadn't given you enough to go on."

Zoe's mouth twitched. A sure sign that she was holding something back.

"Zoe."

Zoe scanned their surroundings and then indicated that Charlie should follow her a ways down the sidewalk. When they were a safe distance from the rest of the law enforcement personnel milling around, Zoe leaned in, keeping her voice low.

"Look, you didn't hear this from me, alright? But the sheriff gets a lot of pressure from the business council to keep any major crimes from hitting the papers during the tourism season."

Charlie's jaw popped open, and for several seconds she was speechless.

"So you're saying they buried it?"

Zoe's head shook from side to side.

"*I'm* not saying anything, because I like my job and want to keep it. But if that's the conclusion you're coming to…"

Charlie scoffed.

"I don't know why I'm even surprised. Of course they buried it," she said, her voice dripping with disgust. "They couldn't have tourists hearing about the sexual assault and kidnapping of a woman at one of our pristine beaches, could they? Something so trivial couldn't be allowed to affect business. Jesus, Zoe."

"Hey, I don't like it either." Zoe shrugged. "But you know how it is. The business council depends on the tourism trade. In turn, the sheriff depends on the business council for endorsements come election time. Politics, baby."

"More like greed. All any of them care about is money and power."

Zoe smiled bitterly.

"You say that like greed and politics are two different things."

Charlie's gaze returned to Rachel Shumway. Whether it had been sheer balls or luck, Charlie worried what would happen if the next girl he tried to take didn't get away.

"He's got a lair somewhere on the island," Charlie said. "Olivia said she woke up in a cinder block building. She thought it was a basement at first, but she doesn't remember there being any stairs. It was near the shore, and she saw the Poseidon's Kingdom Ferris wheel on the skyline when she reached the beach. So a garage or a shed, maybe a boathouse somewhere near the shore. It can't be that hard to find, can it?"

"Oh, no. There are only probably a few hundred buildings matching that description on the island," Zoe mused sarcastically.

Her hopes dashed, Charlie felt herself getting angry again.

"Emma would probably still be alive if they'd done a proper investigation back when Olivia was kidnapped. And now look what's happened. He's clearly getting bolder. With Olivia, he waited until she was drugged. Emma, he waited until she was at least home and alone. But this? This seems like a random grab. First girl he saw, first chance he got."

"That's true," Zoe agreed. "I mean, you'd think with all the attention Emma's murder is getting in the media, he'd lie low, you know?"

"It makes me think he didn't intend for her to die. At least not so quickly." Charlie chewed on that for a moment. "Things went wrong with Emma, and now he's desperate."

"A desperate, murderous stalker," Zoe said, her tone flat. "Just what we need."

"Olivia mentioned a guy she dated. It wasn't a long-term thing. She said the guy was too clingy, so she ended it, and then he got weird. Darren Nesbitt. Can you check out his history?"

"Sure," Zoe said, getting out her phone and typing the name into a notepad app.

"Also, there was a guy sitting at the bar tonight at the Laughing Raven. Real charmer," Charlie said, suddenly remembering the man in the Carhartt jacket. "Neil something…"

She got out her phone and did a quick search of the trucking company he worked for in the hopes of finding his last name listed somewhere.

"Here we go. Neil Kushner."

Zoe nodded and took this name down as well before tucking the phone into her pocket.

They stood in silence for a while as the lights on the tops of the police cruisers lit the world around them in flashes of red and blue.

"We have to find this guy," Charlie said.

"I know. We will."

CHAPTER THIRTY-SIX

Flecks of wetness are suspended in the air everywhere around the car, a mist glistening and glittering wherever the headlights make contact.

He hunches over the steering wheel. A smile playing at his lips. Excited breaths puffing in and out of his nostrils.

He's wide awake now, even as late as it is. Sore eyes wide. Muscles taut. Electricity surging in his brain.

He's back on the hunt.

He waited. Watched. Lurked around the corner from the crime scene like a sleepy spider until the detective left the scene.

And now he stalks again. Pressing forward into the night. Always forward.

Charlie Winters heads toward home, and he follows.

He keeps his distance. Lingering half a block back.

A light drizzle falls from the sky. The windshield wipers keep time like a metronome.

Tick-tock. Tick-tock.

He wants to jam his foot on the gas. Feel the car turn aggressive at his touch. Race right up on her rear bumper. Put a little fear in her.

But not yet. Not yet. All in due time.

The car tires swish over the wet asphalt. Thrumming and sizzling. Flinging tendrils of water into the wheel wells.

Her taillights gleam at the traffic signal ahead. The red glow distorts and smears on the steamed-up windshield before him.

He smears a hand at the window again. Clears a patch of fog away. Feels the chill of the glass as a mild shock against the heat of his body, another reminder of how cold the nights get this time of year.

Charlie steers her Ford Focus down an alley and up a slight ramp into a parking lot pocked with potholes. She parks behind a brick building and quickly climbs a staircase to a loft apartment, hurrying to get out of the rain.

The building itself looks ancient and vaguely industrial, certainly commercial at the very least. A stack of red bricks that might have been a general store in the 1940s or something, though it's hard to be certain from the backside of the place.

He cruises through the alley, puddles sloshing beneath the tires. From there, two left turns place him in front of the building.

The facade of A1 Investigations lies veiled in shadow, all the windows dark for the night. He smiles at the sight, lips stinging anew from remnants of the pepper spray, but he doesn't care.

Maybe there's a better way to put a little fear into her.

CHAPTER THIRTY-SEVEN

True to her word, Zoe called Charlie the next morning with information on the names they'd discussed the night before.

"Let's start off with our bad boy, Darren Nesbitt."

"The one who slashed Olivia Smith's tires after she broke up with him," Charlie said, jogging her own memory as much as Zoe's.

"That's the one. And what a winner he seems to be. We've got felony cocaine possession, criminal trespass, assault and battery, vandalism."

"Any details on those beyond what it says on his rap sheet?" Charlie asked.

"I'm still waiting on a call back from the arresting jurisdictions," Zoe said. "They all happened out of state. Florida and Ohio. Also, his last known address here on the island is no good. I know the building listed here, and it was torn down a few months back to make way for some luxury condos."

Charlie grabbed a blank notepad and a pen and started scribbling.

"Anyway, I figure if anyone can track him down, it's you. According to the Secretary of State records, he drives a red 2012 Camaro, if that helps at all."

"I'm on it," Charlie said, nodding as she walked the note she'd written over to Paige.

Her assistant scanned the words she'd hastily scratched on the pad.

Call Frank and see if he can track down the current whereabouts of Darren Nesbitt. The Water Street address is no good.

Already reaching for the phone, Paige gave Charlie a thumbs up.

"What about the jerkoff I met at the Laughing Raven?" Charlie asked, returning to her desk. "Neil Kushner."

"Kushner is pristine," Zoe said. "Not a mark on his record."

"Not even something minor like drunk and disorderly? Or open intox?"

"No, ma'am. He's squeaky-clean on our end. But maybe you'll dig something up. I assume you're going to look into him anyway."

"Damn right," Charlie said, thinking that while Frank was hunting down Darren Nesbitt, she'd take point on Neil Kushner. "So I've been thinking about the Carnival Bizarre at the Laughing Raven. It's tomorrow."

"Right. They do it every year on Halloween."

"So we have the attack on Olivia, who works there. An attack on Emma, who also worked there. Then last night's attack on Rachel Shumway, who had been there earlier in the evening. All three girls have some connection to the bar, and he used the Labor Day weekend activities as a way to grab Olivia."

"And the carnival would make the perfect hunting grounds," Zoe said.

"If I was a psycho-stalking type already staking the place out, then yeah. It's going to be a lot of people. Very drunk people. He can practically hide in plain sight."

Zoe swore under her breath.

"So what do we do?" she asked. "We could try to convince the Laughing Raven to cancel the party."

"No. He'd just find somewhere else to hunt for his next victim. It's like we said last night: after things went sideways with Emma, the smart thing to do would be to lie low for a while. Instead, he goes out two nights later and tries again." Charlie leaned back in her chair and stared up at the ceiling. "Shutting the party down isn't going to stop him. But if we have a hunch that he's going to stake out the carnival, then maybe we can do the same and catch him in the act."

"It's kind of a long shot," Zoe said. "You said yourself: there's going to be a lot of very drunk people. I've done crowd control at the carnival before. It's a nightmare."

"I know. But I don't have a better plan," Charlie said with a sigh. "Speaking of crowd control, I know the sheriff sends out extra patrols on Halloween. What do you think about pitching the idea of some DUI checkpoints in the vicinity of the party? If we don't catch this creep or at least scare him off, the patrols can keep their eyes peeled for sketchy dudes with unconscious women in tow."

"That's not a bad idea," Zoe said. "I'll go talk to him now. Anything else?"

"Nah."

"OK, I'll call you later with an update."

They hung up, and Charlie opened a satellite map of Salem Island on her computer. Olivia had told her that one of the first things she'd spotted after escaping from her kidnapper was the Ferris wheel at the abandoned Poseidon's Kingdom amusement park, and Charlie hoped she could use that information to pinpoint an area she could search. Unfortunately, the Ferris wheel was one of the most visible landmarks on the island. Charlie could narrow it down a little, since Olivia had been on the beach looking south when she'd seen it, but it meant she was still looking at a section of coastline several miles long.

Charlie chose an area and zoomed in, then tried to access the street view. But the roads on that side of the island were remote, and no street view option was available.

Cursing the limitations of technology, Charlie dedicated herself to a new task. Frank was taking lead on hunting down Darren Nesbitt, which meant that Charlie was left with the Carhartt Prince Charming, Neil Kushner.

It took her less than five minutes to locate not only his home address but what kind of vehicle Neil drove.

"A 2002 Buick LeSabre," Allie said, whistling. "Sweet ride."

Charlie chuckled as she gathered up her bag. She thought maybe she'd head over and check in on Neil. Maybe she'd catch a glimpse of him with red puffy eyes after tangling with the wrong end of a can of pepper spray.

"I'm going out for a bit," Charlie told Paige. "In the meantime, you remember that client from a few weeks back, Mrs. Brecker?"

"You mean the Case of the Cold-Footed Divorcee?" her assistant asked.

Charlie squinted.

"The what?"

Paige smiled, cheeks going pink.

"Oh, I like to give all our cases names like the ones in those old Perry Mason stories. Dutch Carmichael was the Case of the Bogus Billionaire. That woman who thought her daughter-in-law had stolen her necklace was the Case of the Missing Moonstone." Paige shrugged. "So the Case of the Cold-Footed Divorcee would be the lady who wanted proof her husband was cheating, but then he bought her a big fat diamond, which changed her mind even after seeing the proof that he'd been cheating."

"Well, I have a hunch that the cold-footed divorcee is going to try to skip out on the remainder of her bill. Can you call and give her a friendly reminder?"

"Yes, ma'am," Paige said, writing a note to herself in the planner she kept on her desk. "And I don't mean to be a nosy Norma, but I overheard your plan for infiltrating the carnival at the Laughing Raven, and I had an idea."

Charlie smirked a little at the word "infiltrating."

"Yeah?"

"Well, we'll need costumes. To blend in."

Charlie arched an eyebrow.

"We?"

"You let me help last night."

That's true, Charlie thought. But the more she learned about this guy, the less she liked having someone as naive as Paige anywhere near where he might be. Then again, if the Carnival Bizarre was anything like it had been in years past, they were going to need all hands on deck.

"You can help," Charlie said. "And costumes are a good idea. I wouldn't have thought about that until the last minute, and I'd end up having to wear a sheet over my head with holes cut out like Charlie Brown."

"Oh no, you have to get creative on Halloween! That's where all the fun is," Paige insisted.

"I'll check back in this afternoon. If you need me, I have my phone."

CHAPTER THIRTY-EIGHT

Rows of sugar maples lined the streets of downtown Salem Island, and Charlie admired the turning leaves as she cruised down Main Street. She cracked her window to let in a bit of the crisp autumn air. It was a little cold for it, but fall was her favorite season, and she loved the smell this time of year.

Just outside of town, Charlie passed one of the U-pick pumpkin patches on the island. Orange globes dotted the field, and Charlie's mind flashed on a memory of carving pumpkins with Allie when they were kids. Charlie had flicked a seed at her sister, and Allie had retaliated by throwing an entire handful of pumpkin guts back. That had been the last time they were allowed to carve pumpkins in the house.

Classic Allie. Responding to the flicking of a single seed with an entire handful.

"It's called *not fucking around*," Allie said. "I couldn't let you get away with that. I had to show you that if you messed with me, you were going to get everything back a hundredfold."

Charlie slowed and took the next turn. Neil Kushner's abode was the third house on the street, a plain-looking cottage with white siding about a half mile from the main public boat launch on the island. There was a car in the driveway, but it wasn't the Buick LeSabre registered to Neil. This was a white Jeep Cherokee, probably around ten years old.

Charlie got out her phone and after a few minutes of searching discovered another name that came up as a match for the address: Randall Kross.

So, Neil has a roommate.

A smile spread over Charlie's lips. If this Randall fellow was a talker, that might turn out to be even more enlightening than shadowing Neil for a day.

Charlie checked her reflection in the mirror before she got out.

"Put on some lipstick," Allie said.

"What? Why?"

"You want to charm the roommate, right? If you want to give him the old razzle-dazzle, you can't go walking up there with those pale fish lips."

"You have the same lips, you know."

"Exactly why I wouldn't be caught dead walking around without some color. I'm not an idiot."

Charlie emitted an annoyed sound from the back of her throat but ultimately took Allie's advice. She rooted around in her bag and found a tube of dark red lipstick. The name was Blackbird, and Charlie could only vaguely remember buying it on impulse months ago. She must have thrown it in her purse and forgotten about it.

Charlie applied the lipstick and studied her handiwork.

"Much better," Allie said. "I mean, not to harp on about this, but without lipstick, your mouth looks like two maggots trying to hump each other whenever you start talking."

Charlie climbed out of the car and slammed the door, hoping that would shut Allie up. She let her feet clap loudly on the cement of the front steps. Allie rarely tried to compete with clatter.

Pausing outside the front door, Charlie could hear loud sound effects coming from inside. Explosions and gunfire and strange pings and whoops that told Charlie it was coming from a video game.

She banged her knuckles against the exterior screen door, and a few seconds later, a scrawny guy in plaid boxer shorts and an *Evil Dead* T-shirt opened the interior door. He seemed startled to find a woman on the other side and crossed his legs awkwardly.

"Can I... help you?"

"Is Neil here?" Charlie asked, affecting a peppy smile and vocal tone to match.

"Oh. Uh… no. He's at work."

Charlie made a show of furrowing her brow in disappointment.

"I thought so. And he's not getting back from this run until…"

Squinting as if she were trying to remember the date, she waited for Randall to fill it in for her, since she didn't actually have any idea of what Neil's work schedule was.

"November thirteenth," Randall said.

If Neil really was out of town for that long, he'd miss the Halloween bash at the Laughing Raven. But Randall could be mistaken. Or Neil could have lied about his schedule. An alibi that would keep him out of town. Charlie needed more information.

She cocked her head to one side.

"You're Randall, right?"

A dozen lines formed on his forehead and he swallowed, his Adam's apple bouncing up and a down.

"Er… yeah."

"Neil told me about you," she said, smiling. "Could I come in for a minute? I really need someone to talk to."

"Well…"

Charlie didn't wait for an answer. Randall had already broadcast loud and clear that he was a soft touch, and she knew he wouldn't stop her. So she pulled open the screen door and stepped inside.

The place had a dated feel—wood paneling on the walls and brown shag carpet that looked like it'd been kicking around since the late eighties. A large flat-screen was mounted on the far wall with a tangle of cords dangling down like the tentacles of some kind of sea creature.

Charlie sat on the couch and patted the seat next to her. Randall obliged, tugging a crocheted blanket from behind him and covering his lap with it.

"It's just… well, this is embarrassing," Charlie said, fussing with her hair in a way she hoped conveyed self-consciousness. "I really like Neil, but he's just so hard to read, you know? He's got that permanent poker face."

Randall chuckled nervously and scratched his elbow.

"Sure does," he agreed. "I've barely ever seen him crack a smile, let alone laugh."

"The thing is, we were supposed to go out a few nights ago, but then Neil called and canceled on me. He said he had to go out of town on work, but I can't shake the feeling that maybe he was here and just didn't want to see me. And I know how pathetic this must look, me showing up here and asking you all this… but was he working Tuesday or was he here?"

"Oh, he had to work alright. In fact, he's been in a hell of a mood this week on account of his schedule. He got in late Wednesday night from Wisconsin and had to go back out this morning. Basically only had the one day off in between."

If Neil really had been at work through Wednesday, that meant he'd been out of town when Emma had been murdered.

Charlie pretended to look relieved.

"Thank you so much. That just really puts my mind at ease." She stood. "And… I hate to ask this because it sounds so shady, but could you not mention to Neil that I came around? I don't want him thinking I'm some kind of psycho."

Randall smiled shyly.

"Don't worry. It'll be our little secret."

As Charlie headed for the door, Randall called out.

"I didn't get your name," he said.

"Oh," Charlie said, making up the first name that came to mind. "It's Beth."

"Well, if Neil don't start treating you right, give me a call."

Normally Charlie would have thought this sort of attempt was gross, but Randall had such an innocent demeanor that she couldn't help but smile a little.

"I'll think about it."

"Wow," Allie said as Charlie walked back to her car. "I didn't think the little squirt had it in him."

Charlie smirked.

"Me neither."

Charlie sat in her parked car for a few moments, considering what she'd learned. There was always a chance that Randall was wrong or lying to cover for Neil, but for now, it looked like Neil had an alibi for Emma's murder.

"Too bad," Allie said. "I wanted you to take that dickweed down. Hard. No one calls my sister a cheap whore and gets away with it."

Charlie frowned.

"He never said I was cheap."

"Don't delude yourself, Chuck. You're not high-end material. No offense."

Before Charlie could respond, her phone rang. It was Frank.

"Found your Nesbitt fella," he said when she picked up.

"Already?"

"Sitting outside his apartment as we speak."

"That was fast," Charlie said. "I'm impressed."

She could hear the pride in Uncle Frank's voice when he replied.

"I've still got a few tricks."

"Mind if I come by and have a look?"

"Be my guest," Frank said. "But do me a favor?"

"What is it?"

"I only had a smoothie for breakfast this morning, and I'm starving."

"A smoothie?" Charlie repeated, almost choking on the word. "You made a *smoothie*?"

Frank was a firm believer in real food being something that required chewing before it could be swallowed. Her uncle drinking a smoothie was unheard of. She tried to picture him, glass in hand, lips wrapping around the end of a straw. Tried to imagine his cheeks working as he slurped the blended drink into his mouth.

"Can't be done," Allie said. "It requires a suspension of disbelief beyond the scope of what is humanly possible."

"Yeah, well, it's supposed to be a good way to get vitamins and nutrients," Frank was saying. "Also supposed to be filling, but that's a crock."

Charlie chuckled.

"What do you want?"

"A double bacon cheeseburger."

"Wow. No middle ground. Straight from the smoothie to the baconator."

"I'm hungry!" Frank whined. "I think I'm more hungry than if I hadn't eaten anything at all. Substantial breakfast, my ass."

CHAPTER THIRTY-NINE

Charlie rode back into town, stopping off at Bulge Burger on the way to meet up with Frank. A fundraiser for the high school band was set up in the parking lot, and the kids were selling heirloom pumpkins to make money for new uniforms. They had several folding tables covered with squash in an impressive array of colors, shapes, and texture: orange, white, green, tan. Squat, fat, warty, and striped.

Charlie paused at one of the tables on her way back out with the food. She picked out the weirdest pumpkin she could find: a pinkish gourd with large beige warts that made it look like it was covered with peanut shells. She handed a five-dollar bill to a girl with braces and red hair and then carried the bag of food and her new pumpkin friend back to her car.

"This is a new level of dorky behavior for you," Allie said. "Buying weird squash."

"It was for a good cause."

"No, this speaks to something deeper. Some psychological need for hideous fruit things."

A few minutes later, Charlie drove past the address Frank had given her for Darren Nesbitt. His apartment was just off one of the main streets downtown, in an old two-story brick house with a low roof and arched windows.

Charlie spotted Frank's car in front of the courthouse on the next corner. She waved as she passed him by.

There was plenty of available parking on the block, so Charlie found a spot and then walked back to Frank's car.

She handed him the two drinks she'd picked up from Bulge Burger through his window before going around to the passenger side and climbing in.

"Got you something," she said, waiting until he'd finished settling the drinks in the cup holders before handing over the warty pumpkin.

He spun it in his hands.

"What the hell is it?"

"A pumpkin."

He glanced from her to the strange squash.

"Well what's wrong with it? Looks like it's got a bad case of genital warts."

Charlie laughed.

"It's an heirloom," she said.

"Is that what they're calling it now?"

Frank shook his head and set the thing on the dash, freeing his hands to dig into the burger bag.

"Any activity from our friend Darren Nesbitt?" Charlie asked.

"Nothing yet. That's his car parked in the driveway, though. The red Camaro." Frank raised his chin in the direction of the house as he unfolded the paper surrounding his double bacon cheeseburger. "The front door of the place is unlocked, so I took a quick peek inside. There are four apartments. Two downstairs, two upstairs. His is number three. If I'm not mistaken, the second-floor window on the right is his."

Charlie studied both the house and the car for a few seconds but found that there was nothing much to be gleaned from this distance.

She unwrapped her spicy jalapeño burger and took a bite.

Very few words were exchanged for the next several minutes as they shoveled their faces with hot French fries and griddled beef. Eventually, Charlie looked over and found that Frank was eyeballing the warty pumpkin again.

"I used to take you and your sister to the pumpkin patch every year when you were kids, you remember that? We'd get cider and donuts and go through the haunted corn maze."

Charlie nodded.

"You always told us there was five bucks for whoever picked the best pumpkin," she said, smiling. "And then you'd end up saying it was a tie, and we both got the money."

"I can still see the two of you, running through the field, studying each pumpkin as if your life depended on it." Frank chuckled. "Do you remember the time you won the giant pumpkin?"

Charlie dipped a French fry into ketchup and shrugged.

"I remember the pictures of Allie and me sitting on it, but I don't actually remember winning it."

Frank took a swallow of Coke.

"Your dad and I took you girls over to some kind of harvest fair they were doing in Town Square. They had a bunch of stuff set up: a petting zoo, candy apples, hayrides. And there was a contest to guess the weight of the giant pumpkin outside of Henderson's hardware store. I had you and Allie pick the number, and you ended up being only seven ounces off the actual weight." Frank wiped his mouth with a napkin. "I thought it was great until they told me what the prize was: the giant pumpkin itself. I tried to leave without taking it, but Scottie came running over as I was pulling out of the lot, screaming, 'Frank! You almost forgot your pumpkin!'"

Charlie clicked her tongue and fixed her uncle with a reproachful look.

"You tried to leave our prized pumpkin behind?"

"Goddamn right I did. I didn't want to lug that thing around. I even tried to tell Scottie I didn't want it, and he laughed. He said that was too bad, the thing was mine now. So even he wanted to get rid of it."

"How'd you get it home, anyway?"

"Oh, we wrestled it into the trunk of my Civic, somehow. Had to bungee the trunk closed." Frank finished his burger and wadded up the paper. "Have you ever tried to dispose of three hundred pounds of pumpkin?"

"Can't say that I have," Charlie said, smirking.

"An absolute nightmare. Once it started to rot, I had to chop it into pieces with a chainsaw so I could throw it away, bit by bit. I fit what I could in the trash bin on garbage pickup day, but I don't think I got even half of it in there. I might have resorted to dumping some of the carcass in the lake in the dead of night."

They went silent for a time, and Charlie knew Frank was traveling through his memories to a time when Allie and her father were still alive.

Eventually Frank angled his head toward the house in question.

"So what's this Nesbitt guy's story, anyway?"

"There's another girl who works at the Laughing Raven, Olivia Smith. She was attacked last year. Drugged and taken to some kind of… creepy dungeon, for lack of a better term." Charlie pointed at the house. "When I asked about ex-boyfriends, Darren was the name she gave up."

Frank stroked his chin.

"That's two employees from the Laughing Raven who have been attacked."

"Plus the woman he tried to grab last night, who'd been at the bar," Charlie said. "But Nesbitt isn't the only one I'm looking into."

Frank gave his cup a shake, which sent the ice rattling.

"What else you got?"

Charlie relayed her interaction with Neil Kushner at the bar.

"Unlike Darren Nesbitt, Neil doesn't have a criminal record. He's a truck driver, and his roommate said he was out of state on a job the night Emma was killed."

The cup in Frank's hand gurgled as he drained the last remaining dregs from the bottom.

"Our guy might be smart enough to have flown under the radar until now," Frank said. "And the roommate could be covering for him. Or Neil could have lied to him."

"That's what I thought," Charlie agreed. "I've been trying to figure out a way to confirm whether or not Neil was out of town that night."

Frank thought for a moment.

"You know where he works?"

"Yeah."

"You could try the Good Samaritan ruse."

"The what?"

"You make up a story about a mysterious Good Samaritan who stopped on the side of the road to help when you ran out of gas or something like that," Frank explained. "So you call his place of work, and you inquire as to whether or not they had someone in the area on the day in question, because you want to send him some kind of reward or thank you or whatnot."

Charlie grinned.

"OK. And they don't ever get suspicious?"

"Not any of the times I've done it," Frank said. "Since it's a good deed, the person on the other line usually can't wait to help you out. They feel like they're in on a birthday surprise party or something like that."

Charlie got out her phone and found the number for Schnell Shipping, the trucking company Neil worked for. The woman who answered sounded chipper. That was good.

Charlie fed her a bogus story about her elderly mother getting a flat tire outside of Bellevue, Wisconsin, and the chivalrous gentleman who stopped to help. And Frank was right. The secretary ate it up and offered to look up the driver in the computer.

"Well… that's odd," the woman said, her voice faltering.

Charlie felt her stomach clench in anticipation, certain the woman was about to tell her that none of their drivers had been in Wisconsin that day, and Neil's alibi would be shot.

"Did I get the wrong shipping company?" Charlie asked.

"No. One of our drivers was up there, alright. I can see it right here. He was on a run from Detroit to Green Bay from Monday to Wednesday. But I have to tell you, I'm shocked. You see, this fella's got a reputation around here for being sort of a mean S.O.B., if you'll pardon my French. I'm trying to envision him helping a little old lady change her tire, and it just boggles the mind," she said, chuckling. "I suppose my mother was right about not judging a book by its cover."

Charlie knew instantly the woman was talking about Neil Kushner.

"My mother thought his name was Neil, if that helps."

"I guess that settles that then. Neil Kushner, yes indeed. Wonders never cease," the woman said. "Do you have a pen to take his number down?"

Charlie wrote the number in the air with a finger, making the requisite noises after each sequence of digits. Then she thanked the woman and hung up.

"Alibi checked out?" Frank asked.

"Yep," Charlie said, and her disappointment must have been apparent.

"Hey, we still got Mr. Nesbitt over yonder. Not all is lost," Frank said. "I like that little twist you put on it. Your elderly mother. That's a good one."

Charlie put up her hand for a high five.

"I learned from the best."

"So, speaking of Nesbitt, did the sheriff's department ever look into him in connection to the assault on Olivia Smith?" he asked. "Given their history, it would seem pertinent to the investigation."

Charlie scoffed.

"They blew her off. Probably didn't want the story to hit the papers and scare off the tourists."

Charlie expected an outraged response from Frank, but he didn't seem surprised. He only nodded and stared out his window.

"I always wondered what might have happened with Allie's case if it had been the off-season instead of the start of the summer tourism season," Frank said after a few moments.

Blinking in confusion, Charlie found herself momentarily speechless.

"What are you saying?"

He turned to look at her.

"You think this instinct to put business before justice is a new thing for this town?" Frank swiveled his head from side to side. "Salem Island has always depended on tourism for its survival, and young girls disappearing is bad for the trade. It wasn't an accident that they settled on a suspect so hastily. They rushed the charges as fast as humanly possible because they wanted to wash their hands of the whole thing. And if they could have buried it cleaner than that, I have no doubt they would have done it."

Charlie's mind ran in circles as she considered the implications of this.

"You can't be that shocked," Allie said. "It's not like I was the first or the last. Girls disappearing, being raped, being murdered… it's not convenient. It's easier to sweep it all under the rug."

And Charlie knew she was right. She'd seen it time and time again, hadn't she? Police departments rushing through investigations so they could get out from under the sensationalist tabloid headlines. Colleges neglecting to pursue rape cases to avoid damaging the reputation of the institution.

Charlie wondered how many victims had been denied justice because it was somehow considered "not advantageous," and her hands balled into fists.

No matter what it took, Charlie promised herself that Emma's case wouldn't end up like that.

CHAPTER FORTY

The next hour and a half outside of Darren Nesbitt's house were uneventful. While Frank sang along to an oldies playlist and kept his eyes on the house, Charlie went through Olivia's various social media accounts, looking for anything that stood out or might link her attack to Emma's.

Frank was halfway through the second chorus of "Sixteen Tons" when his voice suddenly cut out.

"Is this him?" he asked, turning the stereo down.

Charlie's head whipped around to where a man in a white T-shirt and jeans had emerged from the back door of the house.

"I think so," she said as she watched the man get into the red Camaro. "That's his car."

"Looks like we're going for a ride," Frank said and fired up his own ignition.

They waited until Nesbitt had backed out of his driveway and driven almost to the end of the block before following. Frank was careful to maintain a safe distance between the two cars, and his eyes glittered with intensity as he kept the Camaro in his line of sight.

It occurred to Charlie that her uncle seemed more alive than he had in some time. He'd put on a few pounds and was starting to look more like the old version of himself. The pre-cancer version. But it was more than that. It was the faint scrunching of his eyebrows as he worked. The way his tongue darted out to lick his lips. His fingers clenching and unclenching on the steering wheel.

She thought of the time Frank had invited them over to watch scary movies and then kept excusing himself throughout *Halloween*, only to return wearing a Michael Myers mask and casually carrying a bowl of popcorn or a two-liter of Faygo.

At the climax of the movie, they'd heard knocking at the sliding glass door that looked in on the living room. Charlie and Allie had glanced over and seen their uncle standing there with the mask over his face, tapping a giant knife against the glass.

"Very funny, Uncle Frank," Allie had said with a scoff. "You didn't scare us the first time, and it's not going to work now either."

Maskless, Frank had appeared in the kitchen doorway, drying his hands on a towel.

"What's that, now?"

Allie's mouth had dropped open. Her gaze had gone from Uncle Frank in the house to the mystery person still standing outside the window. Charlie and Allie had started to scream.

Frank had doubled over laughing, and Michael Myers had removed the mask, revealing that it had only been Eric Kilpatrick, a kid a few grades ahead of the girls who lived down the street from their uncle.

And then a more recent event sprang to mind: Frank delivering a swift kick in the ribs to Paige's estranged father. Telling him that if he threatened Paige again, he'd be back. That had been only a few months ago, right around the time Frank had found out he was in remission, and he'd still been somewhat frail then.

That memory in particular made Charlie realize how much progress he'd made in such a short time. The Frank tailing Darren Nesbitt today looked more like the Frank that had pulled Halloween pranks on Charlie and Allie in their youth than the Frank who'd just gone through several rounds of chemotherapy.

It was a short, uneventful drive to the outskirts of Salem Island's commercial district. Nesbitt swung into the parking lot of Starlite Lanes, a bowling alley known for having the greasiest pizza in town. When Frank saw that Nesbitt was heading for the bowling alley, he made a turn into the lot of the gas station next door. They idled there for a moment, waiting to see what would happen next.

After a few seconds, Darren Nesbitt unfolded himself from the driver's seat and walked to the door of the alley, tugging a red polo shirt over his head. The back was screen-printed with the Starlite Lanes logo.

"Well, now we know where he works," Charlie said.

"Yeah. And since he'll probably be here a while, I'm thinking I should take you back to your car. He doesn't need both of us sitting on him all day."

"Bored of me already?" Charlie asked.

He shrugged.

"I'm not paying you to sit on your duff, I can tell you that right now."

"Oh, so that's how it is," Charlie said, pretending to be offended. She glanced at her watch. "I told Paige I'd check back in anyway."

Frank turned the car around and drove back in the direction of Nesbitt's apartment, letting Charlie out next to where she'd parked. Before closing the door, she ducked her head back inside and looked at her uncle.

"Call me if Nesbitt leaves work. I can help tail him if he goes on the move."

"I think you're forgetting who you're talking to."

"Oh yeah, and who's that?" Charlie asked.

Frank's eyes sparkled.

"The guy who taught you everything you know."

Charlie snorted and closed the door. As the car pulled away from the curb, she smiled to herself.

It was good to have the old Uncle Frank back.

CHAPTER FORTY-ONE

Paige was bundled up in a red woolen cloak and clutching a mug of steaming tea when Charlie returned to the office.

"What's this?"

Paige tugged the hood off her head, blushing.

"I got it at that new consignment shop down the street on my lunch break. The My Fair Lady Boutique. Have you been in there?"

"I haven't." Charlie shook her head. "But I was mostly asking if you're alright. You look cold."

"I'm fine. It's my hands mostly. They've been like ice cubes all day."

"Why don't you turn the thermostat up?" Charlie asked, walking over to the digital controls on the wall.

Paige shrugged.

"Oh, I didn't want to fuss with it."

Charlie upped the temperature.

"Well, if you haven't noticed, the windows in this office are all drafty as hell. I keep meaning to talk to Frank about replacing them," Charlie said, staring out the panes of glass. "If it hasn't warmed up in an hour, turn it up a few more degrees."

"Thank you, Miss Winters." Paige blinked and looked at the floor. "The thermostat was off-limits in our house when I was growing up, so I guess I've got a bit of a complex."

"You're here more than I am, most days. I figure that gives you the right to adjust the temperature to your liking." Charlie plopped down behind her desk. "Did you manage to talk to our cold-footed divorcee?"

Paige beamed at Charlie's usage of the nickname she'd come up with.

"I did. She sounded shocked we hadn't received the check yet. Says she put it in the mail at least a week ago, and that she'd be calling her bank and getting to the bottom of it. And I don't mean to be a doubting Dorothy, but I kind of think the whole story was phony."

Scooting her chair out, Charlie sat down and rested her elbows on her desk.

"If you haven't figured it out by now, we spend half our time chasing down clients to get them to pay their bills. At least that's what it seems like, anyway." She sighed. "Put a reminder on the calendar for a week from today. If we haven't heard back from her or received payment by then, it's time to play hardball."

Charlie's phone began to rumble across the desk, and she flipped it over to see who was calling. It was Zoe.

"Are you in the office right now?" Zoe asked, not bothering with the normal pleasantries.

"Yeah, why?"

"I was thinking about what you said last night. About trying to find the place that Olivia was taken to. So I dug up the old incident report from the woman jogging on the beach, the one who initially called the cops, and I think I've narrowed it down to an area of a few miles."

"I did almost exactly the same thing earlier this morning," Charlie said. "Except I only managed to narrow it down to somewhere on the western shore, which wasn't much help."

"Well, how do you feel about helping a gal search for some creepy-looking cinder block buildings?"

"Hell yeah," Charlie said, impressed that Zoe had taken the initiative. But then something brought her up short. "Wait a minute. You're still on duty, which means you got the sheriff to sign off on this."

"That's right."

"But he's the one who wanted Olivia's case buried. I know this time of year is dead as far as tourism goes, but if he starts digging into that case now that Emma's dead, he'll be in even deeper shit than he would have been to begin with." Charlie's eyes squinted down to slits. "Which means he's doing the right thing just for the hell of it, or there's something you're not telling me."

"I might have hinted that a *certain* private detective had gotten her teeth into Olivia's case and said that if he didn't put some man hours into it today, this certain rogue P.I. might go to the press and blab about the whole thing."

Charlie threw back her head and cackled.

"You didn't."

"I did," Zoe said, and Charlie could hear the pride in her friend's voice. "And he took the bait, but he wasn't happy about it. He has this vein right in the middle of his forehead. Gets all twitchy when he's mad, and it looked like it was trying to do the polka today. So don't be surprised if he isn't chomping at the bit to do you any favors for a while."

Leaning back in her chair, a smile spread over Charlie's face.

"I consider that a small price to pay for justice."

"Give me about twenty minutes or so to get my crap together over here, and then I'll come pick you up," Zoe said.

"Sounds good."

Charlie hung up and did a victory spin in her chair. It was good to know she could count on *someone* on the police force in this town to show some initiative.

When Charlie went to find Paige to let her know she'd be heading out again, she found the girl in the back room, whirling around in circles so that the red cloak billowed and flared out around her. The twirling stopped abruptly when she saw Charlie standing in the doorway.

"Oh, Miss Winters!" Paige's cheeks flushed a shade that almost matched the cloak. "I thought you were still on the phone."

Charlie chuckled.

"You look like Little Red Riding Hood."

Paige gasped.

"That's exactly why I bought it! I thought it'd make a perfect Halloween costume."

Charlie reached out and touched the fabric.

"Wow, it's really soft."

"I know. And it's vintage!" Paige's eyes went wide with enthusiasm. "Oh, you should go over to the boutique, Miss Winters. They have really wonderful stuff. I saw a big poofy Scarlett O'Hara dress and a long faux fur coat that reminded me of Cruella de Vil. Lots of interesting pieces you could use for a one-of-a-kind costume, which is so much better than buying one of those cheapo Halloween store get-ups."

Charlie checked her watch. She had twenty minutes to kill, and she *did* need a costume for the Carnival Bizarre.

"Zoe's meeting me here in a little bit, but I guess I could probably go over there and look around for a few minutes," Charlie said with a shrug.

Paige clapped her hands in excitement.

"If Zoe gets here before I'm back, give me a call, will you?"

"Of course," Paige said.

Charlie grabbed a bottle of water from the fridge and headed out the door.

CHAPTER FORTY-TWO

Downtown Salem Island had that turn-of-the-century charm to it: brick and stone buildings stacked side by side with wide front windows and zigzagging fire escapes along the backs and sides. Charlie passed a small café that was only open for breakfast and lunch and then a small garden shop.

She crossed a side street and found My Fair Lady midway down the block. There was an old-fashioned wooden sign hanging over the door featuring a stylized silhouette of a woman in a wide-brimmed hat.

Wind chimes tinkled as Charlie entered. It was a charming place, sort of shabby chic meets retro in terms of decor. Mismatched chandeliers hung from the ceiling, and it smelled like lavender.

The space behind the counter was empty, and Charlie figured the clerk must be in back somewhere. It probably wasn't a busy time of day.

Charlie poked around in the racks, rifling through a row of blouses. There was some cute stuff, but this wasn't what she'd come here for. She scanned the various displays until she spotted a mannequin in a Marie Antoinette-style dress. The costume section.

She shuffled through the hangers nearby, puffy shirts that would work for a pirate outfit. A stretch satin leopard-print wiggle dress.

"That one," Allie squealed. "Pick that one!"

But Charlie already had her eye on a midnight-blue velvet skirt. She pulled it from the rack. It was full length, gathered at the waist, and had sequins all over it in a pattern that matched the constellations in the night sky.

"Aww, come on. How is that a costume?" Allie whined.

"I don't know. I could be a witch. Or a fortune teller," Charlie said, holding up the skirt and admiring the way the sequins glittered in the light. "What was I going to be in the leopard-print dress?"

"I don't know. Some kind of slutty 1960s starlet."

Charlie pinched the small paper tag dangling from the zipper on the skirt. The price wasn't bad.

The counter was still unattended, but Charlie figured there wasn't anything wrong with hopping into one of the fitting rooms to try on the skirt.

She was pleased to find that it fit perfectly. Allie was less enthused.

"That leopard-print dress would have made your boobs look huge," Allie said. "And that's the most important consideration when selecting a Halloween costume, if you ask me. If you're not showing some decent cleavage, then what's even the point?"

Charlie snorted and returned the skirt to the hanger. Whisking the fitting room curtain aside, she stepped through with the skirt draped over one arm. She was pleased to see that someone was manning the cash register now. A blond woman, probably about Charlie's age, in a slouchy white sweater and approximately twenty necklaces. As she approached the counter, Charlie realized the woman was someone she knew. Heidi Oliver, an old high school classmate. It seemed she was running into a lot of old acquaintances lately.

Heidi's face remained blank, which Charlie took to mean the recognition hadn't been mutual. They'd never really been friends, and Charlie didn't want to make it awkward, so she handed over the skirt without mentioning the link between them.

"You have some really great stuff in here," Charlie said.

Heidi studied the skirt, gazing down at the deep blue fabric that pooled like liquid on the counter. She fingered the price tag.

"I'm sorry," she said finally. "This isn't for sale."

Charlie frowned. Glanced back to where she'd found it.

"Are you sure? I found it right on the racks over there."

"Yeah." Heidi pressed her lips into something like a smile but not. "It must have been put out by mistake. It isn't available."

Charlie might have accepted this story if not for the glint in Heidi's hazel eyes. It was the kind of look someone got when they were sure they were about to win the game.

Maybe this was Heidi's thing. Randomly deciding that people couldn't buy things clearly marked for sale. Just because she could.

If she knew who Charlie was, though, if she knew they'd gone to school together, that might change things.

"I don't know if you recognize me or not, but we went to school together." She gestured at herself. "Charlie Winters?"

Heidi grinned now. It wasn't a pleasant expression.

"Oh, I know who you are." She nodded, and then her face went sour. "And I'd actually love it right now if you got out of my store and never came back."

Heidi's tone was so venomous it completely took her by surprise. Charlie stepped back from the counter.

"I don't understand—"

Heidi's jaw seemed to unhinge, and her voice went up an octave.

"I said get the fuck out of my store!"

Her face went bright red as she shrieked. Specks of spittle flung from her lips.

Charlie held up her hands and walked backward a few steps, not sure she should turn her back on this obviously deranged woman. At the door, she turned and pushed out into the crisp air.

Charlie's legs felt numb beneath her as she stumbled out onto the sidewalk. What had just happened?

As she walked back to the office, Charlie replayed the encounter in her mind, starting from the moment she'd entered the shop. Had she done something to offend Heidi? What if Heidi had greeted Charlie when she'd first gone inside, only Charlie hadn't seen, and Heidi had interpreted it as being intentionally ignored? Except that Charlie was certain the front of the store had been empty when she'd gone in.

Charlie reached the cross street, checking that the light for oncoming traffic was red before continuing on. A car approached the light, slowing as it reached the crosswalk. It stopped a few yards from her and honked.

The sudden noise startled her, and coupled with her frustration from the interaction with Heidi, it pissed Charlie off more than it probably should have.

The light was red, for Christ's sake. She had every right to cross now.

She held up her middle finger and glared at the car as she stormed by.

There was a mechanical whirring sound and the car's window began to roll down.

Great. More bullshit.

"Excuse me, ma'am," a familiar voice said. "That particular breed of bird is illegal inside the city limits without proper documentation. Do you have papers for it?"

Charlie halted and changed direction, jogging over to the car.

"Zoe! Shit. I'm sorry," she said, leaning into the open window. "I didn't recognize the car, so I thought you were some jag giving me a hard time for not crossing fast enough or something."

A car pulled up behind Zoe and honked for real this time.

"I was just on my way to pick you up," Zoe said. "Get in."

Charlie scurried around the car and flung herself into the passenger seat.

"The *weirdest* thing just happened to me," she said, buckling her seatbelt.

Zoe chuckled.

"Well whatever it was, you had the meanest case of resting bitch face I've ever seen."

"Do you remember Heidi Oliver?"

"Sure."

"She works in that store over there," Charlie explained. "The My Fair Lady Boutique."

"Right. I remember noticing they were renovating. They had newspaper covering the windows for a few months. I've never been inside. Is it cool?"

"It's decorated really nice. I bet they'll make bank in the summer when the tourist crowd is here," Charlie said. "But that's beside the point. I went in there, because I figured I need a costume for the Carnival Bizarre. And I found this really great velvet skirt I was going to buy. Except when I got up to the counter, Heidi was there, and she refused to sell it to me."

Zoe nodded in such a way that made Charlie think she wasn't understanding the full gravity of the situation.

"I mean, she went *off*. She was practically foaming at the mouth. Total psycho mode."

"Well…" Zoe said, bobbing her head from side to side. "It sounds like she definitely overreacted, but… I mean, you can understand where she's coming from, right?"

Charlie stared at her.

"No." She scoffed. "I cannot. Why the hell would I?"

There was a long pause. Zoe squinted thoughtfully.

And then she said, "Because Heidi is married to Will."

CHAPTER FORTY-THREE

The car rolled down the street, but Charlie could have sworn the entire world had stood still for the split second after Zoe spoke. Charlie stared at her, still not sure she was comprehending what Zoe had said.

"Heidi is married to Will?" Charlie repeated.

Zoe nodded.

"Will Crawford?" Charlie said, just to be sure she wasn't thinking of some other Will.

Zoe nodded again.

"The Will Crawford I kinda sorta dated for a hot minute last year?"

"That's the only Will Crawford I know," Zoe said.

"How did you not tell me this before?" Charlie asked. "A friendly heads-up would have been nice. Like, 'Hey, Chuck, you know the guy you're dating is married, right?'"

"Well, to be fair, they're separated. I guess I should have mentioned that." Zoe shrugged. "But I just assumed he told you. Guess not."

Charlie shook her head.

"I'm going to kill him."

"Well, do me a favor and don't mention that I'm the one who told you?" Zoe said, pursing her lips.

"I won't have to. His wife did all the heavy lifting for you." Charlie banged the back of her skull against the head rest.

Zoe slowed in front of Charlie's office.

"Do you need to run in and grab anything before we head out?"

"No," Charlie said. "I'm ready."

As they rode over to the west side of the island, Charlie digested the notion that Will Crawford had been married—was *still* married—to Heidi Oliver. But as the houses grew more sparse and the landscape on either side of the car shifted from neat rectangles of green lawn to alternating swatches of farmland and wilderness, Charlie pushed the interaction with Heidi from her mind. She had work to do.

They zigged and zagged across the winding, unpaved back roads, focusing on the streets closest to shore. Charlie craned her neck, scanning the surroundings for any white cinder block structures. Zoe drove slowly, but the foliage on the shoulder was overgrown in many places, making the task that much more tedious.

Hitting a dead end just past the crumbling copper-smelting plant, Zoe backtracked to the last intersection. They'd gone half a mile down Beedle Creek Road when Zoe pointed out a cinder block garage on someone's property.

"It's not white, though," Charlie said, studying the mural of jaunty sunflowers that crawled up the sides. "I'd think Olivia would have remembered if it had a mural painted on it. Besides, it looks too well-kept. She described something run-down. Maybe even abandoned."

They drove on, resuming their search, and eventually Charlie couldn't help but bring the conversation back to the incident at the consignment shop.

"I still can't believe Heidi Oliver threw me out of her store. I mean, things with her and Will must have really gone bad for her to react like that."

"Well there's that… and also the fact that you were like mortal enemies in high school."

"What?" Charlie turned in her seat to stare at Zoe. "We were not."

"You seriously don't remember?"

"Remember what?"

"There was a whole boatload of drama because Heidi dated Mark Zalenski for years, but then he started going out with Allie, and Heidi's take was that Allie had stolen him from her or something. They had a big scene at that party at Tommy Morton's house. And you tackled Heidi and dragged her into the water."

Charlie had a sudden flash of Heidi and Allie on a dock, arguing.

Heidi calling Allie a slut.

Allie dumping her beer over Heidi's head.

Heidi shoving Allie.

Allie falling backward and hitting her head on a cedar dock post.

And then Charlie, feeling this overwhelming sense of protectiveness. Of rage.

"Oh." Charlie was quiet for a moment as she processed the memories. "I can't believe I forgot about all that. Allie had to get stitches."

"I'd never seen you so pissed off," Zoe said. "I think if we hadn't been there to stop you, you would have tried to drown Heidi in the lake."

Charlie crossed her arms.

"She started it. I was just defending Allie. If you call someone a slut, you should expect to get a beer thrown on you."

"Well, the way I remember it is that Allie just walked right up and dumped her beer on Heidi's head," Zoe said.

"Really? That doesn't… actually it does sound like Allie. But there had to be a reason."

"Oh, sure. Heidi had been spreading all those horrible rumors about Allie."

Another memory struck Charlie then.

"The hot dog thing."

Zoe nodded.

"Yeah. The hot dog thing."

Zoe brought the car to a halt at a stop sign and a gust of wind sent a miniature cyclone of dry leaves spiraling over the pavement in front of the car.

Allie had been remarkably quiet throughout the conversation, but her voice suddenly erupted in Charlie's head.

"Only Heidi Oliver would come up with something so stupid," she said. "I mean, the idea that someone would masturbate with a hot dog is dumb enough, but the story was that I had done it *in front of people*. Please! I might have been an attention whore, but I was never *that* desperate."

Charlie snorted softly.

A wave of memories washed over her, and she wondered how she'd forgotten about all of it. But of course she had. Most of it had happened only a few months before Allie disappeared, and the tiff with Heidi Oliver wasn't the only thing Charlie had blocked out from that time. Her senior year as a whole was somewhat of a blur.

The memories from that point in her life were too painful. Too close to the wound that had never really healed. It was easier to remember the time long before. When she and Allie had been kids, maybe because those memories had already been set in her mind, like flowers preserved behind glass. But thinking of Allie at the age of eighteen… that hurt too much. She'd had so much spirit, and she'd been right at the brink of becoming an adult. Of starting her life.

The car slowed, and Zoe steered them into a gravel driveway.

"What's this?" Charlie asked, searching for some kind of suspicious-looking building and finding none.

"Coffee break," Zoe said, putting the car in reverse and turning them back toward town. "One of the things they don't tell you about being a cop is that once you pin that badge to your chest, you need a constant stream of fresh caffeine or you'll die."

They stopped off at the Bluegill Diner, famous for their weekly fish fry. At the counter, Zoe ordered an extra-large dark roast with two creams and two sugars and a piece of apple pie to go.

"They have the best pie," Zoe said. "And I'm not saying you have to get the pie, but you *have* to get the pie."

"Well if you're going to twist my arm."

Charlie turned to the waitress and ordered the same as Zoe, only with one sugar in her coffee instead of two.

"I'm going to hit the ladies' room," Zoe said. "If my pie comes out before I'm back, I need you to guard it with your life."

"Wow, are you sure I'm ready for that kind of responsibility?" Charlie asked.

Zoe clapped her on the shoulder.

"I believe in you."

Charlie milled around the entryway near the cash register, her eyes skimming over the Red Wings memorabilia displayed on the wall. When she grew bored with that, she turned away, and as she did, her gaze swept across the tables at the far end of the room.

Charlie froze on the familiar face. Blinked to make sure she wasn't seeing things.

But no. It was him, alright.

Will Crawford sat alone in one of the booths, eating what looked like a patty melt.

And Charlie was struck by a sudden urge to go talk to him. To confront him about never telling her about being married.

"Go give him hell," Allie whispered. "He deserves it."

Usually Allie being so gung-ho about something like this would raise red flags for Charlie. Allie liked to stir the pot, damn the consequences. But just now, she thought Allie was exactly right. Will deserved to have his cage rattled a bit.

Charlie inhaled and marched over to where Will was sitting.

"You're really doing it?" The glee in Allie's voice was unmistakable. "Yes! This is great!"

Will's eyes were down as she approached, reading something on his phone. But when she reached his table, he glanced up and did a double take.

"Charlie," he said, looking surprised to see her. "Hey."

Beyond the fact that he obviously hadn't expected to see her standing in front of the table, she couldn't read his expression well enough to know whether he was glad to see her or not. But she supposed that was a moot point since she wasn't here to rekindle anything.

"What's up?" he asked, gesturing that she should sit.

Charlie remained on her feet, her eyes drawn to the stubble along his jaw and upper lip, distracting her for a moment.

"Told you," Allie whispered. "The beard adds twenty percent to his hotness. It's science, Chuck."

Charlie ignored this and cleared her throat.

"Is there something you forgot to mention when we were… seeing each other, or whatever?"

"Hey, I was very upfront about my raging case of syphilis," he said, smirking.

It was the kind of joke that would have gotten Charlie before. Disarming in its self-deprecation. But she wasn't in the mood for Will's jokes today.

Charlie crossed her arms over her chest. "I'm talking about Heidi. Your wife?"

"Ah," Will said, sucking in a breath. "That."

"Yeah. *That*."

Will shrugged and leaned back in his seat.

"Well, we're separated. And we would be divorced by now if she wasn't such a…" He didn't finish the sentence and shook his head instead. "What happened? Did someone say something to you?"

"Heidi did," Charlie said. "I went into her store, and she flipped out on me."

"Oh. Shit." Will rubbed his eyes. "I'm sorry."

To his credit, he didn't seem even slightly amused by the idea. He leaned an elbow on the table.

"How did she even know about us?" Charlie asked. "We only went out one time."

Will's face tightened into a grimace.

"I might have mentioned it… in passing."

Charlie swore she detected a pang of guilt in his voice, and she seized on it.

"You are so full of it," Charlie said, shaking her head. "You know she hates me, and you told her about us to piss her off, didn't you?"

Will fidgeted with his fork, saying nothing.

"Oh my God," Charlie breathed, taking a step back from the table. "Is that the only reason you went out with me? To stick it to your ex?"

"What? Of course not. I liked you." He pushed up to his feet, moving closer to her. "I still like you."

Charlie held up a hand to stop him.

"Don't even."

Will's arms dropped to his sides.

"Hey, I'm sorry, OK? I'll admit, it was a dick move not telling you. And then I guess I kind of set you up to take the brunt of it." He sighed and stroked his bearded chin. "Heidi has a way of getting under my skin. She's vindictive as hell, and I couldn't resist paying her back a little. But I shouldn't have brought you into it."

Charlie stared at him, judging his remorse. It seemed genuine enough. Finally, she nodded.

"So we're good then?" Will asked.

"I suppose," Charlie said.

He smiled then, looking genuinely happy. Charlie felt something twinge in her chest.

"Why don't you join me?" he said, gesturing at his table. "I've been going over notes from a deposition. Incredibly dull. I'd love the company."

Charlie's eyes lingered on the empty seat in the booth for several seconds. She couldn't deny that she was still attracted to Will, but no. She couldn't go down this road again. Not after he'd betrayed her trust by spying on her. That wasn't something she could just forget.

"Maybe some other time," she said, already moving away from the table.

CHAPTER FORTY-FOUR

Charlie collected the orders for her and Zoe from the counter and went outside to wait by the car. The sun was on its evening descent, and the air had shifted from pleasantly cool to downright chilly. Charlie zipped up the front of her coat, glad she had the hot coffees to keep her hands warm.

Zoe appeared a few moments later.

"There you are," she said. "Thought I'd lost you."

Charlie handed over Zoe's coffee and pie.

"I ran into Will inside. Needed some air."

"Oy." Zoe grimaced. "How'd that go?"

Charlie shrugged.

"He apologized. Asked if we're cool."

"And are you?"

"I guess," Charlie said, shrugging again.

Zoe wolfed down her pie in a shocking amount of time and then put the car in gear. Charlie finished hers on the drive.

"So, we've driven most of the roads in our search area," Zoe said, studying a map on her phone. "I'm not really sure whether we should broaden our scope or go back over the same area again."

"You mentioned that the incident report from Olivia's attack had a location for the original 911 call," Charlie said.

"That's right," Zoe said. "The jogger who made the call told the dispatcher she'd found Olivia not far from the boardwalk on Anchor Bay Beach."

"Maybe we should go down to the beach and search from there instead of from the road."

Zoe nodded. "That's not a bad idea."

A few minutes later, they were parking in a public lot near the beach and taking the boardwalk down to the water's edge.

After turning off the ignition, Zoe donned a baseball hat from the backseat, embroidered with the sheriff's department logo. Charlie dug a pair of sunglasses from her bag, and they were ready.

Their feet echoed hollowly on the wooden slats. Charlie got a whiff of the lake, which always reminded her of the petrichor smell when it rained in summer. It was mostly still today, just a faint ripple here and there where the breeze skimmed the surface. A boat cruised by, its wake slicing a white gash through the blue.

When they reached the edge of the beach, Charlie pointed out the Ferris wheel on the horizon.

"Did the incident report say which direction the woman had been jogging?" Charlie asked.

"No," Zoe said. "We'll have to check the beach on both sides of the boardwalk."

It was decided that they'd walk toward the Ferris wheel to start, and they took off through the sand.

They passed a cluster of rental cottages that appeared to be closed for the season, and Charlie began scanning the low hills and shrubbery that separated the beach from the inland terrain. The fact that many of the small trees bordering the water were mostly bare made the job a little easier, but that would only really help if the place they were looking for was visible from the beach.

"So when you say you and Will are cool, how cool are we talking?" Zoe asked.

"I don't know." Charlie scratched her head. "I don't hate him, if that's what you mean. Why?"

"It's just that he might have mentioned to me that he really regrets how things went between you two," Zoe said, sipping her coffee and glancing at Charlie from the corner of her eye. "And I got the impression he's still hung up on you."

"When was this?"

"Oh, maybe a month or so ago. I ran into him at the Lakeside Tavern, and we got to talking. Had a few drinks."

"Ah," Charlie said, a cynical smile spreading across her face. "So he was drunk. And feeling sorry for himself."

"No." Zoe reached up and adjusted the brim of her hat. "OK, maybe a little. But then I saw him a few days later, and he brought you up again. He asked whether you were seeing anyone."

"And what did you say?"

"I told him that as far as I knew, you were hitting the clubs and banging anything that moved."

Charlie burst out laughing and gave Zoe a playful shove.

"OK, I didn't really say that. I told him if he wanted to know so bad, he should ask you himself. There seemed to be more to it than idle curiosity."

They passed one of the many low-lying marshy areas on the island, populated by cattails and reed and water lilies. Zoe plucked a wad of cattail fluff from one of the seed heads and released it into the wind.

"Anyway, I guess I'm curious if the guy has a chance or not," Zoe said, dusting her fingers off on her pantleg. "You two were kind of cute together, and I don't typically think that sort of thing about straight couples."

"He installed spyware on my computer, Zoe. That's not cool."

"No, it's not," Zoe said. "But at least he only did it to get an edge for a client."

Charlie nearly choked on her coffee.

"And that makes it better?" she asked, wiping her mouth.

"Not *better*. But it's different than if he'd been spying on you for personal reasons. Like if he was some kind of control freak, or he didn't trust you or something like that."

Charlie wasn't convinced and said nothing. She took another slug of coffee while Zoe went on.

"OK, let's say a woman hires you to spy on her husband because she thinks he's having an affair."

Charlie groaned.

"If you're trying to suggest that what he did is the same as what I do as a private investigator, Will already tried that argument on me."

"Just hear me out," Zoe said. "Let's say you're spying on the husband, and you get caught."

Charlie shook her head.

"This scenario isn't believable. I'm too smooth to get caught."

Zoe snorted before continuing.

"Stop being so belligerent and listen, will you? The husband figures you out. And let's just say, for the sake of argument, that he was never cheating in the first place. Who do you think the husband will feel more betrayed by? You or the wife?"

"I get it, Zoe. The wife is the one who betrayed his trust. I was only doing my job, ergo the husband shouldn't be mad at me." Charlie finished off the last of her coffee and deposited her empty cup in a garbage can chained to one of the benches installed on the beach. "The problem is that your hypothetical doesn't exist in the real world. I do this job knowing that if I get caught, somebody's gonna be pissed off, and they probably have a right to be. Because nobody likes it when their privacy is invaded."

"Alright. I shouldn't have gotten involved in the first place. It's none of my business," Zoe said, sighing. "But since I've already stuck my beak into it, can I just say one thing?"

Charlie raised an eyebrow, and Zoe held up a finger.

"Nobody's perfect. People screw up. They do shitty things, sometimes even knowing they're doing it. If they're decent, they apologize. And sometimes—just sometimes—they deserve a second chance."

"Yeah, but…" Charlie said, and stopped. Something beyond the swaying beach grass to their right had caught her eye.

"I'm not saying to do it blindly." Zoe waved her hands. "Or to, like, jump back into bed with Will—"

"Zoe."

"OK, bad wording, but you know what I mean. It's just that I've known him for a long time, and I don't think he's a bad guy. He can be an idiot sometimes, but if you want an idiot-free dating experience, then maybe you should try women instead. Not that women are a walk in the park, let me tell you." Zoe snorted. "I've been seeing this chick from Sterling Heights. Hot as hell but damn if she isn't nuttier than a bowl of granola."

"Zoe!"

"What?

Charlie pointed at the section of a white cinder block building just barely visible over the nearest dune, nestled in the woods.

CHAPTER FORTY-FIVE

They approached the building, moving up the slope to where the hillocks of sand and beachgrass met the flatter land of the beach. Then they picked their way into the edge of the woods. Most of the trees were bare here, or the little structure would have been concealed by the leafy branches.

The shed, for lack of a better term, was built partially into the side of one of the hills. A dingy thing. Cracked paint coated the face of it, with brown and green staining from dirt and mildew. It had a single door and one small glass block window.

Zoe pointed at another building on the property, a crumbling wooden structure with a caved-in roof. Charlie spotted signs near the two entrances, one for men and one for women. It was unmistakably a public restroom.

"This must be part of Camp Kin-ne-quay," Zoe said. "They did good business when Poseidon's Kingdom was still open, but they went bankrupt a few years after the park closed." She crossed her arms. "I wonder who owns this. It's gotta be a pretty valuable piece of land, right off the beach like this."

Charlie nodded, prying her eyes away from the creepy little building to scan the rest of the grounds.

Half a dozen metal fishing boats rusted on a rack beside the structure, and behind that, a pile of old bicycles decomposed in a tangled heap. Rentals for the campground, left behind to rot.

There were plenty of places like this on the island. Abandoned, overgrown with vines and weeds. But this spot had a creepy vibe that Charlie couldn't ignore, and she couldn't put her finger on exactly what it was that made her skin crawl.

They moved closer to the storage building. A fly buzzed past Charlie's face, and she waved it away.

Charlie squinted, trying to see into the small window set in the door, but it was covered with something, blocking her view. Only when she pressed her face to the glass did the something move, and her stomach clenched when she realized what it was.

Flies.

Flies so thick they completely blotted out the view through the window.

And then she smelled it. The same putrid odor from the day they'd discovered Emma's body in the woods.

Death.

"You smell it?" Charlie asked.

Zoe fanned a hand in front of her nose.

"Ugh, yes."

"Is that enough probable cause for you to enter the building?"

"I'd say so," Zoe said, pulling her phone from her pocket and dialing the sheriff's department.

While Zoe reported on what they'd found, Charlie studied the padlock securing the door. It was one of the most common and most basic brands on the market, and if she wasn't mistaken, also one of the easiest to pick. She lifted it to get a look at the stamp on the underside and smiled at the "No. 3" etched on the bottom. She'd practiced on about a dozen of these back when Frank had first taught her how to pick a lock. This would be a piece of cake.

She dug around in her bag and produced the basic lockpick set she always carried on her person, just in case. Charlie had the lock undone in about three seconds. She pulled it free from the hasp and tugged the door wide.

A cloud of flies burst out, freed from their prison. The stench of decomposition intensified tenfold, and both Charlie and Zoe covered their mouths.

"Oh God," Zoe gagged.

Charlie shone a flashlight into the space. The floor was bare dirt, and the walls were crusted over with limescale and lichen.

As the beam illuminated the dingy space, Charlie matched the details to Olivia's description of the place she'd woken up in.

A bare mattress stained and dirty. A headboard from an old metal bed frame with a length of chain extending down to the floor.

And in one corner, a blue tarp covered in dried blood.

CHAPTER FORTY-SIX

Now Charlie stood at a distance, observing the detectives and techs process the scene, and she was struck by a feeling of déjà vu. She felt the same tension, the same uncomfortable roiling in her gut as when she'd watched these very people tackle the crime scene in the woods, where they'd discovered Emma's body. It made sense, since this was surely the place where Emma had been killed.

The bloody tarp was only the beginning of the horrors held in this little storage shed. Several small animal carcasses had been uncovered among a pile of cardboard boxes in one corner. Two cats, one raccoon, and a third critter that was too far decomposed to even identify.

Next came an old gray military trunk, covered in a layer of dust and grime. When the detectives opened it, they found it filled with the most graphic and violent pornography Charlie had ever seen.

Along with the porn, the trunk held a selection of bondage gear and knives. A box of condoms. And in a sealed Ziplock baggy, a collection of Polaroids. All the photos were of girls' bodies, the heads always cropped out of the frame, making identifying the girls difficult at a glance. Charlie couldn't help but wonder if Emma or Olivia were in any of these photos, and if not, who were these girls?

Though she'd been queasy since before they even opened the door, it was after viewing the creepy photos that Charlie tromped out into the bush and vomited up her coffee and pie behind a large maple tree.

She thought she'd feel a little better after that, but the difference was marginal.

Her mind wrestled with the idea of someone capable of such violence. Such hatred and cruelty.

He'd drugged these girls. Brought them here and tied them up. He'd killed at least one of them. How many more might there have been?

The question hung in Charlie's thoughts for some time and was only interrupted by the sound of approaching footsteps crunching through the dry leaves.

Zoe strode over with her hands in her pockets.

"Any luck finding the owner of the property?" Charlie asked.

"Sheriff just got off the phone with her."

"Her?" Charlie repeated.

"Yes, ma'am. Ms. Dorothy Bosch. She's an older lady, lives out in Oregon. Says she inherited the property from her brother after he died six years ago. He'd bought the Camp Kin-ne-quay land as an investment after it had been foreclosed on way back when. Got it for pennies on the dollar supposedly." Zoe shrugged. "Anyhow, she was quite surprised to hear what we'd found. She's wheelchair-bound and has never actually been to Michigan or seen the property in person."

"What about other family?" Charlie asked.

Zoe shook her head.

"The original owner lost his wife and only child in a car accident decades ago. That's why the sister inherited everything," Zoe explained. "And Ms. Bosch is a self-described spinster. No children or other close family members."

"So whoever this guy is, he's basically been squatting here without anyone knowing?"

"That's what it looks like."

Charlie felt sick again. This had been the big break. She'd been hoping to track the property to the killer. Instead it looked like another dead end.

"We've still got truckloads of evidence to go through, though," Zoe said, reading her disappointment. "He left fingerprints. Maybe even DNA. Something out here will lead us to him."

Charlie sighed and hugged her arms around herself.

"Those only help if he's already in the system. We still don't know who he is."

"We just have to be patient," Zoe said, patting Charlie's shoulder.

But Charlie didn't want to be patient. She wanted to find him now. To kick down his door and snap on the handcuffs. She wanted to sit in court and hear the jury declare him guilty. To witness the judge issuing a sentence of life without the chance of parole.

Charlie squeezed her eyes shut.

She wanted him punished for what he'd done to Emma and Olivia and Rachel and any other girls he'd harmed.

Zoe was right, though. There was still hope in finding something in all this evidence that would lead them to Emma's killer.

CHAPTER FORTY-SEVEN

Sharp voices lurch through the speakers. Excited chatter spilling into the cabin of his car.

He listens as he drives, more focused on the voices than the road, cigarette smoke wreathing around his head.

The police scanner tells a tale of dried blood and tarps. Cinder blocks and dead cats and the pervasive reek of death. A probable murder scene uncovered in an outbuilding in the woods, all of it narrated through the blunt, clipped discourse of law enforcement.

His lair. Exposed.

His gut feels cold and runny when he thinks about it. Frigid liquid heaving and spitting inside like an angry sea.

The excitement is plain in the tangle of voices. Visions of forensic evidence dancing in their heads. DNA. Fingerprints.

He doubts they'll find anything that will lead to him. But it's no sure thing.

Again, he does the one thing he shouldn't do. He drives to the scene. Wants to see it. Wants to watch them there, the cops crawling over his den.

He slows as he approaches the dirt driveway. Police cars clog the sides of the road. Parked along the shoulder, passenger sides poking into the brush. Based on the various color schemes decorating the cruisers, several jurisdictions have already descended upon the scene.

Crime scene tape flutters where it cordons off the dusty drive. Its ends are tied off on pine boughs, and the strip of yellow flaps in the steady breeze that perpetually rolls off the water along this side of the island.

Beyond that, the area around the small shed teems with police. Clusters of them move about the structure like ants swarming a hill.

He drives on. Moves on. But his anger isn't so quick to leave this violation behind.

He knows that the Winters bitch is behind this. Meddling whore. She wants to force his hand? So the fuck be it.

CHAPTER FORTY-EIGHT

By the time Charlie got back to the office, night had fallen. Charlie had called Paige from the scene hours ago and told her to lock up on her own, so all the windows at the front of the building were dark as she drove past and turned into the alley that led to the rear parking lot.

Charlie let herself in through the back entrance. After all the bustling action at the crime scene, the office seemed very still and quiet. So quiet that she could hear the hum of the fluorescent bulb over the sink in the back room, which was left on all the time.

Charlie dropped her coat and bag on the counter of the kitchenette and grabbed a can of Arizona tea from the fridge. She fell into one of the dining chairs at the small table and just stared into the darkness for a moment, sipping her drink.

Her lower back ached from being on her feet half the day, and some of that tension eased as soon as she sat down. She and Zoe had begun their search in the afternoon, and she hadn't eaten anything since the pie from the diner, which she'd promptly thrown up at the crime scene. Charlie knew she should remedy that, but she was exhausted and didn't even want to stand up let alone go to the trouble of finding real food.

A half-eaten bag of potato chips she'd brought in a few days ago huddled at the far end of the table. She reached out, removed the clip, and shoved a handful of chips in her mouth.

"Now that's what I call a wholesome meal," Allie said. "Chips and sweet tea."

"When you learn to cook, let me know," Charlie said and crunched down on another chip.

Charlie tried to think of something else. To let her mind wander to other things. Anything not related to this case and that grimy shed. But the Polaroid photos kept invading her thoughts. Naked flesh laid out on a putrid mattress. Skin pale as the moon.

Her appetite vanished, and Charlie folded over the top of the chip bag and pushed it away. She wiped chip grease from her fingers before pulling Emma's file from her bag.

If her brain was going to insist on playing that horror show on a loop, she might as well try to get something out of it. And rereading her notes from her interview with Olivia might jar something loose.

The item at the top of the file wasn't what she'd been looking for, but Charlie paused on it anyway, the bold outlines and crosshatching catching her eye immediately. The drawing Emma had found in her car. She flipped it over and read the back once more.

You could be mine.

Charlie shuffled through the rest of the file and had just found the Olivia notes when she heard something over the rustling of the papers.

Tap, tap, tap.

Her first thought was that it was the sink dripping, but when she glanced over at the faucet, she found it dry. And that wasn't right, anyway. The noise she'd heard had sounded somewhat distant. Coming from the front of the office, perhaps.

She waited for several moments, straining her ears, but she heard only silence. Whatever it was, it had stopped now. For all she knew, she'd imagined it.

Charlie shook her head and refocused her attention on the file. She read the first two lines from the interview with Olivia, and then she heard it again.

Tap, tap, tap.

Her head snapped up. OK. Not her imagination, then.

But what was it?

It almost sounded like someone knocking at the front door. But no one would try to walk in this late. The lights out front were off. And if it was someone knocking, why not knock louder?

Charlie's skin crawled a little as she got up to investigate, even if the rational part of her thought it was probably nothing. A branch knocking against the brick facade. A woodpecker pecking at the roof. A piece of garbage flapping in the wind. Something stupid like that.

She padded out into the front room. Walking across the darkened space, she was just barely able to make out the shape of Paige's desk and the coat rack by the dim glow of the streetlights shining in from outside.

Charlie moved to one of the big plate glass windows and peered out into the night.

Streetlights glowed down on the sidewalk, albeit dimly. Long shadows stretched off the left sides of the buildings across the street.

But there was nothing there. No cars. No movement. Even the crickets were done chirping for the year, succumbed to the cold, leaving a strange hush in their place as fall crept toward winter.

She sighed and chocked it up to being tired and hungry and emotionally drained. She turned on her heel, moving back through the dark front room the way she'd come. She took three steps toward the glowing doorway of the back room.

And then the entire front window imploded in a single loud crash.

CHAPTER FORTY-NINE

Glass burst into the room. An explosion of shards scattering into the space. Strewn over the floor.

Charlie ducked behind Paige's desk, her heart punching in her chest. She peered over the glossy wood tabletop.

One whole pane of plate glass was gone. An eight foot by four foot section obliterated. Leaving the frame naked. Open to the night.

No shots fired.

The words occurred to her even before she realized what she'd been thinking: that someone had shot out the window. But no. There'd been no crack of gunfire. Just the cymbal crash of the glass shattering, and then a dull thump. Something heavy thudding to the carpet.

Charlie turned her gaze to the shards on the floor, searching for that heavy object she'd heard.

A brick.

Someone had thrown a brick through the window.

And Charlie knew who it was.

Him.

Out the window, she caught a glimpse of his silhouette, a dark figure darting across the street.

Charlie snatched the stun gun she kept in the desk and sprinted for the door.

She rushed over the concrete, down the curb, over the asphalt. She banked onto the sidewalk on the other side of the street, racing up the block.

She slowed some as she reached the intersection, the place where she'd last seen him. Eyes scanning everywhere.

A dark smear throbbed in the corner of her eye. He raced through the near blackness, moving off to her left.

She veered that way. Built speed again. Saw the dark shape of the stun gun rising and falling in her pumping right hand.

The form ducked down an alley, and Charlie followed. Feet pattering through mud puddles. Closing on him. His narrow frame focusing into sharper detail now, even in the dark.

Tall. Slender. Angular shoulders with those balled-up deltoids protruding, a grown-up version of a gangly kid.

She felt her jaw clench.

They careened around a dumpster that took up most of the alley. A few more steps, and she'd have him.

She adjusted her grip on the stun gun. Ready to jam it into his back. Pump him full of a few thousand volts.

He cut to the left, changing direction at full speed, heading down a shoulder-width passage etched between two brick buildings.

Charlie tried to follow. Skidded past the opening. Her footsteps went choppy.

Her right shoulder clipped the corner of the building as she rounded the corner. Twisted her. Knocked her further off balance.

And then she was falling forward, arms wheeling.

Charlie stabbed her left foot into the wet asphalt. Planted that leg. Tried to push off and right her balance.

It worked.

For a split second.

Something popped deep in her knee. The joint buckled. A bright bolt of pain flared up and down that limb, and then she felt the sickening sensation of warm fluid flooding everything behind her kneecap.

The pain intensified. Blinding.

Charlie sprawled. Landed hard on her stomach. Scraped over the pavement in a skid. Felt the asphalt scuff her knees and elbows even through her clothes.

She let out a groan.

Lifted her head. The silhouette bobbed in that narrow opening between the bricks, racing away from her.

She pushed herself up on hands and knees. Tried to get back to her feet but her knee collapsed beneath her. She winced at the renewed pain.

His footsteps grew fainter and fainter. He reached the end of the alley and wheeled around the corner.

He was gone.

CHAPTER FIFTY

Charlie hobbled back to the office. Road rash tingled in her elbows where she'd dragged them across the pavement.

She paused in front of the broken window, assessing the damage. It looked wrong, like a smile with one front tooth missing. She wasn't sure how to deal with it in the short term, either. She doubted they had a piece of cardboard large enough to tape over the opening.

Inside, she turned on the lights, staying clear of the glass as best she could. Paige's chair was closest to the door, the girl's red cloak slung over the back. Charlie limped over and fell into it with a sigh before starting an inventory of her injuries.

Her forearms stung like hell, but the scrapes weren't too deep. Her knee was another story. Charlie lifted the leg and bent it to test the joint, wincing at the sharp pain that blazed there. A sprain in one of the ligaments, most likely. Painful but not something that required medical attention unless it got worse.

She got out her phone to call the police, and that was when her eyes fell on the brick. It was partially obscured by a puddle of shadows just inside the window, but she thought there was something stuck to it.

Skirting around the worst of the broken glass, Charlie scooted the chair closer to get a better look.

There was a rubber band wrapped around the brick. Charlie nudged it with her foot, lifting one side.

Her breath hitched when she saw what was there. Jerked her foot away as if shocked and let the brick fall back down.

The rubber band secured a piece of paper to the brick. Plain white paper covered with black crosshatching. It was a sketch, just like the one he'd left in Emma's car.

Charlie swallowed. With the toe of her shoe, she flipped the brick over to expose the drawing fully and gasped at what she saw.

It was a sketch of a girl, bound the same way as the girls in some of the Polaroids they'd found in the killer's lair. Except the heads of the girls in his photographs had all been cropped out of the frame, and this drawing had a face.

Charlie recognized it instantly.

It was Paige.

CHAPTER FIFTY-ONE

He speeds away from the scene. Zigzagging through alleys and back streets. Tires flinging gravel, sloshing through mud puddles.

The car builds up speed until it shudders. Vibrations thrumming through the steering wheel to get at palms and fingers still frigid from the adrenaline rush.

As he pulls onto one of the busier streets close to downtown, he finally slows down to the speed limit. Time to blend in. Another nobody. Another face in the crowd.

No one can see what's behind the mask.

Still his heart quakes in his chest, knocking so hard it feels like his ribcage might implode, splinter the bones like wooden matchsticks.

That was close. Too close.

His shoulders twitch, nervous sweat leaking to soak his hair and plaster it to his scalp.

But then he remembers that window dropping, the image of her shocked face coming to him in slow motion.

The big pane of glass cracking like a sheet of ice. Brittle. All the tiny shards bursting apart and tumbling to the carpet. The bits moved like liquid. A wave of them flowing down. Pouring over each other. Glass flecks tinkling out a thousand chimes.

Property damage to reflect the way he feels inside.

And he could do it again and again. Paint his internal world onto reality in the brightest shades of red.

He lights a cigarette with a shaky hand. Breathes smoke. Euphoria and nicotine intertwining in his blood.

The dotted yellow line flicks past on the road outside. A glowing pulse of color among the black asphalt. Blinking at him. Impatient.

And it hits him then. An epiphany. A dark vision of what the future will hold. Must hold.

Fresh fantasies gleam in his skull. Violent movies that make cold blood surge in his veins once again.

Another grand gesture. A spectacle. That's what he needs. What she needs. What they need.

That's what romance is all about, right? Something audacious to impress the girl. Something dramatic to top what he's just done. Something unforgettable.

He knows just what to do.

CHAPTER FIFTY-TWO

Charlie inched closer to the drawing, wanting to be sure she wasn't imagining Paige's face there rendered in pencil.

But no. It was Paige alright. Charlie squinted, trying to make out some of the details. There was a red smudge on part of the drawing.

Charlie gasped when she realized what it was.

Not a smudge. A hood. A red hood surrounding Paige's face.

Charlie craned her neck around, spying the wool cloak slung over the back of the chair. She snatched it into her hands and held it out in front of her.

It was the red cloak Paige had been wearing earlier that day.

"Oh, shit," Charlie said.

"Yeah," Allie agreed.

Fumbling for her phone, Charlie dialed Paige's number.

"Please pick up. Please be OK," Charlie murmured as the phone rang.

She inhaled sharply when the line clicked, and she heard Paige's voice.

"Hello?"

"Paige, it's me. Where are you?"

"I'm at home." There was a pause. "Is something wrong? I closed up the office just like you said to. Oh goodness… did I forget to lock the back door? I know I locked the front, but I don't remember if I checked in back and—"

"Paige, this is important. Are you alone right now?"

"Well, no. My roommate and her boyfriend are in the other room watching a movie. Why?"

Charlie relaxed slightly.

"Something happened. Something that makes me think you might be in danger."

"Me?"

"Yes," Charlie said. She let out a sigh and then explained the broken window and the drawing she'd found attached to the brick. "I need you to stay put tonight. Do *not* go outside for any reason. I'm going to call Zoe and have them put someone on your house, and then I'll be there in the morning to escort you to work."

"Good gravy, you really think all that's necessary?"

"Maybe not, but I'm not taking any chances." Charlie stared down at Paige's cloak wadded up in her lap. "There are a few things I need you to do after we hang up. The first is to go around the house and make sure all the doors and windows are locked. Also, find out if your roommate is planning on staying there tonight. If not, call me. I don't want you there alone."

"You're starting to scare me, Miss Winters."

"Good," Charlie said. "It's better to be scared than to be stupid. I'm going to hang up and call Zoe, but first I want you to repeat everything I said you need to do."

"Stay inside. Lock all the windows and doors. Make sure my roommate is staying here tonight."

Charlie nodded, wanting to feel satisfied at Paige's answer. But Emma had made a similar promise and that had still gone terribly wrong.

"That's perfect, but I need to make sure you understand me, Paige." Charlie squeezed her fingers into a fist. "I don't want you so much as taking the garbage out tonight. If you hear anything outside or think someone might be trying to get in the house, call the police immediately."

"I understand," Paige said.

Charlie hung up and called Zoe, explaining again what had happened.

"Did you get a look at him?" Zoe asked.

"A little on the skinny side, maybe a touch above average in height, but it was too dark to see anything more than that. He was barely more than a silhouette."

"OK. I'll get a unit sent over to watch Paige's house ASAP, and I'll see who I can send over to collect any evidence. I just saw Detective Sponaugle going to town on a bear claw in the break room."

Charlie shrugged.

"I doubt he left fingerprints on the paper or the brick, but you never know what else they might get off it."

"Roger that," Zoe said. "I'll send Sponaugle your way."

"Thanks."

Despite knowing that the police were already on their way to watch over Paige for the night, Charlie's mind whirred with dark scenarios.

She imagined someone standing outside her bedroom window, watching even now. A shadowy silhouette with his face pressed to the glass.

Charlie tried to imagine what that face might look like, and the first one that came to mind was Neil Kushner. But they'd ruled him out already.

What about Darren Nesbitt?

With a start, Charlie suddenly remembered that Frank was still tailing him, as far as she knew.

She picked her phone up again and called her uncle. When he answered, she blurted the question on her mind without saying hello.

"Are you still on Nesbitt?"

"Yeah, why?"

"You have eyes on him now?"

"Sure," Frank said. "He's just finished enjoying a five-star meal for one at Long John Silver's. Likes both his entree and sides deep-fat fried, apparently."

Charlie's hopes fell as she retold the brick-through-the-window story for the third time this evening.

"Jeez Louise," he said. "Is the kid OK?"

"Paige is safe for the moment. Zoe's sending some units to sit on the house overnight," Charlie explained.

"And what about you?" Frank asked. "How bad is the knee?"

"Sore. I'll be limping for a few days, but other than that, I'm fine." Charlie sighed. "The fact that we just ruled out Nesbitt is kind of a kick in the junk, though."

"True," Frank agreed. "Unless he can astral project or otherwise be in two places at once, it's not him. I watched him eat like eight hush puppies in a row at the exact time you were chasing this guy on foot."

Charlie rubbed her eyes. A sudden gust of chilly night air from the gaping window reminded her of the fact that she had some work to do before she could leave.

"Well, since you're off the hook on the Nesbitt tail-job, can you do me a favor?"

"Yeah, turkey?"

"Can you bring something over that we can use to cover the window overnight? Some plywood or something?"

"Sure thing. There's a measuring tape in one of the drawers in the back room. Text me the measurements of the window, and I'll swing by Home Depot," he said, pronouncing "depot" like it rhymed with "teapot."

As soon as Charlie ended the call, she felt the silence swell around her. With the draft coming in through the open window, it felt even more eerie than before. And with the light on and nothing between her and the darkness outside, she felt exposed sitting there.

Even though her knee was throbbing, she pushed herself out of the chair and shuffled into the back to find the tape measure. It was an awkward task by herself, but she finally managed to get the dimensions of the window and sent them to Frank.

Not wanting to linger in the front office, Charlie returned to the back room and made a pot of coffee. She stood by while it brewed, somewhat comforted by the gurgling noises that broke the quiet.

When the machine had finished brewing, it occurred to her that it was awfully late to be drinking caffeine. Then again, the office was starting to get cold, exposed to the elements as it was. Besides that, it was something to do while she waited for Frank, so Charlie poured herself a cup anyway.

Frank arrived a short time later, and she felt a palpable sense of relief as his car pulled to the curb out front.

Her uncle stepped out of the car with a pizza box in one hand and stood on the other side of the broken window. After studying the mess for a moment, he handed the box through the opening.

"Thought we could use some of Uncle Frank's patented cure for the grumps."

"The grumps" was how Frank referred to any kind of bad mood, which had made more sense when she was six.

"Who has the grumps?" Charlie asked.

"You do."

"Says who?"

"No one had to. I could hear it loud and clear on the phone," he said, coming around through the door. "And now I stand here before you, observing those two frown lines between your eyes. You got those from your mother's side, by the way. That is not a Winters feature. We are stoic and serene, even when we're depressed. Stony-faced, maybe, but that's as far as it goes."

Charlie scoffed as she dropped the cardboard box on her desk and opened the lid.

"I'll try to remain more sprightly the next time someone lobs a brick through our window."

"I know this will make me sound like a cynical bastard, but this could be good for us."

Charlie lifted a slice of mushroom and green pepper pizza. Steam rose from the cheese as the warmth hit the colder air of the office.

"How so?"

"Not the window," Frank said, helping himself to a slice. "But the fact that he seems to have set his sights on Paige."

"Sorry, but how the hell is that good for us?"

"Well, if she's his new target, we can keep an extra close eye on her, but at a discreet distance."

Charlie raised her eyebrows.

"You want to use her as bait?"

"It's not using *her* so much as the particular situation we find ourselves in."

Charlie shook her head, wanting to argue about putting Paige in danger. But if the killer really was stalking Paige, she already *was* in danger.

"We need to talk to her before you start scheming," Charlie said, pausing to swallow a mouthful of pizza. "She needs to know what the risks are."

"Well, of course," Frank said. "We'd only go forward if she agreed to it."

An SUV rolled up behind Frank's car, and Detective Sponaugle climbed out. With his hands on his hips, he whistled at the damage. Inside, he shook hands with Frank and Charlie.

"Heard you were in remission," he said.

"It's true," Frank said.

"Congratulations."

"Thanks." Frank smiled and gestured at the pizza box. "Slice of pizza for you, Detective?"

"You know the rules, Frank." Detective Sponaugle picked up a piece of pizza and took a bite. "We're not supposed to accept offers of food or drink from civilians when we're on duty."

"Right, right." Frank chuckled. "Of course. I respect your level of integrity."

While the detective ate his illicit slice of pizza, he had Charlie go over exactly what had happened. He jotted down some notes and then took photos of the scene from inside and outside. When she got to the part about discovering the drawing attached to the brick, he gloved up and deposited the brick in an evidence baggie.

"Did you touch it?" Detective Sponaugle asked.

"Just with the toe of my shoe."

"I figured you'd know better, but I had to ask," he said. "Had a guy once who found a partial ribcage on his property and called it in, thinking it might be human remains. Dispatcher told him specifically not to touch anything. Guy swears up and down he didn't move so much as a blade of grass while he waited for us to get to the scene. And then a few days later, he posts a bunch of selfies on social media of him posing with it and holding it over his head like some kind of grisly trophy. Turned out to just be part of a deer skeleton, but still."

Charlie chuckled.

"Is it OK if we start cleaning this up now?" Frank asked. "I brought over some plywood to cover this hole until we can get the window fixed proper."

"Why don't you let me give you a hand with that?" the detective said, and he and Frank set about nailing the plywood in place. Meanwhile, Charlie went into the back and got the vacuum cleaner from the broom closet. It was an ancient Hoover from the sixties or seventies and had to weigh more than she did.

Frank and the detective had finished securing the window when Charlie dragged the vacuum into the front office. Frank thanked the detective for his help.

"Anytime, Frank," Sponaugle said.

He climbed into his SUV, waving as he drove off.

"Why do all of the detectives at the sheriff's department treat you like an old drinking buddy?"

"Because I have this," Frank said, pulling his little black notebook from his pocket. "And I've got a piece of dirt on every single one of them."

"Really?"

"No." The book disappeared back into Frank's pocket. "But I do have a list of each detective's favorite booze, and I send them each a bottle every Christmas."

Charlie smirked and bent down to plug in the vacuum cord.

"Let me do that," Frank said.

"Why?"

"So you can go sit on the kid's house."

"Paige?" Charlie asked. "The police are already watching her house."

"Well, no offense to our local boys, but I trust them about as far as I can throw them," Frank said. "When I get done cleaning up here, I'll take your place."

"If someone's going to sit out there all night, it should be me," Charlie argued. "You need the rest more than I do."

"Says who? You've done nothing but cart me around and play nursemaid for the last year. It's my turn to take care of you a little." Frank unwound another few feet of vacuum cord. "If this is going to work, then we'll have to do it in shifts anyway. You already signed up for Paige's security detail for tomorrow morning. That means I'm on tonight."

After a few more minutes of arguing, Charlie agreed to let Frank take the night watch. While Frank cleaned up the broken glass, she went out to her car and drove over to Paige's house.

When she turned onto Paige's street, Charlie spotted the car from the sheriff's department parked across the road. She pulled into a spot about half a block away.

Charlie shut off her lights but left the engine running for the heat.

Her mind went over the events of the evening again. The *tap-tap-tap* sound that she'd been sure she was only imagining. The crash of the brick hitting the window. The dark silhouette hurrying away. It had been a ballsy thing to do. There were security cameras on the street, though she doubted he'd left his face uncovered. Even so, it hadn't even been that late. He might have waited until there was no traffic in sight, but their office was on a busy street. Anyone might have turned onto the road at that moment.

But they hadn't. He'd stayed in the shadows and escaped. Again.

Charlie was still worrying on this when a car pulled alongside her. It was Frank. He rolled down his window and shouted to her across the way.

"Go home and get some rest, turkey. I'll see you in the morning."

"Alright," she said. "But be careful."

"Yeah, yeah," he said, waving her concerns away.

She waited until he'd pulled into an empty parking space down the street before putting her car in gear and turning around.

She rolled up to the next stop sign, knowing she should do what Frank said. Go home and get some sleep. But even if she hadn't had that cup of coffee, she would have been too rattled to go back to her empty apartment with all that quiet.

So Charlie decided to go where she always went these days when she felt lost and alone.

Her mother's house.

CHAPTER FIFTY-THREE

Charlie let herself in through the front door, turning on one of the lamps in the living room before heading for her old room. She put on one of Allie's old mix CDs before plugging in the strand of Christmas lights that hung over the bed. Then she ducked inside the closet and released the hatch on the plumbing access door in the back wall. Allie's old secret hiding place.

Charlie had replenished the bottle of rum a few times now. There were two empties in the small space along with a third bottle that was still three-quarters full. She didn't know why she insisted on hiding it here. She was well past the legal drinking age, and her mother wasn't even living here at the moment. But she supposed she liked keeping one of Allie's traditions alive.

She uncorked the bottle and took a drink, face puckering at the sting of the alcohol in her throat. The rum hit her brain after a minute or two, making her feel tipsy and slow. A smile spread over her face as a small burst of euphoria struck. She felt the tension in her neck and shoulders ease, and she sank down onto the corner of the bed with a satisfied sigh.

But when the artificially warm and fuzzy feelings faded sometime later, Charlie started to get lonely. Maybe it had been a mistake to come here where she was even more alone than usual since Allie never spoke here.

Something shifted outside the window, and Charlie gasped. She set the bottle down and paused the music, tiptoeing over to the window and peering outside. But it was only the bush outside swaying in the breeze.

Still, she couldn't shake the feeling like she was being watched.

"Well, that's a winning combination," Charlie said out loud to herself. "Drunk, lonely, and scared."

As she backed away from the window, she reminded herself that the brick hadn't been for her. It'd been for Paige.

The creepy feeling waned, only to be replaced by worry. But the fact that both the sheriff's department and Frank were watching over the girl eased her mind. She turned the music back on and returned to her spot at the end of the bed.

OK, so she wasn't scared anymore. And she could keep the anxiety about Paige to a minimum. But there was one emotion remaining that she couldn't fix so easily.

Loneliness.

She closed her eyes, and a vision unfolded in her mind like a scene in a movie.

Will whispering in her ear. Brushing hair from her cheek.

Charlie opened her eyes and blinked.

No. Bad brain. Will is over.

Even as she thought that, she remembered Zoe pleading his case earlier in the day. But Charlie wasn't sure she could get past what he'd done. Forgiveness had never been her strong suit.

The rum pumping in her bloodstream seemed to have other ideas, and before she realized quite what she was doing, Charlie had her phone in her hand. Knowing full well she was too drunk for anything good to come of this, she flipped through her contact list.

Her thumb hovered over Will's name. If she could hear Allie right now, she knew what she'd be saying.

Don't be a chicken. Do it. If you don't do it, I'll be super annoying for the rest of the week.

After another few moments of hesitation, of swiping back and forth through the names, Charlie pressed the tiny phone icon and dialed.

It rang and rang. Of course. It was getting late. Everyone else on Salem Island was probably getting ready for bed. She removed the phone from her ear and was about to disconnect the call when she heard a voice come through the tiny speaker.

The voice on the other end was gravelly but not sleepy.

"Charlie?" he asked.

"Sorry," she said, instantly regretting making the call. "It's late. I shouldn't have called."

"No, I'm glad you did. Is everything OK?"

"Not really."

"Why?" Will said, and she heard genuine concern in his tone. "What's wrong?"

"It's too hard to explain right now. Can you... come over?" Charlie glanced around the room, remembering suddenly that she wasn't at her apartment. "I'll text you the address."

"Sure. I'll be right there."

Charlie hung up, knowing she'd probably just made a terrible mistake and not caring at all.

CHAPTER FIFTY-FOUR

Charlie went out to the living room to wait. When she saw the headlights approaching slowly from down the street, she went out onto the porch so he'd know which house to go to.

She watched him park, still sipping at the bottle of rum. His feet crunched over the gravel as he walked up to where she stood.

He was dressed more casually than she'd ever seen him, at least since high school. Jeans and a hoodie under a canvas jacket.

"Thanks for coming," she said.

"It's no problem," Will said, his breath coming out in clouds.

What was she doing? She knew this was a bad idea, and yet she felt powerless to stop it.

Charlie gestured at the door.

"You should come inside."

He followed her into the house and back to her old room.

"What happened to you?" Will asked, noticing her faint limp.

Charlie sat on the floor, using the side of her bed as a backrest. She took another drink.

"It's a long story."

Will tossed his jacket on the bed, sank down beside her, and pointed at the bottle.

"Are you going to share or…?"

She passed it to him. He brought the bottle to his lips and took a long swig. When he finished, he set the bottle down with a *thunk*, liquid sloshing inside.

A Radiohead song ended, transitioning into "Dead Leaves and the Dirty Ground" by the White Stripes.

Will's gaze traversed the room, falling on Allie's *Fight Club* poster featuring Brad Pitt as Tyler Durden. Face bloodied, cigarette dangling from his lip.

"What year is it?" Will asked, blinking as if confused. "Where am I? Whose house is this?"

"This is my old room." Charlie followed his gaze to the poster. Smiled. "*Our* old room. That was Allie's. She was *obsessed*."

"With *Fight Club* or with Brad Pitt?"

"Both."

Will suddenly hunched forward and pointed his thumb over his shoulder toward the doorway.

"So is your mom here or…?"

Charlie snorted at the worry in his eyes, like he was a teenager scared an adult was going to catch him doing something he shouldn't. It was a look that reminded her of Allie, and that changed her expression to a frown.

She reached for the bottle. Took a drink.

"No. It's just us."

Will studied her for a moment.

"Did something happen tonight?" he asked, finally. "Or is this something you normally do? Come sit in your old bedroom and get shitfaced and sad?"

She let her eyes slide over to his, not sure if he was mocking her or not. His hands went up as if she'd pointed a gun at him.

"Hey, I'm not judging. I'm just trying to get a feel for the situation. Whether or not I should be worried about you. And also, I like to know going into this type of scenario what exactly is expected of me, you know? Is it my job to just sit here and get sloshed with you? Lend a shoulder to cry on? Or am I going to need to restrain you later when you decide you must take revenge on the old next-door neighbor who used to wake you up every Saturday during summer vacation at six in the morning with their weed whacker by burning his shed to the ground."

That got a laugh out of her.

"That's oddly specific."

"This isn't my first rodeo," Will said, taking the bottle from her and drinking. He wiped his mouth.

"So? What is it? This is Lance Corporal William Crawford, reporting for duty," he said, saluting. "Ready and willing to do your bidding."

Charlie chuckled.

She stared at him for a beat, her head cocked to one side.

And then she said, "Kiss me."

He didn't hesitate, not even for half a second. He kissed her hard on the mouth, and she tasted the liquor on his lips.

His hands slid around behind her back, pulling her to him.

The combination of the booze swimming in her system and making out with Will made her feel lightheaded. Eventually, she was so disoriented, so lost in the kiss with Will, that when she opened her eyes a few moments later, she was half startled to find herself in her old room.

Will maneuvered onto his knees, inching closer to Charlie in a way that slowly nudged her onto her back, never breaking the kiss. He was smooth, she had to give him that.

Finally they came up for air. Will, straddling her hips, gazed down at her through the hair tumbling into his face.

"Thank you," she said.

"For what?"

"For making me forget about everything for a minute."

"Just doing my job, ma'am," he said with a sigh. "It's a rough line of work, all of this heavy kissing and burning down the sheds of asshole neighbors, but someone's gotta do it."

Charlie held up a finger.

"I never asked you to burn down the neighbor's shed."

"Well that's because we haven't finished the bottle of rum yet. Don't worry, we'll get there. But first…"

He did sort of a slow-motion push-up until the full weight of him was pressed into her. His mouth met hers, and they kissed again. When Will pulled away this time, Charlie smiled up at him.

"Your beard tickles."

"You think it tickles your face?" His finger traced a line from her collarbone down to her waist. He fumbled with the button of her jeans and then unzipped the fly. "Just wait."

His hand disappeared down the front of her pants. Charlie gasped and closed her eyes.

Was she really going to do this? Have sex with Will here? On the floor of her childhood bedroom?

She caught Will's wrist, stopping him before he could go any further.

"You want me to stop?"

She knew what Allie would say.

Grow a pair, Chuck. You want him, don't you?

"Yes," Charlie said.

Will withdrew his hand, rolling away from her. Too late, Charlie realized she'd said it out loud, and he'd thought she'd been telling him to stop.

"Sorry," he said, backing off and moving to sit on the side of her old bed.

Charlie sat up so fast she felt faintly dizzy for a second.

"Wait. I didn't mean that."

"No?" Will ran a hand through his hair. "Because I'm not interested in pushing you to do something you don't want to."

"You weren't. You asked me if you should stop, and I said yes, but I wasn't talking to you."

Charlie reached for him, but he pulled away. Did she know how to kill the mood or what?

"Uh… OK. Who were you talking to then?"

Charlie tried to find a way to explain and finally decided on the simplest answer.

"Myself."

The look on Will's face told her that he remained unconvinced. She went to him, climbing into his lap and pushing him back on the mattress. Charlie removed her shirt and leaned down to kiss him, long and deep.

"You're sure about this?" Will asked when she stood up and started to unbutton her pants.

She paused, gazing down and looking him full in the eye.

"You're not?" she asked.

"Shutting up now," he said and unbuckled his belt.

CHAPTER FIFTY-FIVE

After, they lay in bed, squashed together on the narrow, twin-sized mattress. His skin was warm against hers, a little sticky from the light sheen of sweat.

"Time for part two," he said. "You got any matches?"

"What?"

"Neighbor's shed's not going to burn itself down, is it?"

Laughing, she slapped his arm.

"Are you a pyromaniac or something? What's your obsession with burning down sheds?"

"Not just any shed, OK? Only the neighbor or neighbors who may have wronged you in the past," Will said. "You're telling me you didn't have a single shitty neighbor growing up? The kind who complained about your dog barking too much or that your yard was infecting the whole neighborhood with crabgrass?"

Charlie stared up at the ceiling, thinking about it.

"There was this guy who lived next door for a while when we were in middle school and high school. Allie and me, I mean," Charlie said. "I think his name was Dennis, but we always called him Shirtless Wonder."

"Shirtless Wonder?" Will repeated, chuckling.

"It's probably obvious by the nickname, but he never wore a shirt. Not even when it was ten degrees out," Charlie explained.

"I hate him already," Will said. "So is that our motive? You were subjected to the bare nipples, beer gut, and happy trail of Dennis the Shirtless Wonder one too many times?"

"No," Charlie snorted. "I mean, that *was* pretty bad. But he was kind of creepy on top of that. Always ogling Allie when she was laying out in the backyard, tanning."

"Not you?" Will asked.

"Not me, what?"

"He only ogled Allie?"

"I didn't run around in a bikini top and cutoff shorts all summer like Allie did."

"I see, I see. Well, let's do this then. His shed is toast." Will propped himself up on one elbow. "I'll need a length of garden hose to siphon some gas from the tank, and—"

"He doesn't even live there anymore. Besides, weren't you supposed to be restraining me?"

"What's that?"

Charlie rolled her eyes.

"When you first brought up the shed thing, you asked if you should be restraining me from burning my neighbor's shed down. But somewhere along the line, you seem to have flipped from restraining to encouraging."

Will stared at her for a moment, then reached out and grabbed her wrists. He pinned them over her head and leaned in.

"So the lady wants to be restrained? Is that it?"

"No." Charlie laughed a little. "I'm saying—"

Her words choked off in a squeal as he ran the fingers of one hand down her body while still keeping her arms pinned with the other.

"OK," she said. "Maybe."

"Just maybe?" Will asked, kissing her neck.

He stroked her again, and this time she said, "Yes."

CHAPTER FIFTY-SIX

Waiting. Smoking. Thumbs twiddling at his phone, pretending to text.

He leans against a brick wall in front of a twenty-four-hour coffee and donut shop, the sharp smell of burnt coffee beans thick in the air here. And people circle everywhere. Some filing in and out. Others braving the chilly evening to sit in the small patio just off to his left.

The streetlight's yellow glow gleams down on all of them. Reflects off shiny faces and dirty fingernails and coffee-stained teeth. Ugly people leading desperately boring lives, throwing dozens of donuts down the empty hole of themselves. Glazed. Old-fashioned. Jelly. Cake. Frosted.

His shoulders twitch. He finds it all creepy. Alienating to such a profound degree that it makes his skin shrivel, his gut clench.

The streets will empty out within the next hour or two, though. Salem Island is a town almost entirely in bed by 10 p.m. without fail.

And then it will all belong to him and him alone. A whole city laid out at his feet. Made for him. He sees the empty asphalt paths in his imagination, wants to follow them all night like they might actually lead somewhere this time.

He flicks his eyes up once every thirty seconds or so to look directly at the sandwich place across the street. That's where the target is now, unwittingly partaking in a final meal like some doomed death row inmate.

A puff of laughter jets out of his nostrils at the thought. But he reins himself in quickly. So close now. Can't draw any heat.

This intersection is one of the busiest spots on Salem Island. To him, that's a good thing. Easier to hide in a crowd. No one can see behind the mask anyway. No one.

He caught a glimpse of the target earlier. Sitting at one of the booths in the sandwich place. Eating a Reuben, kraut all hanging out of the side of it. That was twelve minutes ago. Any second now, his prey will come sauntering out that front door, and the hunt will resume.

Hipster doofuses with fat black plugs in their ears talk as they walk out of the coffee shop and pass him by, debating the merits of various coffee roasting techniques. Surely regurgitating something they read in some hipster handbook somewhere, he thinks. They sport matching facial hair and complementary flannel and have probably jerked each other off over the same rare IPAs.

What would they think if they knew how close they were to a killer? An apex predator. Would they feel suddenly tame? Toothless? Weak?

Excitement roils in his gut.

And he flashes to a fantasy. Pictures his blade ripping a new neck. Spiky metal punching a hole in the flesh. Blood spiraling out of the wound like a faucet.

He wonders what Paige will think when she sees what he is doing for her. What he's willing to risk for her. This goes so far beyond hiding an engagement ring in a glass of champagne. This is life and death. Real power wielded. Permanent marks left.

And he wonders what all of them will think, all the people fussing over finding him. He gets a little chill as he pictures it, all of them seeing this spectacle he's about to unleash, knowing that he is out there, knowing what he is capable of.

Movement on the other side of the street. The target sidles out of the restaurant, and after waiting a few seconds, he follows.

CHAPTER FIFTY-SEVEN

He follows the target for four and a half blocks. Creeping. Keeping well back to avoid notice. Flitting and drifting among the shadows like smoke.

His eyes peer out at the world through the sheening black plastic of his sunglasses. Unblinking and fierce. His vision stays trained on the bony shoulders ahead, like a missile locking onto an objective, ready to destroy.

He waits at a crosswalk as the target pulls away. Watches the glowing orange hand command him to wait as the traffic rips by. Feels impatience swell in his gut.

The target's gait seems leisurely. Something deeply relaxed in the motion. A black leather jacket drapes the shoulders, a rumpled hood bulging out from the back with the pale neck sprouting out of it like a stem. Messy hair atop that.

The orange hand gives way to the white walking figure. He crosses the street. Picks up speed to close the gap some.

They move out of downtown. Head into an industrial section of Salem Island dominated by red-brick structures. Empty factories and a couple of sprawling paper mills—the deadest part of the city, a stretch of land that time forgot. Much of it boarded up. Smashed windows staring out from the places the water-stained plywood doesn't cover.

Flecks of glass litter the ground like pebbles. Grit against the concrete under his feet.

A narrow alley takes shape up ahead—a vacancy between the factories. A dark passage enclosed by brick walls.

That would work.

He lets his hand paw at the bulk tucked inside his jacket. Even through the fabric, the blade feels powerful. Vicious. Hard and pointy and aching to open someone up.

He builds speed. Creeps closer and closer. Soon the details of the figure sharpen until every hair on that messy head comes into crisp focus.

And he reads every cue in the target's body language. Sees no worry on display there. No tensing of the upper back. No rigidity in the limbs. No quirk of the posture that portends them turning around any time soon. No sign that they're aware of him at all.

Just that upper body swaying back and forth. Oblivious. Vulnerable.

He licks his lips. Draws his knife. Takes a breath.

He lunges for the swaying form. The metal in his fist ripping in a swooping arc.

The target flinches at long last. Shoulders drawn up high enough to touch the sides of the neck.

But he doesn't turn around until it's too late.

The blade glints yellow. Plunging home. And Robbie Turner screams as it pierces his flesh.

CHAPTER FIFTY-EIGHT

The knife punches into the meat of Robbie's shoulder. Stops dead with an awful scraping sound as it pricks bone.

The stalker rips it free. Swings for the neck again.

But Robbie's thrashing makes him miss. The target dodges back. Feet scuffling on the concrete. Good hand clutching the wounded shoulder.

The slacker's idiot eyes are wild. Mouth open. Screams and whimpers rolling out of him in a choppy stream. Lips quivering, wet with saliva.

This is the loser all the girls seem to go crazy for? A failed drug dealer. A snitch. Doesn't even wash his fucking hair from the looks of it. And somehow they'd all rather have him. They pick him. Over and over and over, they pick him.

A flash of Paige smiling at Robbie burns in his skull, the image blotting out to a deep red as all things seem to in this moment.

Well? Here I am. Here I am. You never noticed me before, but you will now.

He lunges again. Slashes the knife across Robbie's chest. Feels the blade slice at the fabric of the loser's hoodie, but he doesn't think he got through to the skin.

Robbie moans. A feminine sound. Voice cracking. Lips spluttering.

And all he wants is to jam this pointed metal into this little bitch's neck. Into his chest. Into his face. Just stab until he stops squirming.

Robbie tries to run. Stumbling. Confused. He trips over his own feet. Buckles at the waist. Crashes down onto his chest, landing at the mouth of the alley, potholes full of water all around him. He rolls onto his back.

The stalker pounces. Sees that red tint along the edge of things sharpen, like the shadows have turned to crimson tonight. Ready to finish this.

He never sees the punch coming.

Robbie's fist cracks into the side of his jaw. Spins his head to the side. He feels his neck go slack.

Reality dims for a second. The yellow glow of the streetlights dulling to gold. The ambient sound around him muffling to silence.

But his senses sharpen again. The world comes back.

Robbie wriggles beneath him. Tries to scoot back. Free himself. Too late.

He plunges the blade into the slacker's neck and rips. Now it's Robbie's head flung to the side by the force.

The knife bursts out of the flesh. Tearing free all at once. Muscle shredding. Ropes of blood jerked free and flying.

Hot.

Hot blood on his hands. Spattered onto his face. The body heat shocking against his skin.

Robbie gags. Tries to sit up. Steam coils from the wound.

Hot blood gushes down his hoodie and onto his jeans. A throbbing red waterfall cascading down him in spurts. Pulsing.

Robbie's mouth opens and closes like fish lips. Trying to breathe. Eyes blinking over and over.

The stalker shuffles back. Adjusts his grip on his knife.

No longer does he want to stab, thrust, attack. He can only watch in shock.

Blood drains down into the mud puddles. Scarlet clouds blooming in the water, darker than the rest.

Robbie's elbows skid out from under him. His head splashes down into that mix of blood and rainwater.

And then he's still.

Motionless.

Dead.

The killer gapes at the lifeless form. Blinks a few times. Drops of gummy crimson gather and drip from the knife, fall to the pool below. The night is so quiet now, like it's holding its breath.

Good. Good. This is good.

Fresh excitement blossoms in his head. All the lights inside igniting, bursting like fireworks.

The violence is a gift. The violence makes him real.

Stuttering breaths hitch into his chest. He can only sit there a moment and blink and breathe.

He feels how the blood on his hands is already going tacky. A reminder that he needs to get out of here.

He moves to the body. Wipes his bloody blade on a clean portion of Robbie's hoodie.

Somehow he doesn't think the slacker will mind.

CHAPTER FIFTY-NINE

Charlie got back to her apartment in the early hours of the morning and fell deep into a dreamless sleep.

Sometime just after dawn, her phone blared. She opened her eyes to slits, saw it was barely even fully light out, and wondered who would call so early.

She blinked a few times. Confused. Then it hit.

Paige. She was supposed to go to Paige's house so she could escort her to work and relieve Frank.

She bolted upright, and instantly regretted it. A tidal wave of nausea shuddered through all of her, a spiky headache already spearing her frontal lobe. How much rum had she had last night?

Charlie closed her eyes and waited for her bed to stop rocking like a boat. The events of the previous day came to her in snippets. Finding the killer's lair. The brick smashing through the window of the office. Going to her mother's house. Calling Will. And then...

Charlie inhaled sharply.

Jesus, had she really—

"Boned him on your old twin bed?" Allie asked. "Yep. Can confirm. Totes happened."

She snatched the phone off the nightstand and answered it.

"Is she OK?"

Zoe's voice answered her.

"What? Is who— Ohh... Paige. Paige is fine, Charlie."

Relief flooded through Charlie, instantly dialing down her headache and that tight sickly feeling in her middle. She took a big breath. Then she felt her brow knot itself up above her eyes.

If it's not about Paige…

"Charlie, I know you just woke up, and I kind of hate to spring this on you, but… we've got another body. It could be the work of, uh, our guy, and I think you're going to want to get down here."

The hair on the back of Charlie's neck went rigid, and then all feeling left her being, a cold dead numbness creeping over her skin, saturating the meat of her. She sank back to the mattress, finding no comfort in its pillowy touch.

"Another victim…" she muttered, more to herself than Zoe. "He killed another girl. Is she someone from the bar?"

Zoe sighed softly before she spoke.

"Well, no. It's not a female at all, in fact."

Charlie's groggy mind struggled to process these words: not a female. She turned them over in her mind a few times, tried to figure out what logical conclusion they might lead to. Nothing came to her.

"Not a female? Then who?"

"It's Robbie Turner."

CHAPTER SIXTY

Robbie Turner had been murdered in a grim, dank alley that smelled of garbage. It was a dim and depressing place to die.

A white sheet shrouded the body now, concealing it from the view of the crowd of media and onlookers gathering at the police barricade down the street, but Charlie had gotten a good look at Robbie before he'd been covered.

His face was stark white. Bloodless. The raw, gaping wound at his throat matched Emma's. And it suggested Robbie's death had been quick. At least Charlie hoped it had been.

His body was sprawled in that limp, unnatural way the dead had. Toes pointed slightly together. Sightless eyes staring up at nothing.

Charlie's skin prickled with goosebumps, stomach churning. Her face felt hot, and her mouth flushed with saliva.

No. She wasn't going to puke this time.

She closed her eyes and focused on her breathing. In and out. Slow and deep.

The nausea in her gut receded slowly. It was working.

And then she caught a whiff of the coppery blood smell. Not quite the fully rank odor of rotting meat, but a scent that was all wrong nonetheless.

She gagged a little, and then the breeze shifted and the stink faded.

Behind her closed eyelids, Charlie heard the click of a camera's shutter and saw the bright bursts of the flash. The crime scene techs documenting the scene.

When she opened her eyes again, the coroner was bent over Robbie's body, lifting the sheet to complete the preliminary examination. And Charlie's eyes landed on Robbie's hands.

Dried blood caked Robbie's fingers where he'd clutched at his wound. But it would have been too late by then. Much too late.

Charlie turned away. She'd seen enough.

She left the alley, turning away from the gawkers and reporters huddling outside the police tape barrier. She found a small yard next to one of the old paper mills and paused there under a dead tree.

There was a sudden heaviness in Charlie's chest. A seizing feeling in her throat. It was a moment before she realized she was crying.

Which was weird. It wasn't like she and Robbie had been friends, exactly.

But he had been sort of a lovable degenerate. And he certainly hadn't deserved this fate.

After the initial burst of tears, Charlie felt a slight release in tension. She wiped her cheeks and sighed.

"Knock, knock," Allie said.

"What?"

"I'm trying to tell a joke. You know, to bring a little levity to the situation."

"Well, the situation is that this psycho slit Robbie Turner's throat and left him to bleed out in an alley that stinks like old cabbage. I don't think there's any levity to bring to that. Sometimes life sucks, and there's nothing you can do about it. That's just the way it is."

"I don't accept that."

"And that's kind of the point, Allie. *You* don't have to accept anything," Charlie said. "You're fucking dead. It's the rest of us that have to keep going."

For once, Allie didn't have a snappy response.

Charlie heard footsteps approaching and looked up to see Zoe moving down the sidewalk toward her.

"There you are," she said.

"Needed some fresh air," Charlie explained.

"Yeah. I get it. You and Robbie had an interesting history, I suppose." Zoe crossed her arms and gazed up at the sky. "What I can't figure is why he'd pick out Robbie as a victim. I mean, we know he hung out at the Laughing Raven, so that fits. But up until now, he's focused exclusively on women."

Charlie was about to speak, to agree that she found Robbie a strange choice of victim. But then she had a flash of a memory.

"Robbie was there at the bar the night we went to canvass after finding Emma."

"Yeah," Zoe said.

"I saw him with Paige. He had his arm around her. To an onlooker, it might have seemed like they were… I don't know… together." Charlie thought about what Frank had said earlier about stalker behavior and the need to be in control. About how possessive they were over their victims. "If the killer saw that, it would have made him jealous."

Zoe shook her head, holding quiet for a few seconds before she spoke again. Her voice came out hushed and small.

"Crazy, you know? Robbie got killed over nothing."

CHAPTER SIXTY-ONE

A somber atmosphere occupied the office when Charlie and Zoe got back. They pushed through the front door, and Charlie instantly felt a heaviness in the air, a quiet desperation where their collective sense of optimism about the case had once been, as though much of the hope had leaked out of the building, perhaps finding its way through the broken window.

Paige and Frank had been sitting in the front room and stood as Charlie and Zoe entered, grave expressions etched on both of their faces.

"You OK?" Frank said. His face looked so different with that perpetually amused grin wiped off of it, so bleak and funereal and old.

Charlie shrugged and then nodded, not really sure what to say.

Paige's shoulders jerked, drawing Charlie's attention to her. The girl's eyes looked too wide, almost manic. She started babbling.

"It didn't make sense to me. That he'd kill Robbie, I mean. But then I remembered that day we did interviews at the Laughing Raven. I talked to Robbie that day. What if he saw that? What if Robbie died because of me?"

Apparently the girl had spent too much time around the office and was starting to think like a detective.

"First of all, Robbie didn't die because of you," Charlie said. "Whatever the warped reason might be behind it, Robbie died because a very sick person murdered him. For all we know, he knew Robbie from the bar and had some other reason to target him. Either way, the bottom line is that the only person to blame here is the one with the knife in his hand."

"I guess so," Paige said, blinking away the wetness in her eyes.

"Tonight is our chance," Charlie said. "The Carnival Bizarre. He'll be there. Everyone will be there. We'll lay a trap for him, and we'll get him."

Frank nodded.

"Our boy's got his eyes on Paige here. We know he's watching, waiting to make his move, whether we like it or not. Way I see it, it only makes sense to use that to our advantage."

"Bait," Paige said, her voice just louder than a whisper. "You want me to be bait?"

"That's one way of saying it," Frank said.

"Nobody wants you to do anything you're not comfortable with, Paige," Charlie said. "But what Frank said is true. He's watching and plotting, all the time. We can set everything up to keep our eyes on you, have cops and beefed-up security all around you. If we plan it right, it's probably safer than trying to hide."

Charlie had expected Paige to be dubious, but she had barely finished talking when her assistant bobbed her head emphatically.

"Of course I'll do it."

Charlie crossed her arms.

"Paige, I want to make sure you understand the risks."

"I understand. I mean, the biggest risk of all is that he gets away again and goes on doing this to other girls, over and over. Right?" Paige's face was unusually solemn. "I trust you to keep me safe. Just like you did last night."

They all fell quiet after that, but it wasn't the bleak kind of quiet Charlie had felt upon walking in here. It was a determined quiet. Focused. Intense. Ready.

"OK," she said. "Well, we've got a lot to do to get ready, so let's get after it."

*

Charlie waited outside while Paige ran into the My Fair Lady Boutique to buy the velvet skirt, the perfect teamwork workaround to Heidi's skirt-blocking bitterness. The little plan went off without a hitch, much to both Paige and Allie's delight. That set up Charlie's costume for the evening easily enough.

After that, Charlie coordinated with Zoe about getting some undercover police to mix in with the carnival crowd. With a little light convincing, Sheriff Brown offered up a handful of extra officers to work the crowd with a couple of additional patrol cars to stake out the scene from afar.

"You'll brief the deputies before tonight?" Charlie asked Zoe.

"Yes, ma'am. Already have a meeting set. And they've been instructed to wear costumes so they'll blend in with the crowd."

That would be a big help and made Charlie feel a lot better about the plan.

Frank and Charlie took turns drilling safety procedures into Paige, who seemed oddly enthusiastic about each and every aspect of the plan.

"I think we need to talk about the worst-case scenario," Charlie said. "What if he manages to somehow grab Paige and get away from the party? I mean, I figure we'll arm her with one of the stun guns, but that's not enough for me."

"I've got something for that," Frank said.

He dug around in the supply closet, and for the next few moments, all they could hear was the sound of shifting boxes and crinkling bags.

"Here we go." He spun around with a small black case in his hands. "What if we hide one of these on her?"

He opened the clamshell, revealing several thumb-sized rectangles.

"What are those?" Paige asked.

"Tracking chips," Charlie said, nodding. "That's not a bad idea."

"Not bad? I think it's a stroke of genius, personally." Frank flashed a devious smile. "You gotta figure he'll toss her phone, if he's smart. But if she has one of these tucked in her pocket, we can track her anywhere she goes."

A little after lunchtime, Frank's window repairman of choice, Luis, showed up to start working on the front of the shop.

"My word. I still don't understand why anyone would do that," Paige said, shaking her head at the plywood nailed over the broken window. Shards of jagged glass still clung to the metal frame in places, giving the window the appearance of a mouth with long, sharp teeth.

Having just walked back from talking to Luis out on the sidewalk, Frank held up a finger as he responded to her.

"I actually read up on stalking behavior last night." He wheeled one of the office chairs over and sat down. "And while there are a few different subtypes, they play a lot of the same games. Sending letters or gifts. Repeated phone calls. Some of them follow their victims up close. Sometimes it's from a distance—online or in the media if the victim is a celebrity, for example. Sometimes they end up stalking or trying to befriend the victim's friends and family. Stalkers are very possessive. Even the ones motivated by revenge tend to be very jealous. Some of them end up believing they're in some kind of relationship with the victim—that their feelings are actually reciprocated. But it's all very one-sided. The stalker is always the one calling the shots. And that tells me that the whole game is about control. They only want to play if they get to make all the rules."

Frank gestured over his shoulder at the broken window.

"So the message he's sending here is: I'm watching you. I know where you work. I see you, but you can't see me. I can throw a brick through your window, and you can't stop me. No one can."

Charlie felt a twinge of frustration and ground her back teeth together.

"I almost had him, too. I was so close." She glanced down at her knee and sighed. "But the important thing is that Paige is safe."

"Safe and reporting for duty," Paige said, saluting.

As the afternoon crept toward evening, Charlie's mind strayed to Will over and over. Had she made a mistake in trusting him? Would last night lead to something or not, and did she even want it to?

Then a fresh pang of guilt would chase these thoughts from her mind. How could she think about romance after seeing Robbie's corpse in its ghastly final pose? After what had happened to Emma? Knowing the killer was still out there, lusting after Paige, plotting his next move even now?

Each time, a chill crept up her spine, and she got back to work.

CHAPTER SIXTY-TWO

Charlie had Paige wait downstairs while she went upstairs to her apartment and got into her costume. She paired the constellation-covered velvet skirt with a lace-trimmed peasant blouse and a black corset belt. Since most of the Carnival Bizarre attractions were outdoors, she put on a pair of leggings under the skirt and found an old crocheted blanket she could wrap around her shoulders like a shawl. After that, Charlie raided the jewelry box she kept in the linen closet and loaded on all the jewelry she could find.

Charlie studied her reflection in the mirror over the sink.

"Not bad for a last-minute costume," she said.

"I guess it's alright," Allie said with a sigh. "A little underwhelming in the bust department, if you ask me. You only have so many good boob years left, Charlie. You really should try to make the most of it."

Something about Allie's words reminded Charlie of last night. With Will. She cringed a little, some mix of regret and yearning coming over her.

"Hey, it could have been worse," Allie said. "At least Will's hot. Imagine if you'd hooked up with someone gross, like Shirtless Wonder."

"Ew." Charlie recoiled at the thought. "Why would you even say that?"

"I needed someone specifically nasty, and ol' Dennis the Shirtless Menace happened to fit the bill. Remember the time we caught him spying on us with binoculars?"

"Ugh. Yes." Charlie flexed her knee. It still felt a little tight but was much less tender than it had been earlier. "Did he ever... I don't know… act aggressively toward you or anything? Try to get you to come into his house or something like that?"

"Why?" Allie scoffed. "You think Shirtless Wonder killed me, now?"

"Maybe. I don't know. It was just something I've considered at certain points." Charlie picked up a makeup palette and applied a bit of dark shadow to her eyelids. "Not all that seriously. I've probably suspected pretty much everyone over the years."

"Everyone?"

"Pretty much," she said, blending the shadow with tiny circular motions.

"Even Dad and Uncle Frank?"

"No!" Charlie slammed the makeup brush down on the sink. "Jesus. Why would you even say that?"

"You said everyone."

Charlie unscrewed the cap on a tube of mascara.

"Stop messing with my head," she grumbled.

"It's what I do, Charlie. I get in there, and I start knocking shit over and throwing stuff around. Like that time I kicked over your sandcastle."

Charlie froze with the tiny wand clutched in her hand. She'd forgotten about that, but now it all came flooding back. It was the best castle she'd ever made. She'd spent over an hour on it, making it perfect, while Allie bounded around in the shallows with some other kids on the beach.

"Yeah," Charlie said, her voice quiet. "Why the hell did you do that?"

"I don't know, man." Allie sighed. "I wasn't even into building that kind of stuff, not like you were. But then I saw how cool yours was, so I tried making my own. But you were so damn meticulous about everything. Every turret perfectly formed. Every doorway carefully scooped out. Yours even had a moat lined with little pebbles you'd found on the beach. And tiny flags on top that you made from sticks and torn-up gum wrappers. I kept looking from mine to yours, comparing them. And side by side, your sandcastle made mine look like a big pile of dog turds. It made me sad and jealous and pissed off. So I did the only thing I could think of. I asked you to get me a Capri Sun from the cooler and then stomped your castle to oblivion."

Charlie still remembered turning back from the beach blanket to see all of her hard work being destroyed.

"You were a dick," she said softly.

"Yeah," Allie agreed. "But only sometimes."

For some reason, that made Charlie laugh. She laughed until she was doubled over with tears in her eyes. Allie was the only person who had ever made her laugh like that.

She leaned on the sink, staring at her own reflection but imagining she was looking at Allie instead.

"I miss you," she whispered to the room that was empty aside from herself.

"I know."

CHAPTER SIXTY-THREE

With Charlie's costume situated, she and Paige drove over to Paige's house. Charlie gestured at a row of restaurants flitting past outside the car.

"We could get something to eat if you're hungry," she said.

Paige shook her head.

"My stomach feels like a washing machine on the spin cycle."

"Same here," Charlie said.

At the next red light, Charlie glanced over at the girl.

"Are you sure about this? There's still time to back out."

Two small children dressed as superheroes and clutching plastic candy buckets shaped like jack-o'-lanterns crossed in front of the car, accompanied by their parents.

"I'm sure," Paige said, and there was a boldness in her voice Charlie didn't know if she'd heard before. "This is going to sound silly, but I got this fortune cookie last night. The fortune inside said, 'Something momentous is on the horizon.' And I just have the strongest notion that tonight is going to be, you know... momentous."

Charlie turned down Paige's street, admiring the way the orange and red leaves on the sugar maples matched the colors of the sunset. Trick-or-treating on Salem Island went until dark, and they passed by a dozen or so costumed children. Vampires, zombies, fairy princesses, and Charlie thought she saw one kid dressed as a poop emoji.

Allie scoffed.

"In my day, we trick-or-treated after dark," she complained. "None of this 'before sunset' nonsense. They're turning these kids into pussies."

Paige's next-door neighbors had gone all out for Halloween. Their entire front yard was decorated like a cemetery with fake graves and spooky trees and a grim reaper guarding the front door. Fog from a machine oozed between the headstones, lit with an eerie green light.

Charlie and Paige climbed out of the car just as a group of kids scampered up the walk of the house next door. The doorbell chimed, and a woman in a witch costume threw the door wide. Charlie heard the sound of rattling chains and gusting wind as the front door swung open. One of those spooky sound effects tracks, no doubt.

"Trick or treat!" the children screamed in unison.

The woman threw back her head and cackled.

"Be careful what you wish for," she said and began doling out handfuls of candy.

Charlie followed Paige inside a small two-bedroom bungalow like most of the others on the street. Every element of decor inside was dainty and neat, which fit Paige well enough, from Charlie's point of view.

"Would have been pretty awesome if Paige had a bunch of metal and horror posters plastered everywhere," Allie said. "Bunch of gore, and that dripping blood font, you know?"

Charlie ignored her.

"I'll just be a few minutes," Paige said, ducking into her room.

There was a large window in the living room with a good view of the street.

Charlie moved closer to it so she could watch the children move from house to house collecting their sugary bounty.

"No hurry," she said, suddenly overcome with a flood of Halloween memories.

The year Allie had stepped on a board with an exposed nail ten minutes into the start of the night. She could still hear Allie's scream, and then the pained look on her face as she hopped up and down on one foot, saying, "Get it out, get it out, get it out!"

So Charlie had done the only thing she could think of. She'd grasped the board and given it a good yank, pulling the nail out. A moment later their dad had run up and scolded Charlie for not leaving the nail in place. But how could she have known that wasn't the right thing to do? Allie had been scared and frantic.

"Remember Mary Alice?" Allie asked. "That little old lady down the street from us that always gave out king-size candy bars?"

Charlie smiled.

"Yeah. She always had like ten different kinds all laid out on her dining room table, and she'd have us all come inside and pick out what we wanted."

"Mary Alice rocked," Allie said. "Unlike Shirtless Wonder, who tried to give us a handful of pennies from his change jar."

A snort escaped Charlie's nose.

"I forgot about that. Was that why we forked his yard the next year on Devil's Night?"

Allie chuckled.

"Oh man, do you remember how mad he was? It was solid gold. It made stabbing six hundred forks into his lawn totally worth it." Allie let out another wicked laugh. "Halfway through, I remember thinking we should have just egged his stupid car and been done with it. I thought he'd probably just be amused by the forks. I mean, if I woke up and found six hundred forks sticking up from the grass in my front yard, I'd think it was hilarious."

"Yeah, but you weren't obsessed with having the greenest lawn in the neighborhood," Charlie said. "Where did we get all those forks anyway?"

"Jenny Ryan's brother worked at Taco Bell and was a total klepto. Always stealing crap from work. Or maybe it was Jessica

Atwater's brother? Whoever it was, someone gave us a shitload of plastic forks for free."

Paige came out then, dressed in a pale blue dress and the red cloak. She even had a little basket over her arm.

Charlie smiled.

"Well you look adorable."

Paige blushed.

"Oh, thank you, Miss Winters."

"You're only missing one thing," Charlie said, pulling the baggie of trackers from her bag and giving them a shake. "Why don't you shove this one down your sock and tuck another one into the pocket of your cloak, just in case."

When Paige finished securing the tracking devices on her person, Charlie gave her a once-over and nodded.

"Last chance to call this whole thing off."

Paige only shook her head.

"Alright then." Charlie took a deep breath. "Let's do this."

CHAPTER SIXTY-FOUR

There was a line of cars waiting to enter the designated parking for the Carnival Bizarre. Streams of people funneled to and from the main entrance. Most of the crowd leaving seemed to have children in tow—the carnival was an all-ages affair until dark, and then it became an adults-only party. That's when they brought out the more risqué performers and the booze. There'd be booths selling beer, wine, spiked cider, and jello shots. Bands and burlesque dancers would take to the stages set up throughout the grounds.

When Charlie's car finally rolled up to the entrance of the parking lot, a man dressed in a bedraggled clown costume informed them the lot was full.

"There's overflow parking a few blocks down," he said, waving them on. "You'll see the signs."

They drove on, stopping at one intersection to allow a group of women dressed as the Spice Girls to cross to the other side of the street.

Up ahead, Charlie spotted a hand-painted sign with a cluster of black and orange balloons attached that read "Carnival Bizarre Parking." It was only when they got closer that she realized precisely where they were and cringed. The parking lot belonged to the Petoskey Credit Union, which happened to be directly next door to Will Crawford's office.

As irrational as it was, Charlie couldn't help but imagine Will coming outside just as they got out of the car. He'd spot her there and jog over to chat. And he'd want to talk about last night, which would only lead to a very awkward conversation considering Charlie still didn't know quite how she felt about what had happened between them.

Charlie pulled into the lot, hoping to find a spot as far from Will's building as possible, but the attendant waved them into a space practically staring into his office windows.

"You're going to have to move. Overseas, if possible," Allie said. "I mean, if you stay here on Salem Island, it's only a matter of time before you run into him. Better to just cut and run."

Charlie was annoyed at Allie's sarcastic tone, but her sister had a point. She was being ridiculous. There was no way she could avoid Will forever. In a town this small, she'd have to face him at some point. And so what? She was a grown woman, damn it.

But all of Charlie's anxiety had been for nothing. She and Paige left the car and joined the throng of people moving in the direction of the carnival without encountering Will. At one point they stepped off the sidewalk to make way for a woman carrying a squalling toddler in an astronaut suit. His face and hands were stained pink from cotton candy, and apparently he wasn't ready for the party to be over just yet.

Charlie's phone buzzed as they approached the ticket line. It was a text from Zoe, asking whether Charlie and Paige were through the entrance yet. Charlie texted back that they had just joined the line. Zoe replied instantly.

OK. Frank and I will meet you in front of the booth for the palm reader. There's a big light-up sign for it.

The man in front of them in line was wearing a head-to-toe suit made of matted brown fur. She hadn't seen the front of him and therefore couldn't be sure whether he was dressed as Chewbacca, a sasquatch, or perhaps something else entirely.

When they reached the ticket booth, a woman dressed as an old-fashioned cigarette girl exchanged Charlie's cash for two tickets.

Stepping through the archway made to look like an old tattered circus tent was like walking into another time and place. There was a small platform just ahead where a man in a devil costume stood swallowing swords. Beyond that, two women in plague doctor masks juggled flaming torches. Spooky pipe organ music radiated out from the nearby carousel.

Charlie had never been to the Carnival Bizarre as an adult. Only as a kid. And she hadn't remembered it being so elaborate back then. Then again, she would never have seen it after dark, all lit up like it was now. As a kid, she'd come for the rides and the candy and the funnel cakes. Looking around now, Charlie was certain the adults came for the surreal atmosphere.

The music and crowd noise lurched and swelled around them, surging along with the flickering lights. The crisp night air clashed with the collective body heat rolling off the masses of humanity, creating a strange feverish feeling in Charlie. The cumulative effect bordered on sensory overload, especially given the eerie undertone of their plan for tonight.

"Wow," Paige said, clearly having similar thoughts. "I feel like I'm in a dream. I had no idea it would be so… much."

Charlie heard a shrill sound and recognized Frank's whistle. Her head snapped that way, and she spotted two familiar faces under a sign painted to look like a giant hand with esoteric symbols on it.

Frank and Zoe were dressed more or less identically: black suits, black ties, black sunglasses.

"Oh!" Paige said, clapping her hands. "Are you the men in black?"

"We are not at liberty to answer that question, ma'am," Frank said in a deadpan.

"I can't believe you guys coordinated costumes and left me out," Charlie said, pretending to pout.

"Well, I was going to wear the gorilla head from my gorilla costume and be a monkey in a monkey suit, but then Zoe told me about her costume, and I figured two M.I.B.s would be more effective." Frank shrugged. "Did you plant the tracking devices?"

Charlie nodded and held up her phone, which was open to the tracking app and showed that both devices were currently functional. It was a reminder that they weren't here to enjoy the carnival. They were playing a rather dangerous game of cat and mouse. An image of Robbie's lifeless body sprawling in the alleyway flashed in Charlie's mind. She only hoped they were the cat this time.

She turned to Zoe.

"Are the rest of your people here?"

"Roger that. We divided the carnival into four quadrants, and each one is being patrolled by an undercover deputy as we speak." Zoe showed Charlie the radio tucked inside her jacket. "They're on standby in case we need them."

"Good," Charlie said, glancing around at the shifting crowd.

"Where should we start?" Paige asked.

"Well, one of the first lessons you learn when you start fishing with a lure is that you don't catch diddly-squat just letting the bait sit still," Frank said.

Charlie nodded.

"Let's get moving then."

CHAPTER SIXTY-FIVE

They began a slow circuit of the carnival, passing a stage where two women dressed as conjoined twins tap danced to a Cab Calloway song. Meanwhile, the tent across from the stage offered patrons a chance to have their photo taken lying down in a real coffin. The next booth over was filled with baked goods from one of the local bakeries—cupcakes topped with eyeballs and donuts oozing raspberry "blood."

The scent of buttered popcorn wafted their way, and Charlie suddenly felt hungry for the first time that evening. She bought a bag from a vendor dressed as a werewolf to share with Paige, and paused at the next stage, where a woman was in the middle of an acrobatic routine with a giant metal ring.

"How does someone even learn to do that?" Paige asked, transfixed by the performer. "I'd break my neck even trying."

At the end of the act, they joined the rest of the crowd in applauding and then moved on to explore the rest of the oddities and attractions that the carnival had to offer.

"Oh! Bumper cars! I love bumper cars!" Paige clapped her hands, looking even more like a kid than usual in the girly dress and Mary Jane shoes. Suddenly her enthusiasm faded, and she frowned. "Sorry, I keep forgetting that we have a job to do. It's just hard to see all the shiny lights and rides and things and not get excited. I just have to keep reminding myself that we're here to work."

"Sure, but you're playing a role," Charlie said. "The role of the unsuspecting victim. And if the unsuspecting victim wants to ride the bumper cars, then it would be wrong not to."

Paige chuckled.

"I guess that's true."

They joined the line for the ride, and Charlie couldn't help but notice Frank and Zoe getting in line behind them.

"No one can resist bumper cars," Allie said. "Speed, chaos, whiplash. It's the perfect ride."

After bumper cars, Paige's eyes locked on the row of carnival games arranged nearby. After popping eight balloons in the Bust-a-Balloon game, Paige selected a bright pink elephant as her prize.

"I picked the hot pink one because I figured it'd stand out more," Paige whispered to Charlie. "You know, in case he's watching right now and following."

"You're starting to think like a bona fide P.I., Paige."

The girl grinned at the compliment, and then her head swiveled sideways and she gasped.

"Let's ride that one."

Charlie followed Paige's gaze and landed on a ride that looked like a giant spaceship. Multicolored lights blinked and flashed on the sleek metal sides and glowing red letters spelled out "Alien Abduction" over the top of it. As she watched, the ride began to spin like a top. It started slowly at first, but eventually it was rotating so fast that the patterned lights on the outside of it became a blur. Charlie was nauseated just looking at it.

"I'll have to sit this one out," Charlie said. "I get motion sickness from the spinny ones."

Paige's face fell.

"It'll be fine." Charlie shrugged. "I bet we can get Frank or Zoe to ride with you, and then we'll meet up again when the ride is over."

To Charlie's surprise, both Frank and Zoe agreed to get on the whirling contraption.

"I thought you loved rides like this," Zoe said to Charlie while they waited in line.

"You're thinking of Allie," Charlie said. "She talked me into riding one of these. *Once.*"

Zoe laughed.

The spinning ship came to a stop before them, letting out a loud hydraulic hiss. A minute later, the front door whooshed open, and the operator beckoned the next group inside. That was Charlie's cue to duck out of the line.

"See you guys on the other side," she said, watching Frank, Zoe, and Paige enter the faux flying saucer.

The door slid shut, and the ride hummed to life again.

Charlie scanned the crowd, eyes flicking over all those masked faces bobbing and weaving around each other. He was here now, most likely. His face lay behind one of those masks out there—a thought that came with a crawling chill on the backs of her arms.

A voice behind her startled her enough that she jumped a little.

"Well, well, well… what do we have here?"

Charlie spun around. It was Will.

He was wearing a beige bathrobe over a pair of wildly patterned pants, a gray T-shirt, and sandals. He lifted his sunglasses and sat them on top of his head.

Charlie didn't have to ask who he was dressed as. She and Allie had spent one summer watching *The Big Lebowski* on repeat. And despite her misgivings, she couldn't help but smile at the costume.

"Aren't you supposed to be bowling tonight, Dude?"

Will lifted the bowling bag in his hand.

"Just got back from round one of the league tournament." He grinned. "It's so weird to run into you here… I almost called to see if you'd want to come with me, but I didn't know if it would be your thing. I only really came because my niece is one of the performers."

"Oh yeah?" Charlie asked. "Which one?"

"One of the fire-breathers."

"Wow. Where'd she pick that up?"

"I couldn't tell you," Will said, laughing. "She's a good kid, but she's got some weird hobbies."

Charlie smiled. She'd been absolutely dreading this and now here they were, conversing like two normal adults. Everything was fine.

Then Will took a step closer.

"Well, since I ran into you and already admitted to almost calling you, I figure I can drop the 'playing it cool' act." He reached out and took Charlie's hand. "Because I'm kind of dying to know when I can see you again."

Charlie felt her stomach clench. It was true that every time she looked in his eyes, something twinged pleasantly in her chest, but at the same time, a little voice in her head whispered a warning: *You can't trust him.*

Charlie slid her fingers from his grasp.

"Will… about last night…"

"Uh-oh," he said. "I don't like the sound of that."

She pulled the shawl tighter around her shoulders and stared down at her boots.

"Look, that was a one-time thing…"

He raked his fingernails through his beard.

"You're still upset about when I put the keylogger on your computer. Is that it?"

"Well… yeah," Charlie said, thinking that part should be obvious.

When she saw how hurt he looked at this, she sighed.

"I'm sorry, Will. It's just not the kind of thing I can forgive and forget… I've tried. Believe me."

He closed his eyes, tilting his head back.

"So that's it? I screw up once, and I'm branded a dick forever?"

"I don't think you're a dick." She put a hand on his arm. "I mean, we can still be friends."

"Ah," he said, and his smile was bitter. "The consolation prize."

Charlie's arm dropped to her side.

"OK, *now* you're being a dick," she said.

The corners of his mouth turned down into a sneer.

"Well, I apologize if I'm not jumping for joy. It's a little disorienting to be around someone who runs so hot and cold." His jaw tensed, and he looked like he wanted to spit. "I have to go."

He brushed past her, and Charlie let him go.

"That went well," Allie said in an obnoxiously amused tone.

"Please don't," Charlie muttered.

She sighed. She'd expected a certain awkwardness between them, but she hadn't anticipated that Will would be so upset. But she supposed he was right to feel jerked around. She'd initiated all of it. Calling him. Asking him to kiss her. She asked herself again what the hell she'd been thinking.

Charlie closed her eyes for a moment and refocused on her task. She had a job to do here, and worrying about Will Crawford's injured pride wasn't part of it. She could apologize another day.

CHAPTER SIXTY-SIX

When Charlie's eyelids fluttered open, she noticed the Alien Abduction ride had stopped, and people were filing out the exit. Charlie walked over to the rear gate and nearly collided with a man dressed in dark clothes and a hockey mask. Muttering an apology, she skirted around him and spotted Zoe and Frank coming down the exit ramp.

She looked past them, searching for Paige's red cape. Charlie didn't see it anywhere, and her breath caught in her throat. But half a second later, Paige appeared, last off the ride.

They walked back toward the food trucks, and Paige paused to fuss with the hood of her cloak.

"I thought this thing would be enough to keep me warm, but I'm freezing," she said, rubbing her arms.

Charlie waved Zoe and Frank over.

"Paige is cold," she said. "And I am too, honestly."

"Let's go inside the bar for a while to warm up then," Zoe said.

The sidewalk leading up to the front doors of the Laughing Raven had been converted into a tunnel with fake cobwebs and giant furry spiders clinging to the walls. When Frank opened the door, one of the spiders dropped from the ceiling with a shriek.

All four of them recoiled and then laughed at the fact that they'd fallen for such a simple gag.

The interior of the bar was decorated like a spooky forest with gnarled trees and strands of moss hanging from the ceiling lights. A fog machine pumped a steady stream of mist into the space.

There was a band onstage and a crowd of costumed people dancing and drinking on the floor. After a few minutes, everything but the tip of Charlie's nose and the ends of her toes felt warm again, but Paige was still shivering beside her.

"Do you want something warm to drink?" Charlie said, pointing to a nearby table with a large smoking cauldron and a sign that read: "Witch's Brew Hot Cider."

Paige nodded, her teeth chattering together.

"Yes, please."

A witch in a green dress and a purple wig stood behind the cauldron, and she grinned wickedly as Charlie approached.

"One cider, please," Charlie said, holding out a handful of bills.

"Spiced or spiked?"

Charlie thought it was best they all remain sober for the night, so she went for the non-alcoholic option.

"Spiced."

The witch made a show of ladling some of the concoction into a plastic cup.

"This one's on the house, my pretty," she said, winking at Charlie.

It was only then that Charlie recognized Emma's friend behind the false nose and witchy makeup.

"Thanks, Cindy," Charlie said.

"Don't mention it."

Paige took the cup in her hands and blew into the steam. After a long drink, she let out a satisfied sigh.

"Thank you, Miss Winters."

The band onstage finished their set, and then a zombie barbershop quartet did a few songs while the next group set up their gear. Charlie turned her head and spotted a man in a black jacket and a hockey mask hovering a few yards away, the blank eyeholes of his mask pointed at Paige. He was partially concealed by one of the spooky tree props, but when he noticed Charlie looking, he swiveled his gaze in the opposite direction and angled himself so that he was more hidden by the tree's silhouette.

"What's with the creepazoid lurking behind the fake tree?" Allie said.

But Charlie wasn't listening. She was sifting through the events from earlier in the evening. There'd been a man in a similar costume on the Alien Abduction ride. She'd bumped into him when she'd gone to meet up with everyone after her talk with Will. Charlie glanced at him again, trying to decide if it was the same guy, but she couldn't be sure. For all she knew, there were half a dozen dudes running around the carnival dressed as Jason from *Friday the 13th*.

"Yeah, but it's the perfect costume for a murderous stalker, don't you think?" Allie asked.

"You could make the same case for a lot of Halloween costumes," Charlie said.

She got out her phone and texted Zoe.

Guy in hockey mask. Five o'clock.

Zoe's response was lightning-quick.

I see him.

Charlie tapped out another text.

Was he on the Alien Abduction ride with you?

There was a pause before Zoe's reply this time.

I definitely remember a Jason costume on the ride, but I've seen at least 3 tonight, so…

Charlie frowned. From the corner of her eye, she was pretty sure he was watching them again. Beside her, Paige took another sip of her cider, and Charlie's phone buzzed with another text from Zoe.

He seems particularly interested in Paige. Every time she takes a drink, his face jerks that way.

Charlie gulped, remembering that Olivia thought she'd been drugged at the boat party. Was he eyeballing Paige's cider in hopes of dosing her with something?

She fired off another text to Zoe.

Keep an eye on that drink.

Charlie leaned over to Paige.

"The next time everyone applauds, set your drink on the table to your left and leave it there."

Paige smiled, and the next time the group began clapping, she set her cup down so she could join in. Glancing over her shoulder, Charlie found Zoe in the crowd. She gave a single nod to let her know she was watching.

Charlie felt on edge. Practically tingling. Could this be it? Would they be able to lure him in with something as simple as an unattended drink? She hoped so. No, *hope* was putting it lightly. Charlie felt almost desperate for this to work. If it didn't, she wasn't sure what they'd do next.

When Charlie's phone buzzed a few minutes later, she jumped. She dug her phone out and read the text from Zoe.

He's sidled a few steps closer to the drink. Seems jumpy.

Charlie tucked her phone back into the pocket of her skirt, still peeking at the man from the corner of her eye. He'd come out from behind the tree now and was standing just on the other side of the table from Paige. He rocked back and forth on his feet, and every few seconds he swung his head from one side to the other, as if paranoid he was being watched.

Charlie waited for him to turn away so she could risk a more direct look at him. The mask prevented her from seeing his face, but she examined the rest of him, hoping some detail might leap out at her. Black work boots. Black cargo pants. Black Carhartt jacket.

Charlie's gaze returned to the small square label on the jacket.

Neil Kushner had a black Carhartt jacket. And while this one didn't bear the logo of Schnell Shipping, maybe he'd taken a liking to the style and had more than one.

"A business Carhartt and a party Carhartt," Allie said. "Makes perfect sense. But there's one problem."

"What's that?" Charlie asked, not taking her eyes off the man in the hockey mask.

"You ruled Neil out, remember? He was driving a truck to bumfuck Wisconsin or something when Emma was killed."

"Maybe we were wrong. Maybe if we dug into it, we'd find out that Neil swapped routes with another driver or something," Charlie said. "It wouldn't be the first time someone had a solid alibi and then… didn't."

She was still studying the man, trying to decide if his build was a match for Kushner, when a blood-curdling scream came from the other end of the bar.

"Help!" The fear in the woman's voice made the hair on the back of Charlie's neck bristle. "Please, somebody help me!"

CHAPTER SIXTY-SEVEN

They raced toward the entryway of the bar, the area the scream had come from. Charlie could see the door slowly swinging shut up ahead, and the girl's voice suddenly cut out.

Zoe reached the door a few paces ahead of Charlie. She was barking something into her radio as she yanked the door open and burst through.

Outside, Charlie was momentarily disoriented. She'd forgotten about the entrance tunnel with the spider decorations and walked straight into a strand of fake cobwebs. As she untangled herself, she spotted a man lumbering out into the night with a girl slung over his shoulder.

"It's him," the girl screamed. "It's the murderer! He's trying to get me!"

"Sheriff's department!" Zoe yelled. "Stop where you are, and let the girl go!"

The man kept plodding along with the girl in tow. He was a big guy in a lumberjack outfit.

Zoe unholstered her weapon and shouted again.

"Sir! I said stop right there."

By now a sheriff's department cruiser and three of the undercover deputies had arrived. All of the officers had their guns drawn. The lumberjack froze, as if realizing for the first time that he was surrounded by armed law enforcement. His mouth popped open in an almost comical fashion.

"Put her down," Zoe said.

He released the girl all at once, and she tumbled to the ground, landing flat on her rump.

"Ouch! What the hell, Brian?" Then she noticed the cops and the guns, and her eyes went wide. "What is this? Some kind of prank or something?"

The girl's reaction wasn't one anyone had been expecting, and the mood shifted abruptly from one of taut anticipation to confusion.

"A prank?" Zoe asked, lowering her weapon. "You were screaming. We thought you were being assaulted."

"Assaulted?" The girl repeated the word and then let out a drunken cackle. "I was just joking around. I didn't think anyone would take it seriously. Tell them, Bri."

The lumberjack at least had the sense to put on an apologetic face. He had his hands up despite the fact that all of the deputies had holstered their weapons by now.

"We were only playing around," he muttered, shrugging.

"Oh my God, it was a joke!" the girl whined. "What's the big deal?"

As Zoe lectured the pair on the repercussions of crying wolf, Charlie let out a sigh.

"A false alarm?" Paige said from behind her.

"Yeah," Charlie said. "Which I guess is technically a good thing."

"I don't know about that," Frank grumbled. "All these cops coming out of the woodwork for everyone to see?"

Charlie glanced around and saw what seemed like half the carnival crowd gathered around the scene. Even now they murmured among themselves.

Frank shook his head.

"I'd say our cover is blown pretty well to hell."

CHAPTER SIXTY-EIGHT

It was decided that they'd see the plan through to the end of the night, though none of them had high hopes. And the first thing Charlie noticed when they got back inside the bar was that the man in the Jason mask had disappeared. She kept her eyes peeled for a glimpse of the black Carhartt jacket, but he was nowhere to be seen. If he was indeed their guy, it was likely the commotion had scared him off.

When the headlining band finished their final encore, she had to admit to herself that their plan had failed.

"We've still got the DUI checkpoints set up," Zoe said. "We could still get lucky."

"Maybe." Charlie's eyes scanned the crowd inside, which was slowly dwindling even though the carnival wouldn't officially close for another hour. "Can you have a patrol car watch Paige's house again?"

Zoe nodded.

"I'll drive her home and wait there until everything's set, if you want."

"Thanks, Zoe," Charlie said.

Paige yawned beside her.

"I'm sorry, Miss Winters. I really thought something would happen tonight."

"Me too," Charlie said.

As she watched Zoe and Paige head for the door, Frank squeezed her shoulder.

"You're disappointed."

"Well, yeah."

He smiled.

"We knew it was a long shot going in," he said. "This kind of plan always is."

"I just wish there was more we could do other than wait around for something else to happen."

"Ahh, but that was the first lesson I taught you about being a private investigator, wasn't it?" Frank winked. "At least half the job is waiting around."

Her uncle brought a hand up to rub his eyes.

"You stayed up all night last night, and then you were at the office most of the day," Charlie said. "Did you sleep at all?"

"I had a little nap in the evening."

"You need to go get some sleep." Charlie nudged him toward the door. "Get out of here."

"I am pretty bushed, now that you mention it," he said, zipping up the front of his coat. "Just do me a favor and don't go getting yourself all worked up into a state of despair. We'll regroup in the morning. Come up with our next move."

"OK," Charlie said. "Drive safe."

He waved two fingers as he turned to go.

Sleep sounded good, Charlie thought. She knew she should go home. And yet she stayed. She wasn't sure why. She supposed she was holding out some desperate hope that something might happen still. Perhaps the man in the hockey mask would reappear across the room, clutching a vial of mystery liquid over an unsuspecting woman's drink.

Yeah, right.

Charlie knew the real reason she was staying was that she didn't want to go home. Alone in her quiet apartment, she'd have no choice but to dwell on dark things. On their failed plan. On her encounter with Will. On Emma and Robbie.

The party was winding down around her. The earlier promise of the night, the strange magic in the air, was fading. All that excitement and energy fizzling out as people realized that tomorrow was just another day.

The carnival wasn't quite dead, but it would be soon. Charlie climbed onto an empty bar stool and rested her chin on her fist.

She should be glad, on some level. Things could have gone worse. No one had been hurt, at least. Paige was safe. But it was frustrating nonetheless.

"Charlie?"

She perked up at the sound of her name. It was Craig Rattigan. He had on a black robe, and a *Scream* mask was pulled up over his head. He also had a dish towel slung over his shoulder and was just finishing cutting up some limes for drinks.

Charlie tried to think of a phrase from the French class they'd shared, but her mind was shot.

"Hey, Craig."

"Rough night?"

She sighed.

"Yeah. You could say that."

"I guess your plan didn't work out?"

"No, it did not," Charlie said, then frowned. "Wait, you knew about it?"

"Sure. The sheriff came over and briefed everyone at the bar. So we could all keep an eye on things and try not to get in the way of the deputies."

That was annoying. It was supposed to have been a covert operation. There was no telling how word might have spread once all of the employees knew about it. For all she knew, half the crowd at the carnival had known about the undercover deputies.

Craig rested his hands on the bar.

"Can I get you a drink?" he asked.

Charlie considered it then remembered the mistake she'd made the night before. It would be a good idea to steer clear of booze for a while, she thought.

"Thanks, but I probably shouldn't," she said. "If I have a pity party drink now, I might not be able to stop."

"What about some cocoa?" He lifted a thermos and waggled it back and forth. "Non-alcoholic."

Charlie chuckled and raised an eyebrow.

"You just carry a thermos of cocoa around?"

"We have a big pot of it going in the kitchen for everyone working outside."

"Ahh, that makes sense," Charlie said. "The only question now is whether you've got a bag of mini marshmallows hidden somewhere in that robe."

Craig looked confused.

"No. Sorry."

"I'm teasing," she said, reaching out to pat his arm. "I'd love some hot cocoa."

Craig let out a nervous chuckle.

"Oh."

He unscrewed the lid, poured some of the steaming liquid into it, and handed it to Charlie before taking a slug straight from the thermos.

"Thanks," Charlie said, sipping at the small metal cup. It was still fairly hot and sent a warm flush out from her chest. "That is delightful. I bet it tasted really good when you were outside in the cold."

Craig shrugged but said nothing.

"Is this the first time you've worked the carnival?"

"Yeah," he said, and Charlie thought that was all she was going to get out of him.

But then he took another swig from the thermos and wiped his mouth, and the words seemed to spill out.

"It's fun in a way. All the activity. The lights and the noise. The people smiling and laughing and having a good time. You can just kind of stand in the midst of it and feel like you're a part of something big happening. Like the mood is contagious or something." He paused and stared up at the stage that was now empty. "And then other times, like right now, I can see how it's all kind of artificial. Like that feeling of belonging is just a trick of the lights and booze and the loud music. It fools everyone into thinking something truly epic is happening. But at the end of the night, it's gone, and the world goes on, and everything is the same."

Charlie watched him while he talked. He'd always been quiet in school, not a big talker. Always getting in trouble for hiding comic books and graphic novels in the pages of his French book so he could read instead of paying attention in class. She wouldn't have guessed he'd have such complex thoughts going on inside his head.

"Or maybe I'm just a weirdo," he said, and the corners of his mouth turned up into a sheepish half smile.

"Hey, that makes two of you," Allie said. "Two weirdo peas in a pod. You know, you could cleanse your palate of Will, right here, right now. It's painfully obvious that Craig is DTF."

At Will's name, Charlie felt that familiar twinge in her chest. Why couldn't she just forget him already?

"Makes perfect sense to me," Charlie said, and she realized that the brief talk with Craig had snapped her out of her wallowing enough that she was finally ready to go home.

She slid off the stool and handed the empty lid of the thermos back to Craig.

"Thanks for the drink, Craig. You make a damn fine hot choco."

Craig bobbed his head once.

"Anytime."

"I'll see you around," Charlie said.

He smiled, a full grin with all his teeth for once.

"Definitely."

CHAPTER SIXTY-NINE

Charlie had just left the perimeter of the carnival when she spotted a figure in black cargo pants and a dark jacket crossing the street up ahead. She felt a little thrill at the thought that it might be the suspicious man in the hockey mask. She couldn't see if he was wearing a mask, but the jacket looked right.

Maybe Paige had been right after all. Maybe something *was* destined to happen tonight.

If she followed him to his car, she could get a license plate. And with a license plate, she and Frank could run a background check.

She jogged across the road, turning up the side street he'd gone down. The way was dark, with streetlights only positioned at the intersections. For a moment she thought she'd lost him, but then she saw his silhouette up ahead, climbing into a pickup truck.

She squinted, trying to read the plate number, but it was too dark.

There was a mechanical coughing sound as the engine rumbled to life. A second later the taillights flared red.

Charlie hurried closer, her eyes fixed on the license plate, but the letters and numbers were a blur from this distance.

The truck began to pull away. She was going to lose him.

Charlie sprinted down the sidewalk even as the gap between her and the truck widened. She only stopped running when it turned and disappeared from view completely.

The tips of Charlie's fingernails bit into her palms as she squeezed her hands into fists. Had she actually thought she could keep up with a moving vehicle on foot? *Stupid.*

She glanced up at the name on the street sign closest to her. Poplar. The lot next to Will's office where she'd parked was off Maple, but she didn't know exactly where that was in relation to the street she was on. All the streets over here had tree names, and she could never quite keep them straight.

Funny. She'd never thought it would have been possible to get lost on the streets of Salem Island, but here she was.

Of course she wasn't truly lost. She knew the general direction of the parking lot. If she kept walking, she'd eventually find her way.

As she approached the next intersection, she squinted at the name of the cross street. But the streetlight here was out, and she couldn't seem to get her eyes to focus on the letters in the dark.

Was her eyesight going bad? Maybe she needed glasses. Frank had to wear glasses when he drove at night. Could be genetic.

She pulled her phone from her pocket, thinking she could use the flashlight to illuminate the sign. But her fingers felt odd, almost numb, and the phone slipped from her grasp.

"Butterfingers, much?" she said to herself, and it came out much louder than she intended.

She chuckled a little, wondering why Allie hadn't been the one to say it.

"What, are you pouting because I didn't leave with Craig?"

When Allie didn't answer, Charlie took that as a yes.

"The silent treatment," Charlie said as she got down on her hands and knees to search for the phone. "Very mature."

Her phone had fallen into a shadowy area next to a row of bushes planted along a fence. She felt around with her hands, again noting that her fingers felt strange… almost like they were numb from the cold. But she actually felt hot just now. A feverish flush blooming on her cheeks and chest.

The sound of an engine rumbled somewhere behind her. Moving closer. It sounded like the truck she'd chased just a few moments ago, and that thought sent a wave of panic through her. What if it was him?

She continued patting her hands over the grass, frantic now. Her phone. She needed her phone.

The headlights washed over her and then held there. The vehicle had stopped. With one last swipe of her hands over the grass, Charlie gave up on searching for the phone.

She needed to run.

But something was wrong with her balance. She didn't even get fully upright before she tottered backward and landed on her butt.

Jesus. What's wrong with me?

Charlie glanced back at the vehicle idling in the street. Spotted the dark silhouette outlined by the glaring headlights. Standing there. Watching her.

Her heart rate sped up as she remembered the figure outside the office last night. The one who'd thrown the brick. The one who'd killed Emma and Robbie.

Her fear propelled her forward. Sent her scrambling to her feet once more. But she only managed to crawl a few feet before the world lurched around her. Charlie fell again, this time face-planting into the hard ground.

When she tried to roll onto her side, her body refused to obey. Something like nausea clawed at her insides as she realized she was paralyzed.

There was a scrape and then a patter. Footsteps. He was coming closer.

And Charlie realized that it wasn't the truck driver coming for her. Not at all. She knew who it was.

She tried to scream, to call for help, but all that came out of her mouth was a muffled groan.

He bent over her, and the glow of the headlights illuminated enough of his face that she recognized him just before everything went black.

CHAPTER SEVENTY

His skin crawls. His ears prickle, listening for any sound.

He rolls slowly by the carnival as it winds down. Watches the last of the faces through the window. Nobody looks his way.

How many times has he thought that in his life? *Nobody's looking. Nobody's listening. Nobody cares.*

Nobody ever did pay much attention to him. Weird how that weakness has become a strength, how he twisted things to work that way. He walks in the shadows, where nobody's looking, the mindless world made malleable in his grip, at his touch.

He drives. The engine whining a little, quivering out that higher register it hits in the cold weather. The whole car seems to shudder, sends lurching vibrations through the steering wheel.

The heat swells inside the car, though. So much heat. He leaves it cranked. Likes the feel of that dry wind on his face, ruffling his hair, chasing the cold away.

Something loosens in his chest as the bar fades from the rearview mirror. Air comes easier again. Ribcage flexing to hitch in a big breath. He's moving again. Swimming ever forward.

The headlights plunge down empty city streets. Flit over windows gone dark in house after house. The city sleeps again. All the soccer moms and office dads tucked safely in their beds, their families hunkering down, hiding away when the predators come out to snuffle about.

Halloween filled the streets some hours ago. Little ones out in droves. Draped in cheap costumes. Rubber masks. Makeup-caked faces. Bags of fun-size candy bars dangling from their mitts.

Nobody's out now. Nothing all around. Smooth concrete stretching out to where the horizon goes black.

Charlie Winters slumps in the passenger seat. Her lights are out, too, he supposes. Her body made as empty as the streets out here. Smooth, too. Just as smooth as all that asphalt. Smoother.

The thought grips his abdominals and squeezes a hissing laugh out of him. Spit sizzling between his teeth.

He turns his head to the droopy form in the passenger seat. Watches her. The slow rise and fall of her chest. The faintest glistening wetness at the corners of her mouth.

His heartbeat stays steady. His breathing normal. His body hasn't caught up to the excitement he feels, having her here.

This was never part of the plan. But the plan doesn't matter anymore, does it? His impulsiveness has been rewarded.

She is mine now. Mine.

The houses grow sparser and sparser, slowly choked out by the teeming plant life alongside the road. Woods here. Fields populated with corn and beans there.

The car moves out past the streetlights. Into the dark. Out where the stars shine brighter. Glimmering pinpricks that fill the sky.

He crests a hill, and the moon seems to appear there over the horizon like it was hatched just now, just for him and his girl. It's huge tonight, almost full, casting its silvery light over the top of the asphalt.

There's something romantic about it all. A bright honey moon hung up there in the heavens, glinting like a floating coin, meant just for the two of them.

Made for them. Belonging to them.

The moonlight shimmers on corn tassels in the field to their right. All those stalks swaying a little in the breeze, unusually still green and upright this time of year. It's the latest harvest he can remember due to a drought in the spring.

He adjusts his hands on the steering wheel. The excitement making him fidget. So close now.

And he thinks about how many abandoned houses there are once you get outside the city. Homes that have been vacant since the market collapsed in 2008. Sometimes longer.

Boarded-up farmhouses shrouded with overgrown bushes and tall grass. Sagging porches. Leaky roofs. This little slice of the earth that time forgot, that everyone abandoned, that nobody gave a flying fuck about, just like him.

Out where no one's looking. Out where nobody cares.

The cops might have found his other dungeon, but it's no matter.

For this world is full of emptiness. Positively brimming with it.

All of these vacant buildings, and he only needs one. *Just like the girls*, he thinks, hissing out another laugh. All these girls walking the earth, and he only needs one.

CHAPTER SEVENTY-ONE

Charlie drifted toward consciousness, a pounding sound the first thing to filter into her awareness. A steady thud, something urgent in it, something frantic, and yet something familiar as well.

She tried to rouse herself, but the grogginess still held her half under. Paralysis gripped her limbs. Squeezed her eyelids shut. Made her fight for every scrap of consciousness.

She refocused on the pounding, listened to every detail in an attempt to puzzle out what it could be. Footsteps coming for her? She didn't think so.

When the pain hit, she understood.

The headache stabbed in time with the thumping. The sound had been coming from inside, her own panicked blood beating in her head.

That knowledge somehow thrust her toward the surface. Her eyelids fluttered, and she opened them at last.

Fluorescent bulbs glared down at her. Two long tubes set amongst the pale wood of the floor joists overhead. The light seemed to strobe, like the bulbs were vibrating with light. But she couldn't decide if it was real or in her head like the pounding.

More sensory details came to her with each passing second: Her tongue felt bloated and dry like an oversized sponge stuffed in her mouth. Her limbs felt numb. Icy. She moved her arm, found the joint stiff, the limb heavy.

Cold concrete lay beneath her. Its chill seeping into the flesh of her back as she sprawled here. Judging by the degree to which the cool had leached into her flesh, she'd been here a while now.

She was in a basement. Dusty and unfamiliar. An older house, poorly maintained from the looks of it.

She tried to lift her head. Felt reality wobble and reel. Something wrong with her sense of balance. Her head gone light and swimmy, scalp tingling with faint electricity. Better to lie still for a moment.

She felt like she'd had too much to drink and then had popped a few muscle relaxers for good measure. Did that make sense?

No.

Drugged. She'd been drugged. Just like Olivia.

The memories came back then. The Carnival Bizarre. The bar. The hot cocoa Craig had given her.

Craig.

Even through the fog of confusion from the drugs, alarm bells rang in Charlie's head. Craig, who'd known Emma and Olivia because they'd all worked together. Craig, who'd known Robbie too because he'd hung out at the bar.

He'd killed them, and now he was going to kill her, too.

She was seized by mindless fear at that realization. Frozen. Unable to breathe.

But no. Panicking did her no good. She needed to gather her wits. To wake the fuck up.

Just stay focused, take it all in. She took a few deep breaths and scanned the room, or at least what she could see of it from her position on the floor.

Cracks formed haphazard grids on the cinder block walls, paint flaking away everywhere, some of it littering the floor. Tilting her head to look behind her, she found a workbench, and what she saw there made her blood run cold.

A collage of pornographic images had been taped up on the walls over the counter. Gleaming pink body parts, all stuck together. A couple of full centerfolds had been taped up among the rest with strange drawings on them. One girl had a Burt Reynolds mustache Sharpied onto her top lip in thick black coils. Another had wounds added to her throat in jagged red, her mouth and eyes expanded into gaping black pits to exaggerate her fear. Aggressive spirals of black ink tangled over each other to form these creepy depictions, and looking closer, Charlie could see that most of the girls had scared faces drawn on.

But even more horrifying was what lay beneath the magazine cutouts.

Bird heads mounted on metal skewers jutted up from the butcher's block workbench. Three robin heads, feathers almost black, and a pale gray dove in the center of them. They looked wrong. Eyes gone dull and cloudy, the lids around them somehow droopy as though half melted. Tiny beaks protruded from the feathered skulls, frozen in various states of openness. All of them cleaving off to thin metal sticks where the rest of the bodies should have been. They looked like severed heads on pikes outside of a medieval castle.

Her breath heaved in and out now, mouth hanging open, eyes wide. She tried to sit up, get up, get out of here.

But the world turned wobbly again as soon as she lifted her head. Everything spinning and shuddering inside her skull.

Her head thunked back down, heavy as a stone. The wood joists of the ceiling were faintly visible through her slitted eyelids, dark around the edges.

Her breathing rasped in and out. Hyperventilating. She knew this, and still she was powerless to stop it.

When she heard his feet scuffing on the concrete, headed her way, she closed her eyes and played dead.

CHAPTER SEVENTY-TWO

Craig moves through the doorway. Eyes scanning everywhere. Molars clenching and unclenching, making all the muscles quiver in the crook of his jaw.

His gaze falls over the unconscious girl laid out on the concrete. Still out cold. Good. That'll give him time to find what he needs, to make the proper arrangements here in this somewhat improvised situation.

His lair—the one the police picked apart days ago—had all of his best stuff in it. The chains, cuffs, and harnesses. He moved all of them there to the superior location, set back in the trees, totally secluded from the world despite the fact it was about a three-minute drive from town. He even mounted a metal bracket in the cinder blocks, a steel loop he could run his length of chain through, drilled through the concrete with a diamond drill bit and bolted it in place.

His jaw clenches harder when he thinks of what he's lost.

But it's OK. He can make this work. This was once his primary fortress after all. He can still get what he wants, what he needs.

Rope. He knows there is rope here somewhere. Can picture the coiled-up strand in his head, though he can't remember where it might be. His mind tries placing it in different locations.

Tucked on the beige square of carpet remnant in the utility closet. Wound up like a python in a shadowy corner of the basement beneath his workbench. Spread over the wood planks in a haphazard mess somewhere upstairs. None of these seem quite right.

He strides past the girl, moving deeper into the basement. Watches her eyelids subtly shift, her eyes twitching beneath the thin layers of skin, and he wonders what she's dreaming about. True love, perhaps. Well, it's here now. It's found her, hasn't it? For keeps.

He rounds a corner and passes through another doorway. The utility room. An ancient washer and dryer squat in the gloomy corner of the space. The furnace door hangs open, the guts of the thing all spilling out, a tangled mess of wires and a few random mechanical bits having been pulled out.

Behind the furnace he finds what he seeks. Cardboard boxes. A pile of them more than a stack.

He starts digging through the papery containers. Opening flaps. Tossing duds aside. Dust kicking up with his movements. Filling his nostrils with the earthy stench of must, mildew, grime.

Old tubes of caulk and ceramic trinkets and water-stained magazines fill these boxes. Spools of wire. Twist ties. Various glues. Someone else's garbage.

A sound stops his hands just shy of another box. Something thudding in the next room. Her room.

He rushes back through the doorway. Chews his bottom lip as he moves. Expects to round the corner and find the concrete slab empty, the girl—his girl—gone.

His vision wheels around that drywall edge. Eyes open wide.

Her figure still drapes over the cement like a dropped rag doll. Laid out on her back just like before. Still. Motionless save for the subtle shift of her ribcage as she breathes.

It must have been the house settling, the sound. He knows this. And still he watches her there, gives her a good long look before his search resumes.

CHAPTER SEVENTY-THREE

Charlie's eyes snapped open. The world was a blur around her. Fuzzy and soft. All contours indistinct.

But her mind was sharper than before, not so confused, the headache having died back while she lay here. The drugs must have been wearing off, at least a little. She'd played dead, held perfectly still, listened to him shuffle in and out of the room, just barely clinging to consciousness. He'd said something at one point, his voice clear and small, muttering something about them being together forever that made her want to bolt or at least shudder, but she'd stayed strong, held still.

She blinked until reality came into focus. Those severed bird heads sharpened before her again, the wall of warped porn taking shape behind them, and her shoulders quivered against the cement floor as the fear took hold.

She closed her eyes to make the images go away. Let her breath roll in and out. Slow and steady.

Hold on, now. Don't panic.

She listened to her pulse thrumming in her ears. Tried to will her heartbeat to slow down. She had to stay calm. That was the only way out of here.

She knew she should try to sit up, to gauge her condition, but she was afraid she'd get woozy again, maybe even pass out. And the idea of going into that blackness once more was almost as scary as the images on the wall.

But that was OK. She could stay down for now. Think. Plan.

Charlie wiggled her fingers and found that the strange numbness in her limbs and extremities had faded. She balled her hands into fists. Squeezed them tight. She didn't feel the usual strength in her wrists and palms, but it wasn't too far off.

She'd make her move soon, but she needed to figure out exactly where he was first. He'd left around the corner some time ago. Had moved some things around in the next room—cardboard boxes sliding over the cement slab was what it had sounded like to her, but the sounds had cut out some time ago. Was he still over there? Could she slip out now, if she had the strength for it?

No more putting it off, then. The only way she could determine what to do next was to open her eyes and sit up.

Charlie inhaled through her nose.

One.

Two.

Before she could get to three, something scuffed the concrete floor near her feet, and a sigh followed the tiny, gritty sound. A masculine exhalation. Perhaps frustrated. Close. Too close.

Her skin crawled. How long had he been in here with her, hunkering quietly in the shadows?

And then something gripped her by the ankle. Cold fingers wrapping around her skin. They moved her leg ever so delicately, shifted it to the right, and then released her.

Charlie angled her head to look that way at last.

His dark figure huddled there. Slouched over her legs. Hands working at a rope down by her feet.

CHAPTER SEVENTY-FOUR

Charlie ripped her leg out of the loop of rope and kicked for his face. The force of her thrusting quad scooted her rump over the concrete a couple of inches, and then all of that building momentum exploded through her kicking foot.

But her boot missed the mark. Found only empty air.

Craig ducked away from the sole of her shoe, leaning his shoulders back and letting it pass beneath his chin. The rope spilled from his hands, coiled on the floor.

The move threw him off balance. He tilted back on the heels of his shoes. Teetering. His arms shot out to his sides, stretched wide to try to right himself.

No time for a plan now. Her only choice was to fight or die.

Charlie kicked again.

This time her foot caught him on the jaw. The heel connecting under his ear like the head of a hammer.

He flailed upward onto his tiptoes and then flopped onto his back, the crown of his head cracking against the concrete on impact. His jaw slammed shut with a wet squelching sound that reminded Charlie of a dog's mouth.

His eyelids fluttered, and she saw the light wane in his eyes. Dimming but not quite extinguished. Drooping to almost closed.

Craig's movements had gone slow as well. Fingers gripping at nothing. Dumb reflexive motions done out of instinct. Inarticulate and pointless.

His lips parted and Charlie could see a bubble of blood on his teeth where the fall had made him bite his tongue.

She scrambled to sit up. Elbows propping her upper body higher. The world went shaky again as she got her head off the floor, everything quivering enough to slow her but not to stop her.

Her legs bent at the knee. Feet scuffing over the concrete like they couldn't quite get a grip, couldn't quite lift her to a standing position.

Something darted in the corner of her eye.

Craig lunged for her.

His body weight knocked her legs out from under her, elbows skidding away, planting her shoulder blades back into the cement.

He was on her. Straddling her. His crotch mounting her ribcage. His knees found her arms and pinned them down, and then he pulled himself upright.

Charlie didn't see the gleam of the blade until he'd pulled it back behind his ear. It paused there a second. Just over his head. Glittering in the glow of the fluorescent bulbs.

And then he brought the metal ripping down into her chest.

CHAPTER SEVENTY-FIVE

Charlie grabbed the knife. Caught its steel with both her hands. Held its point just shy of her ribcage.

It hovered there, inches above her heart, flailing as the two of them struggled for control of it. Bobbing and swaying. All four hands converging on it.

The blade gashed the flesh of her palms. Razor-sharp metal chewing at the webbed bit of skin between her thumb and index finger. Slicing. Carving.

Pain flashed and popped in her skull, bright and hot. It flushed her face. Beaded sweat along her hairline. Made her grit her teeth.

Instinct tried to make her tear her hands away from that sharp edge, make her fingers release the weapon, but she didn't. Couldn't.

She gripped it tighter. Felt the flesh opening wider, felt the blood slicking her palms, shockingly hot against her cool skin, wet scarlet trailing down the length of the knife's edge. Her body being drained, slowly.

He tried to rip the knife away from her, but she held on. Had to hold on. If she wanted it more, if she didn't let go, she would survive, would live.

If not…

Their eyes locked as the knife bucked in their hands like a flopping fish. No words passed between them, but a connection snapped into place nevertheless. The violence brought them fully into this shared moment, the struggle becoming almost intimate.

Some fierce expression molded itself around Craig's brow, folds and wrinkles and bulging musculature that showed only aggression, only hatred. A mindless, violent, raping face. Ugly and awful.

But Charlie stared straight into his eyes. Unblinking.

She squeezed the blade tighter. Felt the juice gather and drip down, thick red pattering against her torso, puddling on her shirt.

And she brought her good knee up over and over again. Hammered it into his lower back.

She bucked and writhed under him. Tried to shift his weight. Tried to contort herself to land a crotch or kidney shot with her flailing knee.

A hot breath heaved out of him. Rolled over Charlie's face. Flecks of spit seething between his teeth. He clutched her torso tightly between his thighs, squeezing harder in pulses.

The knife squirmed in her hands. Lurching and slipping around. Still tearing up her palms and fingers. Peeling away more and more skin.

Agony burst in bright constellations inside her skull. Motes of blinding light that blotted polka dot patterns in her vision, their brightness ever intensifying as the wounds got worse.

She felt the tears streak down her cheeks, but still, she did not blink. She twisted and wiggled and kept her knee working, pounding into his spine, into the clutch of muscles surrounding it.

A hard buck lifted him finally. Her knee knifed between his legs and found the softness it sought.

His body tensed. Tightened. Hunched. And the strength seemed to leave him all at once, his posture going soft, shriveling like a wilting plant.

The knife pulled back from her hands, and this time she let it go. Craig hugged his arms around his gut, leaning back from her and bending over further.

She wriggled out from beneath him. Gave him a good hard shove. Both hands exploding into his core, striking as much as pushing.

And he toppled onto his side, hands still cradling his groin.

She climbed up on wobbly legs. Lifted herself to a standing position. Something shaky in her sense of balance, her head somehow floating and heavy at the same time. She swayed, but the choppy steps kept her upright.

He leaped for her again. Diving low. Shoulders colliding with her shins.

His swooping knife missed somehow. That arm looping around her ankle.

She vaulted herself back. Both feet jumping out of his grasp. She tipped backward, but the smooth cement wall caught her back, held her up in an awkward lean like the ropes in a boxing ring saving a loopy fighter from hitting the canvas.

Craig crawled for her. Hands and knees clapping and scuffing over the cement.

Her balance righted itself. Legs growing steady and strong beneath her. And she darted forward.

She hurdled his prone form. Weaving past his outstretched arms. Moving past his legs. Turning back once she was clear.

She hurled herself up and stomped on his left Achilles tendon as hard as she could. All of her body weight ground her heel into that thick strand holding his ankle together.

His leg twitched beneath her. Compressed by her weight. Scraping on the concrete. Calf muscle bulging and then going slack.

The connective tissue gritted and popped.

Craig screamed.

CHAPTER SEVENTY-SIX

Pain bursts in his leg, a bright explosion of agony like someone fired an arrow through the back of his foot. Craig clenches his teeth. Head quivering atop his body like a human bobblehead.

Overwhelming pressure floods his ankle. Hot and wet and swelling and angry. Like a tea kettle of boiling water poured into the joint.

He rolls on the floor. Torso thrashing. Limbs flailing. Unable to hold himself still. The pain is too big for that.

His eyes squint shut, tiny muscles quivering and twitching across his face. Breath hissing between clenched teeth.

Something between a whimper and a scream streams from his throat. Vocal cords buzzing and whining. Voice dry and shredded.

The sound of her fleeing brings him back to the moment.

He stops rolling. Belly down on the concrete. Wrenches his head up to look, his body otherwise frozen. Eyes unblinking.

Her slender figure races up the stairs, away from him. Rotting wood cracking under her weight, threatening to give.

She disappears through the darkened doorway. The shadows swallowing her whole.

Two sibilant breaths heave out of him. Frustrated. Seething.

It occurs to him that the pain has receded. Broken and fallen like a cresting wave. Settled down into a steady flare of suffering.

Craig blinks. Stares at the smooth concrete floor.

He needs to move. Pain or not. He needs to move. Now.

He rolls to his back. Feels that bloated joint throbbing down at the end of his leg. A fever pulsing in his ankle, hot fluid plumping it until the skin is as taut as a sweaty hot dog. Turgid. About to blow.

He sits up. His knees fold up into a tent in front of him. He's been careful not to put any weight on the ankle, but he has to chance it now. Has to test it.

Time to find out if he can walk.

He lifts himself. Gets to his feet with the good leg doing most of the work.

He tests the bad ankle. Lowers it to the floor. Leans into it.

Bolts of bright pain flash up his leg. A hurt so intense it blinds him for a second. Blots his vision to black.

It feels like electricity surging through the bones in his calf, in his thigh. Voltage spitting and sizzling through the entire length of his limb and into his hip. Flickering energy. Flash-frying all the meat in there.

But the bad leg props him up. The injured ankle can hold his weight, even if it hurts.

Good. This is good.

Maybe it's only sprained. Or maybe the tendon is only partially torn.

He shuffles forward. Feet scuffing on the cement. Pain shooting up his leg. He's slower than before. No doubt about that.

But this will work.

He drags himself up the steps. Adjusts his grip on the knife.

Time to end this.

CHAPTER SEVENTY-SEVEN

After staring into the fluorescent bulbs in the basement, the dark upstairs was impenetrable. Thick black hung everywhere in front of Charlie. A wall of gloom.

She hesitated at the top of the stairs, stopping just shy of where the darkness took over, and looked both ways.

Something jutted out of the wall to her right, just visible in the glimmer creeping out of the basement doorway. She took a step closer.

Light switches. Two of them.

Her breath caught in her throat. She reached out, air moving into all the opened places on her hand. Stinging and sharp.

She snapped the switches up. Both at once, the clicks loud in the quiet house.

Nothing.

No light.

She flipped the switches up and down a few more times, knowing it wouldn't work. *Shit.*

Charlie swallowed once and pushed herself into the darkness even if some primordial instinct told her not to.

She needed to find a way out of here, light or no light.

She held her arms out in front of her. Feeling her way. Fingers flexing. Wounds opening and closing in a way that made her queasy.

Her heart thundered in her chest, the muscle punching faster and faster, blood pulsing and squishing in her ears.

She found a wall. Felt along its smooth paint with her fingertips, glossy and cool. It would lead her somewhere, for better or worse.

The scent of dust was thick here, earthy and arid, with just a hint of mildew.

Something sharp banged into her hipbone.

She jumped back instinctively.

She waited. Listened. Thought for sure Craig would leap out of the shadows at her, swinging his blade.

Nothing.

She stepped forward. Moved her hands lower to feel where it had been, half expecting it to be gone somehow. It was still there.

Her fingers ran over the metal. Not an edge. A corner. Her bloody hands smeared over the slick enamel of an appliance of some sort.

Then she felt the angular metal of the grates over the gas burners. A stove. She was in the kitchen.

She moved faster now. The glimmer of hope propelling her. Hands fumbling along the wall again.

She found the fridge a few paces later. And as she neared the next perpendicular wall, she could just make out windows with thick bushes and shrubs blotting out the moonlight.

She reached a second wall, butted up against the one she'd been following. Felt her way away from the windows. Swung her arms high and low looking for any sign of a door.

Holding her breath now. Close. She could feel it.

The doorknob brushed the back of her wrist. She squeezed it. Twisted. Her wounded hand screamed in protest.

Cool night air rushed in at her as she ripped the door free of the jamb. Damp wind touching her cheeks, fluttering her hair.

She raced out into the open night.

CHAPTER SEVENTY-EIGHT

Charlie launched herself off a rotting wooden porch, floating, weightless as she rocketed away from the house. Victorious, for this one moment at least.

The ground came rushing at her soon enough.

She landed flat-footed, ankles flexing awkwardly, joints jolted. Her bad knee buckled beneath her.

Then her body toppled, bending at the waist, falling, horizontal. She caught herself with outstretched hands planted in the dewy grass, wounds throbbing, and sprung right back up.

The hulking remains of rusted-out vehicles and tractors were scattered over the grounds, dappled in the pale glow of the moon and stars. A collapsed barn sagged in the distance.

She ran straight for the cornfield dead ahead—rows of spiky stalks stretched out to the horizon. The uneven ground jostled her some, dips and bumps tried to tip her, but she didn't let them slow her.

She just needed to reach that line where the yard ended and the cornstalks reached up over her head.

The corn would conceal her. Swathe her in shadows. Hide her from him.

The wind moaned over the field, blowing in to touch Charlie's cheeks with its October chill. Crisp. The shifting air rasped through the corn, swelling and swaying all those leaves and tassels.

The border where the yard meshed to corn rushed up at her like a finish line. She stood straighter. Picked her knees up higher.

She burst through the first row, stalks sizzling and cracking all around her, the night going darker here and now.

She kept going, kept running. Arms up. Elbows parting the stalks as if she were swimming, making gaps for her to squeeze through.

She crashed her way several rows deep before she turned and ran down one of the aisles. The going got easier finally, and her speed picked up. Her heart banged away in her chest.

Papery leaves reached out for her, tattering flaps of husk that had gone beige and dry as the fall drained its way toward winter.

A hitch developed in her gait. Her bad knee hurt worse and worse, the joint stiffening, popping a little with each step.

And her lungs burned in her chest. Somehow on fire and heavy with the damp night air at the same time. Throat going ragged and raw as her breath plumed in and out.

Black splotches started to blink in the corner of her left eye. Misshapen blots beating along with her rapid pulse. They reminded her of those flickering cigarette burns in the corner of a movie screen just before a reel change.

She ignored the pain, ignored the ever mounting signs of fatigue. Kept going. Picking up her feet and putting them down. Pushing off from the moist soil. Lumbering through the gap between the rows of corn. Fighting for every inch of progress.

A kind of calm overcame her as she ran. A lightness tingling in her chest. Her consciousness whittled itself down to the flicker of stalks rolling by, as if she were floating through the field, just faintly aware of the floppy leaves on each side batting at her shoulders.

When she finally couldn't go on, she stopped. Blinked twice and crumpled to the ground. Curled herself into a ball with her head hugged against her knees.

She breathed. Cool air huffing in and out. And she watched the black splotches dancing in the corner of her eye turn pink and drift around in her field of vision, pulsating figments gliding in slow motion.

She couldn't think of much beyond this moment—her mind unable to hold onto any abstraction for long, focused only on the wind rushing into her chest, dry and harsh where it touched her insides. She closed her eyes. Let her mind go blank.

Just breathe.

She did.

In time her breathing slowed, though it offered no relief to the burning membranes in her throat and chest. Still, it felt good to have her respiration back under some semblance of control.

She pictured Craig as she'd last seen him. Face down on the concrete floor, writhing in agony, screaming over his busted ankle. God, she hoped he'd never walk again.

He'd jerked his head up just as she'd reached the top of the steps. Gaping as he'd watched her run away, a childish look of disbelief coming over his features.

If he's coming, he could be close by now.

She got a hold of herself. Lifted her head.

She listened.

At first, she could only hear the blood pounding in her ears.

Then she heard him.

A whisper through the corn. The stalks rasping and hissing.

He was getting closer.

Not daring to stand up into the moonlight, Charlie crawled a few feet into a deeper shadow—a place where the cornstalks grew tighter, blocking out the moon the rest of the way.

Just as she edged into the darkness, she stuck her hand through something sticky and stringy. She held her fingers up to her face close enough to see the glistening strands wound around her knuckles and stretched over her palm.

A spider web.

Something tickled the back of her wrist. Dainty little pricks like toothpicks faintly jabbing her flesh.

Charlie whimpered under her breath. Chewed her lip a second. She didn't want to turn over her hand and look, but she had to.

She rotated her arm just as a huge spider crawled over her skin. Black and yellow. Bulbous abdomen the size of a buckeye and spindly legs that tapered to minuscule tips. Its sharp little footsteps pricked her skin.

Charlie cupped her other hand over her mouth to stifle herself as she lowered her wrist to the soil. Then she flicked the spider away with the fingernails of her free hand, brushing it off.

The crunch of the cornstalks grew louder. Closer.

She whipped her head back up in time to see him take the first step into her row. Her breath caught in her throat. She didn't move. Didn't blink. Didn't breathe.

Silvery moonlight shimmered through his hair and cast his silhouette in stark relief. She saw the angular jaw, the slightly knobby nose, the stooped shoulders. And beneath these the jagged spike of the knife in his hand. All the details came clear in outline, even if his face itself remained a blackened smear.

Craig's shadow crawled across the ground, reached out all the way to Charlie, a darkness touching her, slicing through her, deepening the murk around her.

She bit the insides of her cheeks. Fought the instinct to shuffle backward again. Move away from the black cloud reaching out of him to caress her skin.

He looked around, turned his head in her direction and held it there for a moment. Then he turned away and stalked down the aisle of dirt, the silhouette of his broad shoulders shrinking. She could see the limp now, the way he favored the stomped ankle, compensating with ginger motions that let the other leg do most of the work.

He hadn't seen her. He was going the wrong way.

He turned to his right. Parted some of the corn with his arms and slipped through into the next row. The wall of corn closed behind him, and he disappeared from her view, though she could still hear him.

She blinked. Let herself breathe again.

As soon as he moved out of earshot, she got to her feet and ran the other way.

CHAPTER SEVENTY-NINE

Lights gleamed in the distance. Small squares of illumination hung up above and ahead of her.

Charlie raced through the corn. Breath whistling in and out of her. Pain throbbing and popping and stabbing through all of her body now. A steady flare of hurt that seemed to ache worse as the night's chill saturated her flesh.

She focused on the glow ahead, which seemed to disappear and reappear behind a curtain of corn as the rise and fall of the terrain changed underfoot. Charlie knew what it was before she got close enough to confirm it.

Windows. A house on a hill. Another old farmhouse, probably. But this one was occupied from the looks of it.

And she knew what that meant. Help. Protection. A phone to call the police. A way out of this endless night.

She veered left, crashing through the last few rows of corn face first, the stalks still crunching, splintering, exploding in protest as she knocked them down and trampled them.

Her legs felt heavier now. Rubbery. Fatigue was settling in. But she kept going. Jaw slack. Mouth dry. A pain in her side like a bamboo skewer piercing her liver. She kept going.

At last she broke free of the corn and zipped through the grass and scrub covering the land beyond the field. The hill slowly filled the horizon ahead of her. A bulky darkness rising up to dominate her field of vision.

She closed on it and began climbing.

She trudged up the incline. The toes of her shoes dug into the soil, tried to find a grip among the wet weeds that covered the hill.

By the time she was halfway up, her legs were dead. Refusing to respond to her commands. She fell onto her hands and knees, but she kept climbing. Her fingers scrabbled over soggy plants, dirt stinging as it worked its way into her cuts.

She inched her way up the hill, weaving and zigzagging toward the top of the slope. She quit looking up. Focused on the ferns and tufts of grass occupying the ground. Clawed her fingernails into the rich black soil.

And then the lip of the hill lay before her, one last bulge to traverse, and the ground flattened out. It felt impossible. Her arms and legs falling into a stagger on the level ground.

She sprawled in the grass. Rolled onto her back. Looked up into the stars and breathed.

Her ribcage heaved. Lungfuls of crisp air sucked into her chest. That pattering patch of blackness at the edge of her vision died back a breath at a time until it was gone.

The chilly dew felt good on her skin. It dappled her neck and hands and seeped into the hair on the back of her head.

The vast heavens sprawled above her, all those pinpricks of light shining through the darkness. The moon looked so big now, stark and milky against the black of the night.

No relief came to her in this moment of rest, though. The heat in her head remained. The agony in her body persisted. Even the twitches assailing her calves refused to give up, popping the muscles and making her feet jerk like her legs had the hiccups.

No rest. No relief. Not until she stopped him for good.

She picked herself up from the soggy ground and ran for the glowing promise of the farmhouse.

CHAPTER EIGHTY

With a fresh jolt of adrenaline coursing through her system, Charlie rocketed across the gravel driveway and moved onto the manicured front lawn. Her dead legs found some of their former bounce as she sped over the final straightaway.

She vaulted up the porch steps to the farmhouse. Ripped across the wooden platform, feet pounding on the planks. Then she stopped abruptly at the front door, leaning her hands on either side of the door frame, leaving red smudges on the white paint.

She lifted a fist. Banged on the storm door. Three cracks that split the night and rattled the door in its frame.

She swiveled her head to look down the hill and back at the dark field. Imagined him emerging from the shadows. But everything was still.

She'd seen no movement in any of the windows on her way up to the house, but the glowing glass panes had made her eyes water after so long in the dark, blurring her vision as she got close. So much light. Apart from a couple of windows toward the back that remained dim, it looked like the whole house was lit up.

Someone had to be home. Didn't they?

Nobody came to the door.

Charlie knocked again. Both fists pounding this time like she was banging on a drum, thrashing out a frantic fill.

The gauzy curtain on the front door billowed, and Charlie stopped knocking. Held her breath. Watched.

A dark shape stepped in behind it. The deadbolt clicked, and then the door swung open.

Overwhelming bursts of emotion exploded in Charlie's brain. Shock took hold. Made her numb. Cold. Confused.

An old man appeared in the doorway, concern folding his forehead into a pile of wrinkles. Gray hair. Loose skin. Caterpillar eyebrows. Saggy wet eyes like a hound dog, deep-set.

He opened the door just less than shoulder-width and stood so his body blocked most of the opening.

Charlie's eyes locked onto his mouth. Watched his lips move. He was talking, speaking loud enough to be heard through the plexiglass of the storm door still positioned between them, but she was too overwhelmed to understand.

He tilted his head. Narrowed his wet eyes. He seemed to understand that she was in trouble, perhaps even that she wasn't hearing him. His eyes dipped, lingered on her bloody hands.

"Ma'am?" he said. "Ma'am, are you OK?"

Her thoughts reeled. Her mind somehow both overflowing with words and blank at the same time.

She needed to get inside, but how could she explain it all? Her tongue tapped at the roof of her mouth. She found her eyes looking past the old man, scanning what little of the living room she could see for some place to hide.

"He's going to kill me," she said. Her throat was so dry that it came out in a croak, just louder than a whisper.

"What's that now?" He crushed his eyebrows together, more wrinkles adding themselves to that stack of pancakes he called a forehead.

He couldn't understand. No one would understand.

Her panic swelled. Fresh sweat prickled along her hairline.

It wasn't over.

Crazy throbs of current thrummed through her. Made her itch. Made her shoulders squirm. Made her shift her weight from foot to foot.

If she couldn't explain it, couldn't solve it with words, she needed to act. Needed to get inside, to hide. Now.

"He's after me," she said, frustration plain in her voice this time. She gestured at the empty night behind her, as though that might clear things up for him.

He looked out into the darkness for a second, and then he shook his head.

"Now, hold on just a minute here, hon," he said.

But she couldn't do that. Not anymore.

She tore open the storm door and shouldered past the old man, pushing into his house.

CHAPTER EIGHTY-ONE

"Ray, who was it?" a woman's voice called from the back of the house.

Charlie ignored it. She stumbled through the living room, rustic plank flooring and Shaker-style furniture barely registering in her conscious mind, eyes scanning everywhere for a place to hide.

It wasn't over. She knew it wasn't. He was still out there. Chasing. Hunting.

He would be here soon.

She entered a back hallway. A squat older woman stood in a bright kitchen off to Charlie's right, and a darker room was visible through a doorway to her left. The kitchen was too well lit, so she went left.

"Who the— Oh, hon. You're bleeding," the old woman said behind her. "Ray, she's cut the dickens out of her hands."

"I know," the old man said. "Said someone is trying to kill her, Mabel."

Charlie fumbled into the dark space, finding a bedroom cast in shadows. She could hide under the bed, maybe.

"Honey, come on. We've got to call the police."

Police. Yes. That made sense. More sense than hiding.

The old woman, Mabel, took Charlie by the elbow and led her back toward the light of the kitchen.

"He drugged me," Charlie said. She was breathing heavy, her voice a hoarse croak. "And he was… he was going to kill me."

Mabel nodded slowly, rubbing Charlie's back, genuine concern in her eyes as they shuffled into the kitchen.

"You just sit down and breathe, honey," the old lady cooed. "You're OK now. I'll get you something to drink and call the police. Water OK?"

Charlie didn't say anything. Just stared at the glossy tabletop, eyes locked onto the two shimmering spots where the lights reflected, while she watched the old lady totter around out of the corner of her eye.

Mabel ran a glass of water under the tap and placed it on the table before her.

"Drink this. You'll feel better."

Then she waddled to the landline phone mounted on the wall and dialed 911.

Charlie lifted the glass to her lips. The cold water felt incredible in her parched throat. She guzzled it down in a matter of seconds.

Charlie's bloody palm stuck to the glass like a suction cup, and she pried it off with some effort. She stared at the bloody red daub left on the glass, an oblong imprint with scarlet creases running through it, realizing only after several seconds had passed that Mabel was talking on the phone.

"I haven't managed to get her name. She seems out of sorts. Says she's been drugged, and there's quite a bit of blood."

Movement through the doorway caught her eye, and she turned to look.

Ray took a small key to an ornate wooden cabinet in one corner of the living room. He unlocked the case, and then he reached out of Charlie's view, hands disappearing behind the open cabinet doors.

When his hands came back out, a wooden shotgun stock was clutched in them. The steel barrel kept coming out of the cabinet for what felt like a long time. Impossibly long.

Ray pulled the lever and broke open the shotgun, angling the open barrels away from the stock. He plopped a shell into each barrel. Clacked the weapon shut again.

Then he leaned the barrel of the gun up over his shoulder and looked out at Charlie in the kitchen. He gave her a nod.

"If he comes out here after ya, like ya said he would… Got somethin' for him. That's all."

CHAPTER EIGHTY-TWO

He twists the knob while all their backs are turned. Creeps through the unlocked door. Stays light on his feet as he steps into the farmhouse.

His heart thuds. His tongue and throat taste like battery acid.

His skin vibrates around the knife in his hand. Feels like it's sending voltage into his palm and fingers. Prickling energy radiating off the thing, surging into him.

Keeping low, Craig moves to the dark room to the right of the living room. Moves away from the people, away from the kitchen where he saw the old woman guide Charlie.

He slips himself behind a decorative case full of owl figurines. Back against the wall. Gut sucked in.

Concealed. Not invisible by any means, but concealed.

He waits in the shadow there. Listens. Squints his eyes to sharpen his senses.

Water runs in the kitchen, the pitch rising as it fills a glass, and then it cuts off.

"Drink this," the old woman says to Charlie. "You'll feel better."

The layers of drywall between them muffle her voice but only a little. Her sound makes the hair on his arms stand up. So close now. So real now.

He pushes the thoughts away. Feels his breath pass over his wet lips and shudder into his lungs.

The two ladies are in the kitchen. Confirmed. Far enough around the next corner that he can't quite see them.

He doesn't know where the old man is just now. He could be in the kitchen with them, but maybe not. He needs to know that before he can make a move.

He licks his lips. Doesn't want to be here. Too much risk. Too many moving parts.

She can identify him now, though. That's the problem. Unmanageable.

It leaves him no choice. Nothing to lose.

If Charlie Winters lives, he's done. Better to take the risk. Better to die trying to kill her than give up.

The woman speaks into the phone now, her voice making him jump. She's calling 911, but he has time. Way out here? The Podunk police might take half an hour or more to drag themselves to some farmhouse in the sticks.

Ol' mom and pop might need to go, too. But Charlie is the only thing for now.

Something scuffles in the living room to his left. Shoes chafing at the carpet. Making the floorboards groan.

Craig glances that way. Squints harder.

The old man passes by the doorway and heads out of view. Shuffling toward the opposite side of the living room.

He stares down at the knife in his hand. Half expects to see sparks flying off the thing with the way it's shooting biting current up his arm.

He drifts across the room. Gliding. Soundless.

He edges behind a door there. Nose all pressed into the crevice so he can watch the old man through the gap between the door and jamb.

The old man pulls a shotgun from a gun case. An old double-barrel.

His throat gulps involuntarily as he lays eyes on the weapon. Then gulps again as the old man loads it.

The farmer turns. Leans the gun on his shoulder. Faces the kitchen doorway. He lifts his reedy voice.

"If he comes out here after ya, like ya said he would… Got somethin' for him. That's all."

The farmer's half smile slowly fades from his lips. He hesitates. After a second, he speaks again.

"Anyhow, I'll go out now. Have a look around."

The old man turns and heads for the front door. He flicks up a bunch of light switches just as he hits the doorway and then closes the door behind him. The porch creaks under his feet as his figure bobs across the well-lit space, and then he's gone.

An icy chill spreads over the flesh of Craig's body.

Just like that, he has his chance.

He hauls himself out from behind the door. Slow. Careful not to jostle anything.

He creeps through the darkened den. Moves for the glowing rectangle ahead: the doorway leading to the kitchen, where the women are.

He comes up on the open doorway at an angle. Trying to get a look at the dining table he glimpsed around the corner. Not wanting to come at the doorway straight on where the light would expose him.

If Charlie is still there, he can't see her. Not yet, at least.

He crouches low. Dares to lean his head into the doorway.

Craig's eyes slide over glittering linoleum. The little reddish squares in the flooring are made to look like brick with gray lines of grout etched between them.

Then he looks at the mess of legs under the table, finding those of the chairs surrounding it alongside the cylindrical supports of the table itself. All wooden. No human legs.

He skulks the rest of the way into the kitchen. Crossing the threshold. Feet leaving the carpet to stride onto the fake brick tiles.

Still careful. Still quiet. Still slow.

The kitchen is empty. A water glass smeared with fresh blood rests on the table.

Fuck.

He stops. Listens.

Nothing.

How did they slip away without me hearing?

He tries to remember the old woman's phone call. Did she hang up? He can't remember hearing it. Maybe the shotgun distracted him.

Wait. Doesn't the 911 dispatcher usually ask a caller to stay on the line?

He scans for the phone. Eyes crawling up the walls.

He finds the landline unit mounted on the wall next to the refrigerator, but the handset isn't on the hook.

His eyes trace along the coiled beige cable running out of the bottom of the unit. It trails around the next doorway, wrapping itself out of view.

Craig licks his lips again. Fingers tightening around the knife's handle.

The women must be just there. Around the corner. The phone cord drawing a squiggly line that will lead him straight to them.

It's too perfect.

He stays low. Walks forward in a crouch. Shoulders hunched.

He leans out through another doorway. Peers into a dimly lit space. After staring at it a second, he can make out part of a king-sized bed, a dresser, a painting on the wall. Must be the master bedroom.

His eyes follow the phone cord again. That spiraling white line ends on a nightstand just next to the bed. The handset rests on it.

He still can't see Charlie or the old woman, but they must be here.

He hears voices. They're muffled but certainly female. Just ahead. Somewhere beyond that bedroom doorway.

He smiles. This is it.

Just as Craig creeps out of the kitchen, a gun cocks behind his back. He freezes mid-step.

"Drop it," the old man says.

He looks down at the knife quivering at the end of his arm. It no longer seems to swell energy into his hand. He drops it.

The weapon bounces and skitters away from him. Out of arm's reach.

"Nice," the old man says. "Now hands up, Bucko."

He hesitates a second. Then he puts his hands up.

"There," the old man says. "It's all over."

CHAPTER EIGHTY-THREE

Fear trembles in Craig's upraised arms. Throbs in the muscles along his neck bone. Writhes inside his skull.

He stares straight ahead, unable to see the gun at his back. His eyes latch onto a painting on the far wall of two owls perched on a branch.

This couldn't happen, but it did.

A small sob just louder than a whisper escapes him. Makes a popping sound on its way past his lips.

He can't let it end this way.

His eyes fall away from the owls. He scans the floor, seeking the knife. It's tumbled over the carpet, tucked itself halfway under an end table, far out of reach.

But maybe he could leap for it. Try something. Anything.

The old man jabs the barrel of the shotgun into the small of his back as though to dissuade him of this notion.

"Walk," the old man says. The farmer is so close that he can feel his old-ass breath on the back of his neck.

He takes a few paces into the living room. Passing within a few paces of the knife and then moving even further away from it along the way. Cursing himself inside. Not that the blade would do any good against the brutal force of the shotgun at close range.

"That'll do. Stop there, just in front of the couch, and then turn around and face me. Slowly. And keep your hands up nice and high."

He follows the orders. Lifts his hands slightly from where they've sagged at the elbow. His arms are tired. All of him is tired. He wheels around while the old man drones on.

"Police'll be here before long. I figure we can wait on 'em here in the living room. If you're smart, we'll keep everything real peaceful-like between us in the meantime."

Craig focuses on a dark spot in the folded corner of the farmer's mouth and wonders if he chews tobacco. It wiggles when he speaks, a sheening obsidian fleck of something or other.

The old man's faces hardens as he keeps talking. Brow all crushed together. He stares Craig in the eyes.

"Any funny shit out of you, and I'll put a load of buckshot in your ass. Believe that."

Charlie and the old lady trail out of the bedroom. Their footsteps stop abruptly in the doorway, both their eyes wide.

He makes eye contact with Charlie for a split second, and a jolt of adrenaline pours into his bloodstream. Makes his scalp tingle and his hands go cold.

She's right there, and there's not a damn thing he can do about it.

"Ray?" the old woman says.

"Just stay back, Mabel. I got 'im here. Everything's under control. Where you two been?"

The old lady gapes a moment before she replies, blinking hard as her eyes bounce from the gun to Craig and back again. Her mouth hangs open for a few seconds before she finds words.

"I patched the girl's hands up," Mabel says. "Best I could, anyhow. She'll probably need stitches and what have you. Cuts are deep, some of 'em."

He glances down at the gauze wrapping Charlie's hands as the old bitch talks. Red patches are already visible on the white fabric. He wounded her but not enough to count for much.

He sees the old man's head turn. He wants to see Charlie's bandages as well.

Big mistake.

Craig lurches for him. Outstretched arms grasping for the end of the gun. Finding it. Fingers lacing themselves around the barrel.

The old man recoils. Startled. He stumbles back a step before his reflexes kick in.

The farmer's arms flap once, and then he tightens his grip on the gun. Upper body flexing.

He squeezes the trigger.

The shotgun booms.

But the barrel lifts in Craig's hands. Angled up.

The gun bucks in his hands. A thrashing, violent thing that fights him. Jerking. Straining.

He keeps a hold of it. Pushes the barrel higher.

The whoosh of the blast ruffles his hair. Hot and close. A snort of flame accompanying it like dragon's breath.

The shell's pellets pepper the ceiling somewhere behind him. Patter where they punch through the drywall. Harmless.

He thrusts his whole body forward. Shoving with his arms. Driving with his legs.

He jams the walnut stock straight back into the old man's shoulder. Jolts him off his legs.

And then he wrenches downward on the weapon as hard as he can. A ripping motion like he's swinging an ax.

The downward force wobbles the old man. Topples him forward. Just about pulls him to his knees.

The gun jerks free of the farmer's grip. Plucked cleanly.

He turns the gun around. Points it at the farmer. Finger hovering over the trigger. Aching to squeeze. To vent most of this old fuck's brains out the backside of his shattered skull.

But no.

Only one shell left, one chamber still loaded.

The girl knows his name. She has to go first.

Everything else can come after.

He pivots to the doorway, where Charlie stood seconds before. Swings the gun that way.

Empty.

No.

A breath hiccups into him. Feels like a strange bubble in his throat.

He stalks toward the back of the house. Feet stomping over the carpet. Pounding on the wood beneath. No longer quiet.

He reaches the kitchen just in time to see Charlie Winters disappear out the back door, fleeing into the night.

CHAPTER EIGHTY-FOUR

With all the floodlights on, the big backyard was lit up like Main Street. The broad beams shimmered through oak branches and pine boughs, made all the trees look like they were glowing.

Charlie flung herself down the four concrete steps that comprised the back porch and wheeled hard to her left, moving away from the light.

With her banged-up knee, she didn't think she could make it to the next cornfield, which began on the other side of the yard—a straight shot from the back door of perhaps fifty yards.

There was a chance she could outrun him, now that he was limping, but outrunning the gun was another matter. She couldn't risk it.

She needed to stay out of the light.

A barn perched on the small rise up ahead. The top half formed a black silhouette against the stars. Maybe she could find a weapon there. Make a stand.

His footsteps thumped down the porch steps somewhere behind her, interrupting her thoughts. She could hear the odd rhythm of his limp as the soles of his shoes clapped down on the cement, but he seemed to be moving with some speed.

She lifted her knees higher. Pumped her muscles harder.

But he was already gaining on her. Closing on her.

She couldn't outrun him for long. She needed to think.

Her eyes snapped back to the barn up ahead. Closer now. The details filling in as she ran.

Darkness swallowed most of the structure, but the floodlights lit the face of the red building enough for her to see that the door hung partially open.

A place to hide? A place to die?

Either way, she'd run for it. She didn't think she had much choice.

She sprinted along the edge of the floodlight's glow, the line between light and dark. Her gaze stretched way out in front of her, dancing over the gambrel roof, over the red and white detailing on the wooden plank siding, over that gapped place where the door hung open about shoulder-width.

She pushed herself. Chewed up ground faster and faster. Felt more than saw the glistening wet grass sliding by underneath.

Pain flared everywhere—hands, legs, gut, and lungs. White-hot knitting needles stabbing up and down her body. Nerve endings screaming in agony, begging her to quit.

She ignored all of the hurt. Dropped the world. Ran.

She could hear his breath behind her now. Heaving through his mouth.

She ducked into the barn, and the dark closed around her. She shuffled a few steps over the dirt floor, needing to get away from the open door, away from the light.

Dry air surrounded her as she moved deeper into the barn, and the smell of hay filled her nostrils.

Her eyes started adjusting to the darkness. Form slowly taking shape in the void.

Wooden stalls came first, their angular shapes rising up on both sides of her. If there were any animals here now, she couldn't see them.

Exposed beams coagulated on the ceiling above—the bony structure of the building laid bare. No help there.

Then scraps of hay filtered in, bits sprinkled over the floor below like confetti. The specks made a path that led to a pile of hay in one of the stalls ahead.

She scrambled forward. Heart punching at the walls of her chest. Eyes scanning for any weapon.

And then she spied it. A handle and pointy bits leaned up against one of the stall dividers next to the pile of hay.

A pitchfork.

CHAPTER EIGHTY-FIVE

Craig's feet jostle beneath him as he mounts the hill. He slides a little on the wet grass, but the shotgun helps him balance. He holds the weapon sideways, like a tight-rope walker's pole hanging out on each side.

He watches the girl's figure vanish into the shadowed cleft where the barn door lies open a crack. The darkness lurches and swallows her.

But this only makes him smile.

She's penned herself in now. Confined herself to this wooden structure. Put herself on a path that only leads one way.

Like a hog forced down the kill chute, hooves scrabbling in a useless fight against the inevitable. Time has come for the piggy's purpose to be served. A few steps from now, it'll get its brains battered in to become someone's breakfast delight.

That's the way of this world, he thinks. *The meek and the strong. Meat on the plate. Blood on the teeth.*

Always. Forever.

Mine. Just taking what's mine. That's all.

He picks up speed.

He's got her now.

CHAPTER EIGHTY-SIX

Charlie squatted on the dusty floor. Got low. Positioned herself just in front of the open barn door.

This would either work or it wouldn't. No second chances now.

After looking things over, she scooted back a little. Moved out of the wedge of light that crept in through the gapped door and painted a yellow glow onto the dirt floor, lighting up flecks of hay.

Sweat wept from her temples. Stung where its salt touched the corners of her eyes. She tried to blink it away, squeezing her eyes shut hard a few times, but it didn't seem to help any.

Then she swung the pitchfork in front of her so that the business end faced the open door, still shrouded in shadows. She angled the end of the handle into a divot in the dirt before her and braced the tilted wooden stick against herself, balancing it on one knee, wrapping both bandaged hands around it.

She'd need to hold steady. Absorb the blow.

She stared into the breach where the two wooden lips of the door parted. She could only see a narrow slice of the grass beyond the building from this angle. The rounded hilltop that sloped downward out of view.

And the sky stretched out to the horizon above that. Dark and stars and a slice of the moon just glowing away. The night always seemed deeper this time of year, like the darkness got bigger and colder when the fall arrived.

His footfalls sounded out there in the night. That odd rhythm of his limp making them distinct as they trod over the wet grass, a pitter-patter not unlike a horse's gallop. More of a slap and drag than the standard *rat-tat-tat* of footsteps.

Her eyes got wider. Staring still through that open doorway, at that slab of sod on the slope, at that vast sky flecked with the bright of the stars.

Waiting. Ready. Hoping. Hoping he burst in at speed. Two strides into the barn should do it. Maybe three.

Please. Please let it work.

His figure rose up over the hilltop. A silhouette. Backlit by the floodlights mounted near the house so his front half remained a dark smudge, his face a black smear without detail.

Sweat streamed out of every pore on Charlie's body now. Her breathing scraped in and out of her, hot and somehow heavy in her throat.

That silhouette grew larger as he rushed for the barn.

He showed no signs of slowing.

Charlie tucked her chin. Squeezed all the muscles in her core tight to brace for impact.

Then she tightened both of her tattered hands around the wooden handle of the pitchfork. Felt the wounds reopen under the bandages.

He burst through the door. Lifted the shotgun to his shoulder just as he moved through the doorway.

He ran full speed into the pitchfork.

Stopped dead as he hit it.

Impaled.

The tines speared his gut just below his belly button. The four metal prongs disappeared into his flesh. Jabbed into his torso at a slightly upward angle. Curving.

It stood him straight up as though lifting him onto tippy-toes.

The handle butted into Charlie's body when his weight hit. Its stubby wooden end lifted from the dirt, scraped over her leg, pounded into her abdomen with an audible thud. It tried to stab her, too, to shove its way through her.

But she fought it. Shoved it back down into the dust, back down into that divot where the earth could help her push back against his weight.

And his neck and limbs jostled at the end of the fork. Jerked hard by the sheer force of the impact. A shudder shook through him, made him look floppy like all the puppet strings holding him up had gone limp for a split second, only to be yanked hard a moment later.

His arm flexed. The shotgun boomed before him. A jet of fire snuffling out of the barrel.

The buckshot scattered above Charlie's head in a starburst. One of the pellets careened low enough to skim her left cheek. Hot metal grazed her skin, but the rest thunked into the wood somewhere behind her.

And then the recoil flung his arm, wrenched the weapon free from his hands. Plucked it. Spun it.

It tumbled, rattling against the pitchfork handle on the way down. Clattered to the floor.

A cloud of dust billowed up between them. A gray puff faintly visible in that weak light streaming through the door.

Everything else went still. Nothing stirred but that spreading plume of dirt.

He gasped. A wet breath sucked into his throat, torso shuddering.

His hands clutched at the wounds in his belly. Fingers squirming in the wetness there, which looked black in the low light of the barn.

Then his toes scraped on the floor. Legs churning. Calves pistoning. He wasn't quite able to touch his heels down to solid ground, no matter how he twisted himself.

Giving that up, he arched his back. Laced his hands around the sides of the pitchfork's head. Elbows fanned out to the sides. He tried to push himself off the curved metal skewers. Body quivering with the strain. Wounds sucking and squelching against the tines of the fork.

Finally, he gave in. Surrendered to his fate.

His bloody hands slipped off the fork. One then the other.

A big breath heaved out of him. Deflated him.

He let his weight go slack. Torso slumping forward. His limp limbs dangling like a rag doll's.

Tears quivered along the bottom rims of Charlie's eyes as she beheld this profane image: A slouching human figure dangling at the end of a pitchfork. Black wetness pulsing out around the prongs of the fork. Stooped shoulders arching over the handle. Head bobbing on the craned neck, hovering not so far from hers.

He coughed. Grimaced. Tipped his head back into the light.

And Charlie could see the blood on his teeth.

CHAPTER EIGHTY-SEVEN

Charlie clung to the handle of the pitchfork, refusing to let go. Afraid he might spring back to life if she did. She held on until her arms began to quiver with exhaustion, and even then she didn't so much let go as the tool seemed to slip from her grip.

Craig's body hung there for a moment, still propped upright by the long handle. And then the far end of the pitchfork shifted in the dirt. The body tipped sideways and landed with a thud on the barn floor.

His right arm flung outward as he fell in a heap, grazing Charlie's ankle. She gasped and recoiled, thinking he was still alive, still grasping for her. She scrabbled away, kicking her legs wildly in a manner that sent her scooting backward over the floor. She didn't stop until her shoulder blades connected with the wall of the barn.

She stared at him, watching for another sign of movement. But he lay as still as a stone, and she realized it must have been the momentum of the fall that had propelled his arm out like that.

In the distance a siren screamed. One and then another and soon there were so many she couldn't make out a single voice amongst the chorus. Police. The police were coming.

Relief sent a fresh flood of tears streaming down her face, hot and salty and stinging the place where the buckshot had grazed her cheek. She tried to stand but found that her legs were made of jelly. She'd used up her last bit of strength in the fight, and now she felt empty. Hollow.

She supposed she'd just have to wait here for someone to come find her. It wouldn't be long now. The sirens were getting louder.

She felt something warm and wet on her hands and was momentarily startled to glance down and find them splotchy, swollen and devoid of fingers.

What had happened to her hands?

Her thoughts, which had been racing only a few minutes before, seemed like they were coming in slow motion now.

Then she remembered the bandages the old woman had applied. Gripping the pitchfork with such ferocity had reopened all of the cuts. The gauze was so soaked with blood now that only a few patches of white remained.

Charlie gagged and dry-heaved for several seconds, but nothing came up. She was well and truly empty.

The sirens outside built to a crescendo and then seemed to cut out all at once. Replaced by voices. Shouting and car doors slamming. All the noises sounded like she was hearing them through water. Murky and quavering.

She tried to call out, but her voice came out weak and small.

She was fading. The combination of blood loss and the drugs and the exertion conspiring to pull her into the murky darkness of unconsciousness. She closed her eyes. Drifted for what felt like a long time, hours maybe, though it surely could have only been minutes.

A scuffing sound outside the barn startled her out of the fog. Her eyelids peeled back, and she saw a silhouette darkening the aperture of the partially open door. Tall. A man's shape. Broad shoulders and long arms.

Charlie tried to speak again.

The man shoved the barn door aside. When he saw Craig lying there in a lifeless heap, he brought a fist to his mouth.

"Oh, Jesus."

And Charlie thought the voice seemed familiar. Her mind sought out a match. Not Frank… Not the sheriff… But who?

With his gaze sweeping past the corpse on the floor, the man took one step into the barn and spotted Charlie. She squinted.

Saw Will Crawford's face in her mind. But that couldn't be right. Will wasn't police.

"Charlie?" he said, eyes going wide, and it sounded so much like Will that something twisted in Charlie's chest.

He leaned his upper half outside the door and shouted back down the hill.

"She's in here!"

His feet thudded over the bare dirt of the barn, shuffling around Craig and kneeling when he got close to her.

Charlie closed her eyes, trying to clear the image of Will. She was seeing things. Hallucinating because of whatever Craig had slipped her. Because Will couldn't be here. That didn't make sense. She was going to open her eyes, and Will would be gone, replaced by some deputy she was vaguely acquainted with.

When her eyelids parted, the man had shifted, his features concealed by the thick shadows inside the barn.

"You're OK now," he said. "Everything's going to be OK. I've got you."

He leaned in and hooked an arm around her, pulling her upright.

"Can you walk?" he asked.

She nodded and took two steps before her bad knee buckled. The man caught her before she went all the way down, scooping her up in one smooth motion and carrying her the rest of the way.

The fabric of his jacket was cool against her cheek. It felt clean. She breathed in. Christ, he even smelled like Will.

They passed through the door and outside. The floodlight on the barn shone down so brightly that Charlie had to squint. She tilted her head back, wanting to see the man's face once and for all. To identify her rescuer.

It was Will Crawford.

She swallowed against the dry lump that had formed in her throat, forcing his name to her lips.

"Will?"

But he wasn't looking at her.

His face was angled toward the house, calling out to the police and paramedics swarming the property. And then they were surrounded by what sounded like a hundred voices all talking at once, babbling and squawking. A dozen or so hands latched onto her. Pulling her away from Will even though she clung to him, not wanting to let go.

The gripping, scrabbling arms yanked her down. Something clanged beneath her. The surface somehow soft and hard at the same time. A rough hand shoved her down onto the stretcher, laying her out flat. She didn't like that. Didn't like being forced down like that.

She started to struggle as a plastic mask was drawn over her face. Cold air blasted her nose and mouth. She heard another familiar voice, a woman's voice—Zoe?—telling her it was fine, that they were trying to administer oxygen, but it was too much, all the people and the noise and the pushing and the pulling and the grabbing.

She fought harder, squirming against the groping claws. There was a sharp prick on her arm, and the fight seemed to go out of her all at once. Consciousness fading. Spiraling out of her like bathwater down a drain.

Blackness.

CHAPTER EIGHTY-EIGHT

The first thing Charlie saw upon awakening was a pair of fluorescent light fixtures mounted to the ceiling, and her thoughts went immediately to the lights in Craig Rattigan's basement.

She panicked, her mind still foggy and confused.

Bits and pieces of the night came back to her. Terrible, haunting images.

The head of a dead bird on a stick. The flash of a knife. Blood on her hands. The gleaming points at the end of a pitchfork. And the awful sound they made against bone and flesh.

She'd escaped. She'd won. Or had it all been a dream?

Charlie blinked several times, trying to clear the haze shrouding her vision. Her surroundings sharpened with each flick of her eyelids.

The ceiling above the lights was some kind of acoustic tile. The basement had been open joists.

There was a shifting sound beside her. Something like a vinyl chair cushion squeaking. And then Uncle Frank's face filled her field of vision.

"Hey, turkey." He smiled down at her. "You awake for real this time?"

She tried to answer but found something restricting her mouth. She clawed the oxygen mask off and managed to force out a weak, "Yeah."

"Water?" he asked but didn't wait for an answer before tilting the head of her bed slightly upright and shoving a Styrofoam cup in her face.

She'd figured out by now that she was in the hospital and decided not to waste time asking stupid questions like, "Where am I?" or, "What happened?" She was thirsty.

Her lips found the straw. It seemed like it took tremendous effort to get anything into her mouth, but as soon as the cold liquid hit her tongue, she felt more awake. More clearheaded. She sucked greedily at the water until Frank yanked the cup out of reach.

"Go easy now," he said. "If you drink it too fast, you'll make yourself sick."

Charlie swallowed. Her throat still felt thick and scratchy and wrong, but better nonetheless.

"That's a myth. Like getting cramps if you swim too soon after eating."

Frank chuckled.

"Well, there's a whole crowd of people waiting to talk to you. Detectives, for one. But Zoe's outside. Paige, too." He glanced over at the door. "Only the thing is, they've saddled you with a Nurse Ratched type, and she's being quite strict about adhering to visiting hours. I only got in because I'm next of kin."

There was a familiar gleam in Frank's eye, and he rubbed his hands together like a mischievous raccoon.

"But I think if we sneak people in one at a time, we can keep her from getting too suspicious. I'll be back."

"Wait," Charlie said, only wanting him to give the water back, but he was already gone.

Seconds ticked by. Charlie stared at the cup of water on the bedside table. She was still so thirsty.

She sat forward a little. She could just barely graze the Styrofoam container with her fingertips, but her hands had been wrapped in fresh bandages. They looked like they belonged to the Stay Puft Marshmallow Man. Giant white fluffy things made of gauze and tape. And utterly lacking the dexterity required to maneuver the cup closer.

A loud voice rang out from the door.

"Oh, Miss Winters!" Paige halted just inside the door and clamped a hand over her mouth. When she spoke again, it was a whisper. "Oops. Frank told me to be quiet, and here I am, screeching like a wombat."

"Hi, Paige."

"It's just that I'm so glad you're OK," she said, coming around to the side of the bed. "Does it hurt?"

Charlie wasn't sure what Paige even meant until she pointed at Charlie's marshmallow hands.

"No. I think I must be on something. What everyone calls 'the good shit.'" She gestured at the cup. "Can you hand me that water?"

"Of course!"

Paige passed her the cup. Charlie fumbled with it for a moment, finally using her chest to balance the bottom of the cup and her hands to tip it toward her face.

"I was so worried when I got the call. Everyone was in a panic." The words seemed to rush out of Paige all at once, each sentence running into the next. "We looked everywhere for you, at your apartment and the office and then your mom's house. Then we found your things on the ground, and it was hard not to assume the worst. And all I could think about was how it was supposed to be me."

Charlie had no idea what Paige was talking about, but she was too busy chugging ice water to pause to ask, and Paige went on.

"Except I thought of my fortune cookie again, and I knew everything had to be OK, but then the longer I thought about it, I thought that maybe there was a way the fortune cookie could still be right, but in a bad way. Momentous could mean disastrous, you know? That's when I really started to worry. But we didn't give up, we kept searching and searching and—"

"Searching for what?"

But Paige's eyes had darted over to the door. She threw herself to the floor.

"Shoot. I think that's the nurse. Is she gone?"

Charlie saw only the empty hallway beyond the door.

"Yeah."

Paige popped up again.

"I should go and let someone else have a turn."

"But—" Charlie started to say, but Paige had already slipped out the door.

Charlie drained the last of her water while she waited.

Zoe came in next, looking tired but triumphant.

"I swear you've got more lives than a cat, Winters." Zoe took the chair Frank had been in before, scooting it closer to the bed. "But I have to formally request that you stop getting yourself into these situations. A girl's heart can only handle so much."

"No promises." Charlie tried to wink but a bandage over the wound on her cheek hindered the move. "What was Paige talking about earlier? Something about everyone searching. Didn't the old lady give the address when she called 911? And also, are the old couple OK?"

"They're fine. We were looking for you for a while before that, though."

"You were?" Charlie asked, finding a new pocket of water in the cup and slurping it up. "How did you know I was gone?"

"Will called me. He saw your car in the parking lot next to his place. Said it was the only one left, even hours after the carnival had closed down. He was worried."

"So he *was* there," Charlie murmured.

"Come again?"

Charlie felt her cheeks flush, like she was embarrassed for some reason.

"I thought I'd dreamed that it was him finding me in the barn," she explained.

Zoe shook her head.

"No dream. He was there, alright. And you fought like a banshee the second he let you go and we tried to put you on the stretcher. They had to sedate you. Do you remember that?"

"Sort of. Those drugs really messed me up." Charlie tried to scratch an itch on her arm but found it impossible with the bandages on her hands.

Zoe shifted in her seat, fidgeting.

"So uh… I don't know if you want to get into this or not, considering everything you've gone through tonight," Zoe said, pausing to clear her throat. "But I feel like it's something you have a right to know."

Charlie stared at her, not liking the look on her face.

"What is it?"

"Well, the guy… the one who attacked you, that is…"

"Craig?"

That brought Zoe up short.

"Wait… you know him? Like from before today?"

"Well, yeah. We went to school with him."

"We did?" Zoe's brow furrowed. "Was he in our class?"

"No. A grade behind us."

"Huh. I do not remember him. At all. Weird," Zoe said, shaking her head.

Charlie realized they'd gotten off track.

"You were about to tell me something about him?"

"Oh, right. Crap." Zoe puffed up her cheeks and blew out a breath. "It's just that I figure the way you left things, you probably assumed that he was dead? And he's… uh… not."

"He's not dead?" Charlie repeated, feeling like a pile of worms had started wriggling in her stomach.

She couldn't help but imagine him managing to slip away in the commotion of her rescue, like Michael Myers at the end of one of the *Halloween* movies.

"But is he… I mean, you got him, right?" Charlie asked, almost afraid to hear the answer.

"Oh yeah. Of course." Zoe let out a nervous chuckle. "And I'll admit that I wished on my lucky star that he'd croak on the way to the hospital, but no dice. The doctors say it was close, though. You skewered him good."

Charlie cringed, an image of blood foam spritzing from Craig's mouth after he'd impaled himself on the pitchfork springing to mind. It was several moments later before she realized Zoe was still talking.

"… in the mood for it, he's here. If you want to see him, that is."

"Craig?" Charlie recoiled at the idea.

"No," Zoe said, making a disgusting scoffing noise with her throat. "*Will.*"

"Oh. He's here?"

"Yeah." Zoe's forehead wrinkled. "That's what I was just saying. He's out in the waiting room with everybody else."

Charlie licked her lips. They felt chapped and raw.

She thought about how she'd refused to give him a second chance, even after he'd apologized over and over again. Because she didn't know if she could trust him. She'd completely blown him off at the carnival. And then he'd done this. Seen her car in the empty lot and been worried enough to raise the alarm despite the fact that she'd more or less told him to get lost. And she thought maybe that was enough, not to undo what he'd done, but to finally set things right between them.

"Yeah, I'll see him."

Zoe grinned, nodding. "OK."

"Cut it out," Charlie said, sighing.

Zoe pasted an innocent expression on her face.

"What?"

"That smile. You're matchmaking again."

Zoe pushed to her feet.

"I'm just gonna go ahead and send him in before you can change your mind."

As soon as Zoe had disappeared into the hallway, Allie spoke up for the first time since the carnival.

"It's funny that Zoe doesn't remember Craig, don't you think?"

"Funny?" Charlie said. "And where the hell have you been, anyway?"

Allie ignored the second question.

"Yeah, I mean… can't you just imagine a guy like that fearing obscurity more than anything? Going unnoticed? Being forgotten? He's so fucking unremarkable you barely remembered him, and you remember everything."

"I guess," Charlie said. "I don't really feel sorry for him, though."

Allie snorted.

"Believe me, neither do I. Dude's a *loser*. I'm just saying, he probably goes around feeling sorry for himself, blaming the rest of the world for his complete lack of a personality."

"The female half of the world, anyway," Charlie said.

"Good point."

There was a faint knock at the door, and then Will ducked into her room.

"Hey," he said, smiling self-consciously.

"Hi." She patted the bed with one of her mitts, gesturing that he should sit down next to her. "I think I owe you my thanks, but also an apology."

"No, you don't. I barely did anything."

"That's not true. You didn't have to call Zoe." Charlie stared down at her bandaged hands. "Especially not after the way I acted at the carnival."

"Of course I called Zoe. I was worried about you. Just because I was a little pissed off doesn't mean I stopped caring about you." He shrugged. "Anyway, it's a moot point. By the time we'd found you,

you'd already saved yourself. You didn't need me to do anything. The fact that I called Zoe ultimately doesn't matter."

"It matters to me," Charlie said. She suddenly felt tears in her eyes and had to wait a few seconds before she could go on. "And it means that what happened in the past maybe doesn't matter so much anymore."

Will cocked his head to one side, squinted at her.

"Is that a roundabout way of saying you forgive me?"

Charlie nodded.

"Like, for *real* forgive me? For everything? The spyware? Heidi? The fact that I may or may not have once set fire to a neighbor's shed? All of it?"

"Yes," she said, laughing a little. "Clean slate."

"Wow. OK. So not to get ahead of myself—and maybe this is a totally inappropriate thing to ask right now—but does this mean you'd go out with me again?"

"Well, yeah. I thought that was implied."

"Oh, excuse me for not picking up on the subtleties of the conversation," he teased. "I suppose it was also implied that I should kiss you now."

Charlie rolled her eyes.

"Duh."

EPILOGUE

Charlie was cleared for discharge the next morning, and one of the nurses on duty came to help her change into a pair of scrubs. Her outfit from the night before had been taken as evidence by the police, but even if it hadn't, the clothes had been so caked with dirt and blood that Charlie figured them for a total loss.

When Zoe pushed a wheelchair into the room, Charlie frowned at it. "What's that?"

"It's hospital policy," the nurse explained.

"What's the policy?" Charlie asked. "No walking allowed?"

The nurse chuckled as she guided Charlie into the chair.

Zoe wheeled her outside to where her car was idling at the curb. Again, she and the nurse insisted on manhandling Charlie out of the chair and into the car.

"You realize that the bandages on my hands don't impede my ability to walk at all?" Charlie complained.

Zoe reached across and buckled Charlie in.

"Frank is at his place, getting the spare room set up for you," she said.

Charlie sighed.

"I told you guys that I'm fine."

"Says the girl who can't even buckle her own seatbelt," Zoe said. "Stop whining, and let us help you."

Charlie made a *hmph* sound but stopped arguing. They stopped off at the pharmacy to pick up her prescriptions—mostly pain meds of varying intensities and antibiotics to keep the wounds on her hands from getting infected.

"You hungry?" Zoe asked, gesturing out the windshield at the line of fast-food joints across from the pharmacy. "We could get some food while we wait for your prescriptions to be filled."

The black-and-white logo of Steak 'n Shake caught Charlie's eye.

"I'm not super hungry, but I'd kill for a milkshake right now."

"Milkshakes it is," Zoe said, steering them over to the restaurant.

A few minutes later, they were back in the pharmacy parking lot, sucking down ice cream disguised as a beverage.

"Oh, hey." Zoe snapped her fingers. "You were right about Craig Rattigan having gone to school with us."

Charlie raised an eyebrow.

"Uh, no shit. Did you think I was making it up?"

Zoe shrugged.

"No. It's just that I really had no recollection of him. I even dug out my old yearbook and looked him up. He was right there in black and white. But even that didn't jog my memory." Zoe drummed her fingers on the steering wheel. "Seems weird, is all. How many times must that happen in life? A hundred times? A thousand? All those people passing us by, close enough to touch, but they flit past like moths, and we barely notice them at all."

"Craig Rattigan is more of a cockroach than a moth," Charlie said. "But I know what you mean."

Zoe nodded.

"Speaking of which… his mother is coming down to the station today."

Charlie lost her grip on her milkshake and just barely managed to avoid spilling it in her lap. She swung her head around to face Zoe.

"She is?"

"Yeah. I asked Detective Sponaugle if he minded you observing, and he said it was OK. But I didn't know if you'd be up to it."

"Of course I am. When does the interview start?"

Zoe squinted at the clock.

"In about fifteen minutes."

"Let's go." Charlie thunked one of her bandaged mitts on the dashboard. "Chop-chop."

Scratching the side of her neck, Zoe blinked over at her.

"You don't want to go to Frank's first? Take a shower? Change into some actual clothes?"

"If it means missing the interview with Rattigan's mother, then no."

"It doesn't even occur to you to rest and recuperate, does it?" Zoe asked. "I mean, you fought off a knife attack last night with your bare hands, but God forbid you take a day or two to get back on your feet."

"Are you going to take me to the station, or do I have to bail out of your car and hobble over there myself?"

"Alright, geez." Zoe shook her head. "But can we at least wait until your prescriptions are ready?"

Fifteen minutes later, Charlie and Zoe watched from behind the glass wall of the observation room as Craig's mother settled into a chair in the sheriff's department interview room.

Carol Rattigan looked small sitting behind the large empty table that took up most of the space. She had a cloud of graying hair surrounding her face and wore a floral-print turtleneck over khaki pants.

According to Zoe, Craig's father had died three years ago, and Mrs. Rattigan had used the money from the life insurance policy to retire early to a suburb outside of San Diego. She taught Sunday school and did genealogy reports for people as a hobby.

"I don't know what to say," Mrs. Rattigan said, clutching the bottle of water Detective Sponaugle had brought her. "Until I saw that it was indeed Craig in the hospital bed, I was convinced that you had him confused with someone else. I just couldn't fathom my son being involved in all this."

"Why don't we talk a bit about his childhood," Detective Sponaugle said. "Did he ever show any aggressive behavior as a boy?"

Mrs. Rattigan shook her head.

"No. Nothing like that. Craig was a good boy. Always polite. Obedient. Reserved, even. He did his chores and mowed the lawn without much fuss. Of course I know that's only part of raising a child, but I thought we'd done good." Her jaw began to quiver. "I'm sorry. I don't know why I'm crying. I'm not the one he hurt. Not directly anyway. But this is… this is all very upsetting to hear."

Things were quiet in the interview room for several seconds as she gathered herself. When she spoke again, her eyes glistened with unspilled tears.

"I keep going over it in my head, around and around. It can't be my Craig. There must be some mistake. But I saw the proof myself. The only logical explanation is that he did these things." She paused, swallowing, and her voice shook faintly as she continued. "So then I try to think of something, anything that might explain it. An incident in his childhood. A time I wondered to myself about him. But there isn't anything. He was… normal. He always *seemed* normal. So was I just blind? Did I miss something I shouldn't have? Is this my fault?"

"This isn't an interrogation, Mrs. Rattigan," Detective Sponaugle said, his voice soft. "No one is pointing the finger at you or accusing you of anything. I asked you here to get a better picture of who Craig is and was as a person, OK?"

He waited for her to nod.

"So can you tell me what kind of activities he was into? Hobbies, interests, that kind of thing."

"Well, Craig loved comic books and drawing. He was always doodling in the margins of his schoolwork." She smiled a little at that. "He was quite good. So good that one of his art teachers in school wrote him up a recommendation letter that got him into the College for Creative Studies in Detroit. And we were just delighted by that."

Her smile faded.

"But he dropped out after the first year. He didn't like the structure. He was used to drawing whatever he wanted and didn't want to have to do figure studies and hand-lettering exercises. He failed a few of his classes because he just stopped showing up." Mrs. Rattigan sighed. "That was one of the only arguments I can ever remember having with him. His father and I were so disappointed. To us, it felt like he was giving up at the first sign of adversity. He said he hadn't liked any of the people there anyway. Called them pretentious snobs."

"What about his social life?" Detective Sponaugle asked. "Did he have any close friends? Girlfriends?"

"He had a few friends. Other boys who were into the same things. The comic books and video games. But they drifted away after high school, and I don't think he made many friends at art school." She shrugged. "He didn't really date much. I remember he went to a school dance once with a gal but he was quite adamant that they were 'just friends.' I will admit that I wondered sometimes if he was gay and just too afraid to tell us. But then this past year, he said he'd met someone. A girl named Emma. He told me all sorts of things about her. And I thought it was wonderful. He sent me a picture of her. And now I've come to find out…"

Mrs. Rattigan put a hand to her lips, but it did nothing to stifle the sob that burst forth from her mouth.

Charlie remembered the way Emma had broken down that day in her office. How the emotion had surprised and overwhelmed the girl, and then Charlie in turn.

She felt the same lump in the back of her throat. The same stinging in her sinuses.

Charlie backed away from the window and headed for the door that led to the hallway.

Zoe followed her out.

"You OK?"

"Yeah," Charlie said. "I just need a break."

Zoe glanced back toward the door of the observation room.

"Kinda wild, right? I mean, you'd think she'd have something worse to say than he dropped out of art school. I was expecting her to say that all the family pets mysteriously went missing when Craig was ten. And that he used to perform weird rituals on his sister's Barbie dolls."

Charlie crossed her arms.

"Does he have a sister?"

"No, but you get what I'm saying."

Before Charlie could respond, the interview room door opened. Mrs. Rattigan came out, dabbing her eyes with a tissue. She halted abruptly when she saw the hall wasn't empty, and Charlie saw her taking in the hospital scrubs and bandages.

Mrs. Rattigan took a step closer.

"Excuse me, are you…" Seconds ticked by as she struggled to find the words. "Are you the one that Craig hurt?"

Charlie swallowed and nodded.

The woman pulled her arms close to her body as if she were trying to make herself smaller.

"I know an apology from me probably means very little, but… I can't help but feel responsible somehow. Like I missed something."

Charlie looked down at the puffy gauze concealing the wounds on her hands. She wasn't sure what to say to this woman. No one had taught her how to address the mother of the man who had tried to kill her.

"Some people are very good at hiding what's inside," Charlie said.

"Thank you, but… I think you're wrong." Mrs. Rattigan let out a quavering breath. "I think a mother should know. I didn't know, but I should have. I should have seen it. And I just want you to know that I'm sorry. I'm so sorry."

Charlie thought of Craig Rattigan then as a stone striking a still pond and sending ripples across the entire surface. The actions of one man had altered the lives of so many: Mrs. Rattigan, Charlie, Paige, Olivia, Robbie, Emma. Some of them were gone forever. None of them would ever be the same.

It was unfair, really. An imbalance. There was so much good in the world, so many people who lived their lives never harming anyone else. And yet one bad apple like Craig Rattigan could come along and cause so much destruction. So much pain.

"That's why we fight," Allie said. "Someone's gotta keep an eye out for the cockroaches."

And suddenly Charlie knew what to say. She rested one of her marshmallow hands on Mrs. Rattigan's arm.

"I don't think you owe me an apology. But I won't refuse it either. If you need my forgiveness, you have it."

The woman started to cry, and Charlie found herself moving closer to comfort her. As Craig's mother sobbed into Charlie's shoulder, Charlie thought that Allie was right. Someone had to fight. But someone also had to be there to tend to the wounded. To reassure the survivors that they would get through it.

A NOTE FROM L.T. AND TIM

Thanks for reading *Watch Her Sleep*. Pretty stalker-y, right? If you enjoyed it, feel free to sign up for the Bookouture Vargus/McBain list at the following link. They'll keep you posted about new releases in the series.

www.bookouture.com/lt-vargus-and-tim-mcbain/

Want to hang out with us? We love hearing from readers. Join our personal email list to hear about all of our other books and reading recommendations. Sign up for that here:

http://ltvargus.com/mailing-list

Oh, and if you have a second to leave a review, we'd really appreciate it. Just a couple sentences about your experience reading *Watch Her Sleep* would mean the world. Reviews help us find new readers and keep the lights on.

That's all for now.
L.T. Vargus and Tim McBain

ltvargusbooks

@ltvargus

ltvargus.com